IT **WRONG**
TO TRY TO
PICK UP GIRLS
IN A **DUNGEON?**

VOLUME 9

FUJINO OMORI
ILLUSTRATION BY **SUZUHITO YASUDA**

YEN ON

NEW YORK

IS IT WRONG TO TRY TO PICK UP GIRLS IN A DUNGEON?, Volume 9
FUJINO OMORI

Translation by Andrew Gaippe
Cover art by Suzuhito Yasuda

This book is a work of fiction. Names, characters, places, and incidents are the product of the author's imagination or are used fictitiously. Any resemblance to actual events, locales, or persons, living or dead, is coincidental.

DUNGEON NI DEAI WO MOTOMERU NO WA MACHIGATTEIRUDAROUKA vol. 9
Copyright © 2015 Fujino Omori
Illustrations copyright © 2015 Suzuhito Yasuda
All rights reserved.
Original Japanese edition published in 2015 by SB Creative Corp.
This English edition is published by arrangement with SB Creative Corp.,
Tokyo, in care of Tuttle-Mori Agency, Inc., Tokyo.

English translation © 2017 by Yen Press, LLC

Yen On
1290 Avenue of the Americas
New York, NY 10104

Visit us at yenpress.com
facebook.com/yenpress
twitter.com/yenpress
yenpress.tumblr.com
instagram.com/yenpress

First Yen On Edition: September 2017

Yen On is an imprint of Yen Press, LLC.
The Yen On name and logo are trademarks of Yen Press, LLC.

The publisher is not responsible for websites
(or their content) that are not owned by the publisher.

Library of Congress Cataloging-in-Publication Data
Names: Ōmori, Fujino, author. | Yasuda, Suzuhito, illustrator.
Title: Is it wrong to try to pick up girls in a dungeon? / Fujino Omori ; illustrated by Suzuhito Yasuda.
Other titles: Danjon ni deai o motomeru nowa machigatte iru darōka. English.
Description: New York : Yen ON, 2015– | Series: Is it wrong to try to pick up girls in a dungeon? ; 9
Identifiers: LCCN 2015029144 | ISBN 9780316339155 (v. 1 : pbk.) |
ISBN 9780316340144 (v. 2 : pbk.) | ISBN 9780316340151 (v. 3 : pbk.) |
ISBN 9780316340168 (v. 4 : pbk.) | ISBN 9780316314794 (v. 5 : pbk.) |
ISBN 9780316394161 (v. 6 : pbk.) | ISBN 9780316394178 (v. 7 : pbk.) |
ISBN 9780316394185 (v. 8 : pbk.) | ISBN 9780316562645 (v. 9 : pbk.)
Subjects: | CYAC: Fantasy. | BISAC: FICTION / Fantasy / General. | FICTION /
Science Fiction / Adventure.
Classification: LCC PZ7.1.O54 Du 2015 | DDC [Fic]—dc23
LC record available at http://lccn.loc.gov/2015029144

ISBNs: 978-0-316-56264-5 (paperback)
978-0-316-44244-2 (ebook)

1 3 5 7 9 10 8 6 4 2

LSC-C

Printed in the United States of America

OLUME 9

UJINO OMORI
USTRATION BY **SUZUHITO YASUDA**

BELL CRANELL

The hero of the story, who came to Orario (dreaming of meeting a beautiful heroine in the Dungeon) on the advice of his grandfather. He belongs to *Hestia Familia* and is still getting used to his job as an adventurer.

HESTIA

A being from the heavens, she is far beyond all the inhabitants of the mortal plane. The head of Bell's *Hestia Familia*, she is absolutely head over heels in love with him!

AIZ WALLENSTEIN

Known as the Sword Princess, her combination of feminine beauty and incredible strength makes her Orario's best-known female adventurer. Bell idolizes her. Currently Level 6, she belongs to *Loki Familia*.

LILLILUKA ERDE

A girl belonging to a race of pygmy humans known as prums, she plays the role of supporter in Bell's battle party. A member of *Hestia Familia*, she's much more powerful than she looks.

WELF CROZZO

A smith who fights alongside Bell as a member of his party, he forged Bell's light armor (Pyonkichi MK-V). Belongs to *Hestia Familia*.

MIKOTO YAMATO

A girl from the Far East. She feels indebted to Bell after receiving his forgiveness. Former member of *Takemikazuchi Familia* who now belongs to *Hestia Familia*.

HARUHIME SANJOUNO

A fox-person (renart) from the Far East who met Bell in Orario's Pleasure Quarter. Belongs to *Hestia Familia*.

EINA TULLE

A Dungeon adviser and a receptionist for the organization in charge of regulating the Dungeon, the Guild. She has bought armor for Bell in the past, and she looks after him even now.

CHARACTER & STORY

The Labyrinth City Orario——A large metropolis that sits over an expansive network of underground tunnels and caverns known as the "Dungeon." Bell Cranell came in hopes of realizing his dreams, joining *Hestia Familia* in the process. After being saved by the Sword Princess Aiz Wallenstein, he became infatuated with her and vowed to grow stronger. As he ventured into the Dungeon, he fought fierce battles beside the supporter Lilly, the smith Welf, the girl from the Far East named Mikoto, and the renart Haruhime as a member of *Hestia Familia*. With more allies at his side, Bell sets foot into the Colossal Tree Labyrinth for the first time and meets a vouivre girl who can speak using language. Is this a sign of a storm on the horizon…?

TSUBAKI COLLBRANDE

A half-dwarf smith belonging to *Hephaistos Familia*. Currently at Level 5, Tsubaki is a terror on the battlefield.

BETE LOGA

A member of a race of animal people known as werewolves. He laughed at Bell's inexperience one night at The Benevolent Mistress. However, he recognized the boy's potential after witnessing Bell's battle with a minotaur.

FINN DEIMNE

Known for his cool head, he is the commander of *Loki Familia*.

OTTAR

An extremely powerful member of *Freya Familia*.

SYR FLOVER

A waitress at The Benevolent Mistress. She established a friendly relationship with Bell after an unexpected meeting.

MIACH

The head of *Miach Familia*, a group focused on the production and sale of items.

HERMES

The deity of *Hermes Familia*. A charming god who excels at toeing the line on all sides of an argument, he is always in the know. Is he keeping tabs on Bell for someone......?

TAKEMIKAZUCHI

The deity of *Takemikazuchi Familia*.

CHIGUSA HITACHI

Another member of *Takemikazuchi Familia*.

OURANOS

The god in charge of the Guild, he also manages the Dungeon.

DIX PREDIX

Captain of *Ikelos Familia* and ill-tempered hunter of rare monsters.

HEPHAISTOS

Deity of Orario's most well-known and respected familia of smiths, *Hephaistos Familia*. She has loose ties with Hestia dating back to their time in the heavens.

LOKI

Deity of Orario's most powerful familia and has a mysterious western accent. Loki is particularly fond of Aiz.

RIVERIA LJOS ALF

High elf and vice commander of the most prominent familia in Orario, *Loki Familia*.

FREYA

Goddess at the head of *Freya Familia*. Her stunning allure is strong enough to enchant the gods themselves. She is a true "Goddess of Beauty."

ALLEN FROMEL

A cat person who belongs to *Freya Familia*.

LYU LEON

An elf and former adventurer of extraordinary skill, she currently works as a bartender and waitress at The Benevolent Mistress.

NAHZA ERSUISU

The sole member of *Miach Familia*. She gets extremely jealous of other women who approach her god.

ASFI AL ANDROMEDA

A very gifted creator of magical items. She is the captain of *Hermes Familia*.

OUKA KASHIMA

The captain of *Takemikazuchi Familia*.

WIENE

A vouivre girl Bell meets in the Colossal Tree Labyrinth of the Dungeon. Can speak.

IKELOS

God of *Ikelos Familia*. Desperate for entertainment, his moral scale is based on whether something is interesting or not.

PROLOGUE

CHANCE
MEETING

© Suzuhito Yasuda

Sharp, labored breaths rang out.

The ceiling, walls, and floor in this area of the labyrinth were all tree bark. Moss thickly covered its surfaces, illuminating the passageway in a bluish-green light. It gave the impression that not a soul had ever set foot in this part of the Dungeon. The reverberations of distant monster howls made leaves tremble, prompting beads of silver to dribble off sundry fantastical flora.

In this giant tree labyrinth that was completely removed from the world up above, a lone shadow ran with every bit of energy it could muster.

The figure had supple, delicate limbs that closely resembled those of a young girl. Azure-silver hair glistened in the light of the moss.

Besides its long, silky tresses, the being possessed skin of a bluish-white hue.

The many scales covering its shoulders, lower back, and the long ears framing its face, tapering to even finer points than those of elves, were similarly colored. But the most notable feature by far was the glimmering crimson jewel embedded in its forehead.

Blue-white skin and a crimson jewel were just the first of many features that proved this creature was a monster.

Thump, thump, thump! The monster held its thin, branch-like arms against its chest as it ran through the Dungeon.

Why?

It was bleeding.

Claws, fangs, and blades had inflicted many wounds on its body. Deep-red blood trickled from open gashes with every step. The attacks had ripped entire scales from its shoulders, dyeing its cerulean skin completely red.

Why?

Terror showed in its eyes. Confusion. Grief.

Several water droplets accompanied the blood on its way to the floor below. The clear liquid flowed from the monster's stunning amber eyes as its thin throat began quivering.

"Why...?"

The sound that escaped from its small lips was not the crude howl of a monster but a single hoarse, mournful word.

The voice was like that of a sobbing child. As if disdaining the sounds strung together to make a word, the barks of monsters echoing through the labyrinthine Dungeon closed in. The lone figure's bluish-silver hair and slim shoulders trembled in fear.

Sorrow had distorted its face, which was out of place on a monster and attractive enough to leave a person breathless.

The monster—the "girl" was crying.

Why, why is everyone...?!

She was alone.

She was only a newborn, recently delivered from the Dungeon walls, but everything she had encountered rejected her.

She had memories of her birth, of breaking out from the wall before falling to the floor. Still unable to tell left from right, she wandered the Dungeon, trying to make sense of her dim surroundings. While she was anxious at not knowing her location, she picked up a familiar scent—one of her own kind. Her instincts drove her to follow it.

It led her to a different corner of the Dungeon, where a creature much larger than herself stood. She approached it to ask:

"Where am I?"

The creature's response was a monstrous roar. After raising its voice in anger, the monster slashed her with sharp claws.

Skin torn, she ran away without understanding why.

As confusion seized her body, the red blood seeping from her wounds and the first-time sensation of pain inspired terror in the newborn.

Since then, she had been attacked again and again. The beings that shared her scent, no matter their shape or size, threatened her life. There were no exceptions. She fought desperately to hold back something that threatened to flow from her eyes as her injuries continued to increase.

Rushing out from the depths of the Dungeon, the exhausted "girl" next encountered creatures of a completely different species.

They were humans equipped with swords and bows.

Accompanying them were a fairylike male and female. The long-eared pair nestled close together, protecting each other.

She approached them, unaware that her eyes betrayed her envy.

Not wanting to startle the newcomers, she hid her sharp claws from view and opened her mouth to speak.

"Help me."

In an instant, a blade opened a new wound on her body.

The group appeared more confused and shaken than she, but most apparent was their terror as they rejected her.

Faced with this new animosity, she fled once again. The men scattered as they swung their swords, and the pale-faced women readied their bows with muffled shrieks.

Arrows streaked at her from behind as her tears finally spilled over.

Pain. Suffering. Sadness.

The scales on her back deflected the arrowheads but cracked with each impact. Her torn, lacerated shoulders felt as if they were on fire. The world excluded, alienated, and rejected her; it had branded her an outcast.

She questioned herself over and over. *Why, why?*

Cries of *I'm scared, I'm so scared* slipped from her mouth.

Her weeping did not stop.

What...am I...?!

No matter how many times she asked, the Dungeon, her mother, gave no answer.

She fled for some time, but in the end her pursuers appeared again. Astonished by her beauty, they adopted unfamiliar expressions as they gruffly yelled, "Stop!"

The hunters, wetting their lips and gazing sadistically at her, had no reason to halt their advance. The madness in their eyes as they stalked her was far uglier than anything she had seen from her fellow monsters. She tried to escape on her two slender legs, having already learned to fear everything.

The reason she was regarded as a beast lay in the latent power she used to shake off her pursuers, dodge other monsters in the Dungeon that continued to attack her, and race through the arborous path alone. The lonely echoing *tap, tap, tap* of two feet hung in the air of the seemingly endless Dungeon.

Translucent tears spilled from her amber eyes again.

"Ahh!"

A downward slope.

She lost her footing like a child and tumbled heavily down the hill crisscrossed in tree roots.

After falling to the very bottom, the "girl" noticed she had injured her leg. She couldn't stand.

Distant monster howls and the footfalls of people prompted a shiver in her body. She examined her surroundings before setting off, dragging her immobile leg along. Her wounds had already clotted enough to stem the flow of blood, allowing her to hide her trail. In one corner of the Dungeon, she found a single tree and an abundance of plants. Using the leaves as a shelter, she hid within.

Her back pressed to the wall, she held her breath. Trembling, she squeezed her badly injured body tightly with both arms and fought back against the endless waves of terror.

Then she realized something was approaching.

Her breath caught again.

She could hear steps coming closer and closer with each passing moment. The crescendo of footsteps made her recall the biting pain of a sword, almost as though the memory itself radiated heat, paralyzing her with horror.

Her body shook uncontrollably.

Her cheeks still wet, another wave of fear crossed her face.

Looking up at the human figure drawing near, the girl hugged herself with all her might.

Then.

The "girl's" tearful eyes looked up as the newcomer appeared.

"A monster…a vouivre?"

White hair and rubellite eyes.
In a dim corner of the Dungeon, she had a fateful meeting with one boy.

CHAPTER 1
AN IRREGULAR GIRL

It all started with a certain quest.

"Firebirds are overflowin' on the nineteenth floor. Little Rookie, you're gonna lend us a hand, too."

We, *Hestia Familia*, had just arrived on the eighteenth floor when the adventurers of Rivira came to us unexpectedly with a request.

From time to time, there are unpredictable outbreaks of many monsters unique to the Dungeon. These erratic, unusual phenomena are referred to as Irregulars.

The specific species involved this time had been confirmed as firebirds, a rare kind of monster normally found on the nineteenth floor and below. Just like its name suggests, they have the appearance of birds and predominantly use flame-based attacks. This is a problem because the nineteenth floor is the start of the "Colossal Tree Labyrinth" in the Dungeon.

Apparently these firebirds can turn an entire area into a sea of flames if left unchecked. What's worse, I've heard they sometimes come up to the eighteenth floor—which should be a safe point—and soar through the wide-open skies, putting even the lakeside town of Rivira in danger.

Upper-class adventurers who stage expeditions from Rivira weren't about to let their base go up in flames, and we had arrived just as they were setting off to exterminate the monsters. The residents were seeking help in suppressing the outbreak and soliciting every upper-class adventurer who happened to be passing through.

The war against Rakia had ended three days ago. Having returned to our regular activities in the Dungeon, we had finally made it all the way to the safe point without relying on anyone else for the very first time. Lilly was quite unhappy when this quest was forced on us upon arrival, but given the handsome reward and the fact that a flock of firebirds in our way made it impossible to comfortably progress any farther, she grudgingly gave in.

The adventurers of Rivira provided robes made of burn-resistant salamander wool as an advance payment to all cooperating participants. Meanwhile, the organizers temporarily assigned me to a different party because of my high agility. They wanted to finish the monster subjugation as quickly as possible, so I was deployed in a group that stressed speed.

With my salamander-wool robe wrapped around my shoulders, I left Lilly, Welf, Mikoto, and Haruhime for the time being and followed my assigned group of burly adventurers through the entrance leading to the nineteenth floor.

Just when I thought things were going well, I realized I had ended up separated and alone.

The Colossal Tree Labyrinth was completely different from the other floors I'd seen before, and I had no experience with its structure and paths. Since we were chasing after and sometimes running away from firebirds in unfamiliar territory—not to mention my possibly detrimental position at the rear of the formation—the other adventurers totally left me behind.

I found myself in a deserted corner of the Dungeon, trying to get my bearings, when it happened.

I glimpsed something that resembled a human silhouette.

It dragged an injured leg along the ground and hid itself in the lush undergrowth of the Dungeon, suggesting it was attempting to evade pursuit.

At first, I thought it was an injured fellow adventurer and started running over in a panic, but then I suddenly felt as if something was off. With as much caution as possible, I approached.

Then—

"A monster...a vouivre?"

I'm shocked by what I see.

It's a humanoid monster with delicate, slim limbs and bluish-white skin. When I spot the jewel in its forehead that could be mistaken for a third eye, I reach back into my memory and find a type of dragon called a vouivre.

"Vouivre."

On par with the unicorn, it's known for being the rarest of rare monsters even in the Dungeon.

I've heard it's known to appear between the nineteenth and twenty-fourth floors, and its drop items, whether scales or claws, fetch tremendous sums on the market. However, these are nothing compared to the red gem set in their foreheads, known as "Vouivre's Tear." Its value promises such immense riches that adventurers often refer to it as the "Prosperity Stone."

But extracting the jewel from a vouivre's forehead causes it to go berserk—and slaying the dragon inevitably shatters the precious item. There are records of innumerable adventurers who have been cut to pieces trying to obtain one. Vouivres are a species of dragon, the greatest monsters in the Dungeon, and their combat strength is unmatched.

Usually, vouivres would have a humanoid upper body with a snakelike lower body, like lamias. Overall, they resemble women attached to a dragon tail, but…

…Is this really a monster?

The creature's face seems surprisingly human, and there are *tears* leaking out of its breathtaking amber eyes.

It's not wearing anything at all, just the bluish-white skin it was born in.

I notice it has thin legs where the dragon tail should be, and a pair of modest breasts sits on its chest.

Apart from its complexion and scales, it could very well be a girl about my age.

"…, …!"

The vouivre…is crying.

Arms wrapped tightly around its trembling body, it looks up at me from its spot on the floor.

Like it's forgotten that it's a monster, showing fear like a person.

I don't believe it, comes a whisper from a corner of my mind.

I can't even think clearly. My confusion is only building. Even seeing it with my own two eyes, I simply can't understand.

I mean, monsters are our enemies, after all.

Monsters are born killers, baring their fangs at us and taking every chance they get to attack. They possess such atrocious destructive urges that there's no room for reason or emotions to intervene.

Monsters are, well, monsters.

—*At least they should be.*

I don't feel any of the hatred and disgust that a monster is supposed to summon within me.

These enemies unconditionally drive us to fight back, but I can't sense even a fragment of the instinctual animosity I would expect.

Right now, it's the exact opposite. I'm reluctant to thrust a sword at this humanoid figure before me.

I've never seen a monster like this.

"Uu, aah......!"

"!"

The vouivre's eyes are glued to the tip of the Hestia Knife. I quickly hide it behind my back. *The hell are you doing?!* I scold myself. The tiny bit of relief passing over the monster's face bewilders me even more.

Is this specific vouivre a subspecies?

A product of sudden mutation that could be considered an Irregular itself?

It's hurt...No, it's wounded.

There are several places on its body caked in dried blood. I can see spots on its shoulders where scales have been violently ripped or broken off.

Only weapons can make injuries like that. Likely, it was adventurers who attacked it. Whatever the case, the badly wounded vouivre is looking up at me in terror and desperately trying to put more distance between us. But its back is already up against a wall, and no amount of retreating will help.

I can't move.

Monsters are the purveyors of death and destruction.

One should never befriend them, and certainly not extend a helping hand for any reason.

But I'm standing here, trapped in the vouivre's gaze, peering into those amber eyes that definitely carry emotion. I can't finish it off... Slowly, I back away.

At an impasse, I decide that acting like I never saw it is the best option and then run away pathetically.

Turning my back on the vouivre, I leave the place behind me.

"......?"

The human gone from her line of sight, the vouivre looked around with a mystified expression, tears still filling her eyes.

The Dungeon was eerily silent. Frightened by what she might see, the girl glanced at her surroundings before slowly standing up.

Placing both hands on the Dungeon wall to take some weight off her injured leg, she started hobbling along the passageway.

Suddenly, with a *thud*—

The sound of flapping wings descended behind the injured vouivre as a crimson bird appeared from a side tunnel branching off the passageway. The firebird was over two meders long from end to end, with narrow bloodshot eyes and a massive, gaping beak.

The vouivre girl froze as she felt heat closing in on her from behind. The airborne creature had found its latest victim.

As the firebird aimed at her a stream of fire more powerful than a hellhound could ever produce, she tried to kick off the ground with her slender legs, but it was too late.

The flames dancing in the back of the firebird's beak lit up the vouivre girl's face, about to spew forth—

"—Aghh!"

—I brandish my Hestia Knife.

I sprint and leap forward to attack, the blade carving a bright violet arc through the air before splitting the firebird in two.

The disrupted fire attack breaks apart in midair like fireworks. Its magic stone is cleaved apart, so the firebird crumbles into ash, and its remains are blown away.

The vouivre collapses to the ground beneath the cloud of sparks and smoldering soot as I land.

…*Damn it.*

Now I've done it.

Staring at my Hestia Knife, which I'm holding in a reverse grip, I hunch over in despair.

I couldn't bring myself to take off after leaving this place behind, so I doubled back and watched the vouivre from a blind spot. Then I found myself dashing out of my hiding place once the firebird attacked.

The horror on the monster's face—no, "her" face—spurred my legs to move on their own.

All alone in the heart of the Dungeon…

After being attacked by adventurers, it only makes sense that she's afraid of us now.

But to be assaulted for no reason at all by her fellow monsters?

Yes, I know thinking like this will only cause problems. The rational, levelheaded part of me keeps telling me to not do something so stupid. But my hands already went ahead and did it anyway.

I grip my bangs with my free left hand, clenching my hair as I walk toward the stunned vouivre.

She's in pretty much the same position as before, looking up at me.

Trembling with fear and confusion, she gazes my way as if clinging to the faintest ray of hope. I let go of my hair and slowly lower my hand with all sorts of thoughts running through my mind—and then I smile weakly at her.

I can't do it.

No matter what happens.

I can't kill her.

"—It's okay. Don't be scared."

I kneel beside her so that our eyes are on the same level. Then I relax my face and smile again.

Her eyes open a little wider, almost as if she understands what I said.

Even tamers, who bend monsters to their will using a combination of strength and pain, would never do something this downright stupid. Growing increasingly reckless, I examine more closely the various injuries covering her body.

Her shoulders are in terrible shape, and her broken leg is hideous. I reach into my leg holster and take out a Dual Potion made by *Miach Familia*.

The vial containing unknown liquid in my hand must've startled her, because her whole body flinches when she sees it.

"Nothing to worry about. This is called a potion—"

"Po...tion...?"

—She spoke.

I don't know how many times common sense has been obliterated today, but this one tops everything. Her voice is still ringing in my ears.

I was simply speaking to her about what I was doing to soothe her nerves, not expecting a response. Now I'm frozen in place, and a dry, empty laugh escapes from my mouth.

At any rate, I open the vial and wonder if potions have any effect on monsters at all as I pour it over her shoulders. Relief swells in my chest as I watch her open wounds begin closing beneath the dried blood. She, on the other hand, seems surprised.

High potions can mend a broken bone, but...apparently they can force it to heal at the wrong angle if it isn't set properly. The same is true for other healing items and magic—they can cause permanent damage when used without proper preliminary treatment. While I have no idea how to deal with injuries the "right" way, I tear off a piece of salamander wool for a bandage and wrap it around her leg using my knife's sheath as a splint.

"......"

"......"

I pour the remainder of the potion over the rest of her injured body while kneeling beside her. Now that the vial is empty, the two of us stare at each other in silence.

The long silver-blue-haired girl seems to be flustered. Holding her hands together in front of her chest, her surprisingly clear amber eyes quiver while her delicate mouth opens and closes every few moments.

As I do my best to ignore the heat building in my cheeks and keep my eyes off her completely exposed breasts, I know there's something different about her.

I encountered harpies when I was stranded in the Beor Mountains not too long ago—they looked human, too, but also hideous. Those creatures were definitely monsters. But this girl—she looks so much like us, and the mysterious air around her is completely different from the harpies'.

A strange monster…A strange girl.

Something catches in my throat as I try to comprehend the being that's somewhere between person and monster sitting in front of me.

"—Keep looking! It can't have gotten far!"

Human voices.

Rough, angry shouts echo down the passageway toward us.

The vouivre girl shrinks in fear. The trembling that had all but stopped comes back with a vengeance.

Terror fills her eyes as the footsteps draw closer to us. I don't say a word as I take off my salamander-wool robe and fling it over her shoulders.

I just finish hiding all her bluish-white skin beneath it as several heavily armed adventurers turn the corner.

"Hey, you there! Did you see a vouivre girl pass by?"

A group of four men and women rush up behind me with the leader yelling at the top of his lungs. I stay facing the Dungeon wall.

I've got a bad feeling about this.

It's not difficult to guess their relationship with the vouivre girl. If I don't protect her now, then…

I can tell they're already suspiciously glaring at the girl hiding beneath my robe. Taking hold of the small, trembling hand beneath the red fabric, I desperately rack my brain for a solution.

Time slows to a crawl. I can hear the agitation in their voices and feel beads of sweat dripping down my face. Glancing down—I see the empty vial still clutched in my grasp. That's it!

It's risky. I just hope my acting skills are up for the task.

"Forget about that, do you have any potions on you? She's been hit by a firebird and got burned bad, real bad!"

Fixing my gaze on the form against the wall, I put as much panic in my voice as I can.

The empty vial, the shaking body beneath salamander wool, the singed ground and foliage left over from the firebird explosion—everything here tells the story. Their eyes shift to me, narrowing.

My desperation must be doing the trick, because they sneer at me before turning on their heels. They don't want to get involved with my problem and are much more interested in tracking down a rare monster. The adventurers sprint away.

Once I'm sure they're gone for good…I let my shoulders relax.

"W-we should be okay now…"

I whisper to the trembling robed figure, and she timidly pokes her head out from the fabric.

I'm sure that never in her wildest dreams did she expect an adventurer to heal her rather than deliver the killing blow, let alone protect her from other adventurers.

I saved a monster—how would I react if I saw someone else do that?

…No, I don't want to think about it.

I can't help but sigh as the vouivre girl still shivers in fear of the adventurers, even though they're gone.

"Um…Can you walk?"

I stand up and offer her my hand.

Staying here only puts her at risk of being found by…well, anything. Those adventurers could double back, and she'd die a pointless death.

She looks at my outstretched hand and then up to my eyes…then nods slightly.

Her trembling hand reaches out and comes to rest on my palm. It's cold, surprisingly so. I curl my fingers around it and gently pull her to her feet.

She's probably about 150 celch tall. After making sure she's completely hidden by the salamander-wool robe, I pull her arm over my shoulder as we take our first steps.

Sounds like there's a battle over there…Okay, we'll head this way for now and figure out what to do next on the way…

Now that I'm separated from my assigned group, I have no idea how to get back to the entrance.

There's no choice but to follow my ears back to what I hope are other adventurers on the same quest, fighting firebirds along the main route. After that, it'll all be a matter of following the map that Lilly practically jammed into my pocket before I left. My only hope is to find the landmarks on the map, follow them out, and avoid being seen as much as possible.

Hoping that we don't encounter any truly ferocious monsters on the way, I support my injured companion so she doesn't have to put any weight on her broken leg. If worse comes to worst, I'll pick her up with both arms and book it.

"…"

The strange girl-monster hunted by both man and beast watches silently as I ward off bugbears and mad beetles blocking our path with my Swift-Strike Magic, Firebolt.

Her moist eyes glisten. "Khaa…" She's sobbing, I think.

She turns toward me a few moments later, burying her face between my neck and shoulder. A little nose presses against me, and I can feel her warm breath on my chest. I know I'm in the Dungeon and losing focus is a one-way ticket to the grave—but my cheeks are on fire.

So delicate…and soft.

Even if she does have the body of a normal girl, getting hot under the collar in a situation like this is a failure as a man and an adventurer.

Did I save the vouivre because she's pretty? Was it her appearance that made me extend a helping hand? If that's the case, I'm already beyond help.

What would Gramps, the one who always told me to save damsels in distress, say if he saw me now? Would he praise me?

…I have an inkling that this is the one time he'd groan.

I've gone far off the deep end, doing what I just did.

Saving a monster.

Then she whispers:

"……Thank you."

Needing a moment to get over this new surprise, I look down at her. She gazes back up at me with tears in her eyes.

Her head is slightly tilted beneath the robe's dark-red hood. In that moment, I feel something that can't be put into words—a warmth that only people can share.

How do I respond? Should I respond? An endless string of thoughts races through my head as she watches me uneasily.

Her pure, childlike innocence makes all the contradictory feelings melt away. I force a smile.

"It'll be okay."

I give her another smile to try to put her at ease, and she returns the gesture with a tiny one of her own.

She closes her eyes and presses her body against me again, and I wrap my arms around her.

My mind is made up. I'll protect this girl who can smile like the rest of us.

There's only one problem…How am I going to explain this to Lilly and the others?

It took a while, but we found our way back to the main route on the nineteenth floor.

Guided by the simple map in my hand, we hid from adventurers and monsters at every turn until we spotted the light from the eighteenth floor's crystal ceiling. At last, the exit.

"—It is true! A monster spoke to me!!"

"Why do you not believe us?!"

We follow the path that connects the eighteenth and nineteenth floors and come out at the base of the Central Tree located at the center of the area. Several adventurers, including the ones from Rivira, are standing around the roots.

Two elves, a man and a woman, are pleading their case to the group.

Their insistence does nothing to convince their skeptical audience. I glance to my side to check on the vouivre girl and see her grab at her shoulder. Her amber eyes lock onto the elves in fear.

"Yeah, yeah. Hey! You there, get these two a place to rest their heads. Dreamin's fine when you do it on a pillow, so make sure they find one."

"Bors, please believe me! That monster, it really did…!"

The unlikely story of a talking monster is raising more than a few eyebrows, but no one will take it seriously if Bors, the man at the top of Rivira's hierarchy, can't be convinced.

However, the elves' pleading gives us a distraction. We quickly slip out from the tunnel entrance.

"Mr. Bell!"

"Are you unhurt?!"

"Damn, you know how to make a guy worry."

"Hi, guys…"

Hardly anyone else spares us a glance as we make our exit, but as soon as we're clear of the other adventurers, the rest of *Hestia Familia* spots me and comes toward us.

I can hear the relief in their voices as Lilly, Mikoto, and Welf reach us first. Maybe they heard I was separated from my group?

"……? Um, Master Bell, who might this be…?"

Haruhime catches up to them with a relieved smile, but then she points out the girl wrapped in salamander wool at my side.

Well, here goes. "Follow me…" I lead everyone away.

Rather than returning to Rivira, I head east, deeper into the forest. Lilly gives me a suspicious glance as we make our way among the crystals and dense trees that fill this area of the safe point.

I keep going until I'm absolutely sure the other adventurers are out of sight and earshot. We've come pretty deep into the forest by the time I turn to face everyone.

We form a circle in the middle of a small clearing that's surrounded by the sparkle of rock formations.

"Now then, Mr. Bell, please inform us exactly who this is. Don't tell Lilly that you've dragged us into a new mess by rescuing another girl!"

Her words are sharp as knives. She walks up to the girl at my side. I think she's got the wrong idea here…Planting her feet, Lilly tries to get a glimpse under the robe's hood.

"Ah." A weak sound comes from beneath the cloth as the frightened girl steps back. Lilly takes another step forward, and the girl slips in an attempt to retreat farther.

The broken leg! I reach out and catch her—her hood falling away in the process.

"!!"

Time freezes.

The exposed bluish-white skin and the jewel on the vouivre girl's forehead come into view. Lilly and the others are dumbstruck, but they're ready for battle with weapons drawn in no time flat.

Lilly springs backward as Welf grabs hold of the greatsword strapped to his back and Mikoto wraps her fingers around the hilts of two blades hanging from her waist.

Haruhime's green eyes open wide with shock as she covers her mouth with both hands.

Everyone is immediately on edge, and I'm too stunned to react. Beside me, the vouivre girl goes stiff as a board.

"…You've got some explaining to do, Bell."

"Lady Haruhime, please come this way."

Welf's eyes never leave my new companion while he speaks. I've never heard him sound so intimidating. At the same time, Mikoto positions herself in front of Haruhime, hiding her from the vouivre girl.

Just as they've always been, my friends are extremely wary of monsters.

"W-wait! Everyone, please! This girl, she's…!"

"Get away from it, Mr. Bell!! What's going on in that head of yours?!"

Lilly cuts off my attempt to explain, practically screaming at me as she aims her bow gun. Her chestnut-colored eyes are brimming with reproach and confusion.

"Did Mr. Bell bring her along because she has a pretty face?!"

"N-no, it's not like that…!"

"Lilly can't be blamed for thinking this is a monster fetish!"

Monster fetish.

Just as the name suggests, the term *monster fetish* describes those who have an abnormal sexual attraction to anthropomorphic monsters like harpies and lamias. In the mortal realm we live in, it's the ultimate insult.

This is how deeply the hatred for the Dungeon's inhabitants runs in our hearts.

"Mr. Bell, monsters are monsters!! Even tamed ones aren't worth that kind of attention! They're—our enemies!!"

Sensing the panic in Lilly's voice, plus Welf's and Mikoto's reactions, I can tell this isn't going well.

Fiends and people can't see eye to eye—that's always been our relationship. I can't blame my friends for this. It's expected.

Monsters have been killing our ancestors since the Ancient Times. Caught in a spiral of death for millennia, they could never live peacefully with us.

Welf's completely focused on the girl while Lilly presses me for answers in his stead.

"This is no dog or cat!! Mr. Bell, please get away from it!!"

"Bell."

"Sir Bell."

I step in front of the vouivre girl, shielding her from Welf, Mikoto, and Lilly's bow gun. The three of them beg me to get out of the way. Only Haruhime, unaccustomed to direct confrontation, stays silent as she watches.

I've never been on this side of their blades before, and I'm at a loss. I can't do anything, but I refuse to stand down. I will protect her.

The vouivre girl appears terrified of Lilly and the others, but a spark of light shines in her eyes as she looks up at me.

"…Bell?"

A chorus of gasps fills the air the moment that word leaves her lips.

"Ah, um, yes…That's my name."

"Name…?"

"Y-yes. I'm Bell."

"Bell…Bell is name…Name is…Bell?"

My friends need a moment to process what just happened. They stare at the girl as she plays with the sound of my name.

The talking monster leaves everyone speechless.

Their intense focus now broken, the four of them watch her with blank astonishment.

"Bell, Bell."

She squeezes my finger with one hand, repeating my name as if she's figured out what the word meant.

Just "Bell, Bell," over and over as though trying to burn it into her memory. The girl leans in closer to me, bluish-white skin pressed against my armor.

As if I'm the only thing she can count on in this world.

"The monster…spoke."

"This has gotta be some bad joke."

Mikoto and Welf whisper in disbelief.

At the same time, they begin to lower their weapons.

Confusion is setting in. The open display of weakness so uncharacteristic of other monsters would do that to anyone.

"Master Bell…what transpired between the two of you…?"

Voice unsteady, Haruhime has built up the courage to step forward and ask. I couldn't be more grateful.

"I found her…on the nineteenth floor. She was hurt really bad… Adventurers and monsters both attacked her…She was trembling… crying."

I explain my reasoning for bringing her with me as clearly as I can.

Her leg, limp and useless, dragging behind her. My emotional struggle in the face of those amber eyes.

Welf, Mikoto, and Haruhime consider the girl clinging to my side, now with a better understanding of what she's been through.

"I...I'd like to help her."

"...Should word get out that we're harboring a monster, *Hestia Familia* is finished..."

Lilly, who's been silently quivering all this time, feebly shakes her head after I disclose what I want to do.

Even though I know it puts the familia at risk—the one I'm the head of, no less—I apologize to everyone for my selfishness while sharing my true thoughts.

"Even so, I can't just abandon her."

As pitiful as I sound, I keep my eyes focused on Lilly. She bites her bottom lip.

A few moments pass. Lilly's gaze starts to shift, almost as if she can see a shadow of her former self in the vouivre girl.

Memories of the day the goddess and I saved Lilly must be running through her head—and she slouches over.

"Just...do what you want..."

She lowers her right hand, pointing the bow gun at the ground.

Welf and Mikoto also relax, completely lowering their weapons. The tension subsides.

Finally able to breathe again, the girl apprehensively observes our group.

The threatening atmosphere might have lifted, but now no one knows what to do—least of all Haruhime, who's in the middle of it. No one's moving; there's just lots of eye contact.

Putting aside the fact that I've dragged my own familia into uncharted territory and caused problems for everyone, I propose a plan of action.

"She'll be vulnerable to adventurers and monsters if she stays in the Dungeon...I'd like to take her home. I also want to hear what our goddess has to say."

Besides protecting the vouivre, I'm also interested in Lady Hestia's opinion. And if she can tell me what exactly this girl is.

Welf, Mikoto, and Haruhime don't object. They just give me absentminded smiles and reluctant nods, as if their necks are covered in rust.

Lastly, Lilly lets out a long sigh.

"If we are returning to the surface, it needs to be at night. That'll ensure there are as few adventurers around as possible…We should aim to exit Babel at a time when no one will be watching."

Whatever we do, we can't let anyone else know that we're sheltering a monster. With that in mind, it makes sense to resurface when adventurers are too busy drinking in bars to notice us. Lilly's advice is a lifesaver.

I know she's not happy about this, but even so, she's doing everything in her power to help me. I don't know what I'd do without her as my supporter.

"Sorry, Lilly. And thank you…"

"…Lilly's given up. Yes, do whatever you want because no matter what you say or do, Lilly can't bring herself to leave you to your own devices."

She turns away, a bit red in the face. Is she sulking?

Even though I feel sorry for putting her in an uncomfortable position, I'm happier that my friends have sided with me.

I'm extremely grateful to Lilly for saying what she did.

Welf and Mikoto appeared a bit lost at first, but seeing Lilly's reaction brings a smile to their faces.

"Surface…?"

"Yes. Let's go to where we live."

I smile at the nervous girl squeezing my finger amid my friends' smiles and Lilly's red-faced pouting. She stares at me for a few moments before a tiny smile appears on her lips.

Plop. She falls against my chest, burying her face in my neck.

Stumbling backward, I catch her small frame before raising my eyes to the ceiling far above.

I can see the countless blue and white crystals overhead among the leaves. With every passing moment, their glimmer weakens, signaling that night is falling.

The gigantic white tower was shrouded in darkness.

Situated in the very center of the Labyrinth City, Babel stretched high toward the heavens in the middle of Central Park as day became night. All over the city, a lively tumult developed around the bars as the multicolored illumination of magic-stone lamps replaced the sun.

The vibrant city's energy never waned, even at night. The streets of the Shopping District were still full of people, and a lewd atmosphere was descending on the still active areas of the Pleasure Quarter, where some' were trying their best to help the neighborhood recover. On the bar-lined outskirts of the main streets, drunken women danced with deities on the road as though they were at a ball. As always, the white tower watched over the nightlife underneath it.

Adventurers returning to the surface after a long day in the Dungeon went their separate ways to blow off steam at their favorite watering holes. One party watched group after group ascend the spiral stairwell before finally making the ascent themselves.

A white-haired human was at the center of this group of six. Swiftly climbing the sparsely populated staircase, they arrived at the Dungeon entrance located in Babel Tower's basement.

Quickening their pace, the group passed beneath a beautiful mural depicting a clear sky on the ceiling.

Little did they know that hidden in a corner of the artful design was a small blue orb that twinkled as they went by.

"—We have a problem, Ouranos."

A voice echoed through a dark stone chamber built to resemble the temples of old.

The only source of light was four burning torches in the center of the chamber. The dancing flames illuminated a blue crystal set atop a pedestal as well as the owner of the voice.

A black robe completely covered the mysterious figure. Absolutely no skin was exposed. This person wore black gloves decorated with intricate designs over both hands. It was as if a shadow had come to life.

Even its voice gave no hint as to whether a man or a woman was speaking. The hood of its robe hovered over the blue crystal as the figure continued to speak.

"*An intelligent monster* has encountered a party of adventurers. They are leaving Babel now."

The blue crystal displayed an image: a view of the tower's basement from the orb in the ceiling.

A white-haired boy was clearly visible beneath the crystal's surface, as was a girl wrapped in salamander wool.

The black-robed figure knew immediately that the girl pressed up against the human was, in fact, a monster.

"Are they working with the monster?"

"I don't believe so…From what I can see, they appear to be protecting it."

A different, majestic voice echoed through the chamber from the vicinity of the four torches while the black-robed figure focused on the blue crystal.

The dancing flames cast flickering light on a towering stone throne-like altar in the darkness and highlighted the imposing, elderly deity sitting on it.

Well over two meders tall when standing, the deity, clad in a robe of his own, displayed no emotion as he continued asking questions.

"Fels, who are the adventurers?"

The black-robed figure—Fels—responded right away.

"Bell Cranell, member of *Hestia Familia*."

In the crystal display was a familiar combination of white and red.

The elderly deity frowned at this revelation, his blue eyes narrowing.

"Little Rookie, now a household name in the city…And one of Hermes's favorites."

"What is your divine will, Ouranos?"

"…Wait and observe."

The elderly deity quietly closed his eyes at the question and didn't reopen them until he answered.

"Are you certain? For better or worse, *Hestia Familia* holds the attention of the populace. Should anything happen…"

"These are Hestia's followers. There is no connection between them and the hunters we pursue. But most of all…"

The deity's gaze fell on the blue crystal. He studied the human's face for several moments.

"I want to know. Can Hestia's followers become the catalyst for change…? Can they provide *them* with hope?"

A heavy silence followed. The figure's hood shifted forward, indicating a nod.

"As you will, Ouranos. I shall follow."

Crackle! A spark burst from one of the torches.

"Dispatch 'eyes.' Keep a close watch on Bell Cranell, his familia, and the monster."

"Yes."

Inside a peaceful chamber of stone…

…a black robe swished as it disappeared into the darkness.

CHAPTER 2
**DAILY LIFE WITH
A VOUIVRE GIRL**

We surface pretty close to midnight.

Just as Lilly had predicted, Babel and Central Park are practically deserted when we arrive. We don't stick around, and the side roads and back alleyways provide the perfect cover for us as we stay out of sight on our way toward home.

The bars are loud, as are some houses in the residential areas—the vouivre girl jumps in surprise at the lights and sounds of civilization. Although it's a challenge to keep her calm in a city overflowing with noise, we eventually make it safely back to Hearthstone Manor.

"Mr. Bell, please wait here with her. Lilly will have Lord Miach leave first."

She tells the vouivre girl to stay out of sight next to the manor's back gate while everyone else enters through the front.

Miach Familia was kind enough to housesit for us while we were in the Dungeon today. Lord Miach is one thing, but the situation will get tense if the chienthrope Nahza or his two new followers, Daphne and Cassandra, see the vouivre—just like what happened earlier with my own familia. While they're friends of ours, Lilly and Welf thought it might be a good idea to keep them in the dark about the monster girl. I agreed.

The salamander wool–covered girl and I hide in a dark spot behind the manor for a few minutes. At last, I hear voices come from the other side of our home and fade in the distance. Lord Miach and his followers are gone.

Haruhime and Mikoto run out the back door to collect us moments later.

"Sir Bell, who should inform Lady Hestia…?"

"…I will. Please let me tell her."

"Are you certain…?"

They're clearly concerned as they open the iron gate to the back garden.

The girls take up positions one step to the left and right of our visitor. I'm the one who invited her here, so I should be the one to explain. I glance down at the vouivre girl and marvel at how much her leg has healed on its own—this is what monsters are capable of. Even so, I tighten my grip to support her.

"Hey, hey. Welcome back!"

The goddess greets us in the living room with her customary smile.

"Well, Bell! This is unusual, you coming in through the back door by yourself. Miach's already gone home. And who's this—?"

She looks at us with bubbly curiosity, only to suddenly fall silent.

Welf and Lilly arrive and see all of us frozen with our mouths nervously clamped shut. The goddess's sky-blue eyes are locked on me.

Time slows to a crawl as her gaze shifts to the girl at my side, hiding beneath the robe.

"—Bell, what is *that*?"

Her expression changed completely. Our goddess hadn't asked "who" but "what."

Overwhelmed, I silently pull back the girl's hood.

"……!!"

Bluish-white skin, amber eyes, and a garnet-like jewel in her forehead.

Hestia gulps hard at the girl's fantastical appearance.

Meanwhile, our visitor is terrified of the deity staring at her. She wraps her thin arms around me in response.

"…Explain what happened for me."

Surrounded by her familia, Lady Hestia takes a deep breath to steady her voice and looks at me with unblinking eyes.

In the living room, I recount the details of how we met.

Lilly, Welf, and the others have all pulled up chairs around our round table. I'm sitting with everyone else, next to the vouivre girl. The goddess retains a gentle expression while listening to me and doesn't say a word from start to finish.

"…What should we do, Lady Hestia?"

Lilly asks the goddess for a decision as soon as my story ends.

The vouivre girl has a strong grip on my right arm and won't let go. Our goddess is deep in thought, arms crossed over her chest until she slowly opens her eyes.

"…Please don't tell anyone else. We'll wait and see."

She makes eye contact with each of us in turn, even the strange girl at my side.

"I'm going to be brutally honest with you all, but I really don't know how to take this. I can hardly believe it…"

The goddess stares at our unexpected guest for a few moments as the blue-skinned girl quivers in fear under her gaze.

A talking monster has violated everything we thought we knew about the things that lived in the Dungeon.

Furthermore, the goddess's admission that even the all-knowing deities aren't truly omniscient has left all of us speechless.

"Monsters and you children of the mortal realm…are enemies. Two entities fated to fight each other. I know that to be true, but I can't turn my back on someone capable of so much fear."

"So that means…!"

"Yeah, she can stay here for now."

Protecting those in need is the goddess's way of showing affection.

Her willingness to kindly reach out to any child fills my heart with relief. Her decision triggers many different reactions around the table, from sighs to grimaces. But no one speaks out against the decree.

The goddess hops out of her chair with a little grunt of effort. I can see the anxiousness in her eyes, but she still gives the vouivre girl a gentle smile.

"So, do you have a name?"

"…Name?"

The vouivre girl dons a curious expression as she leans in closer to me.

"…Bell?"

"No, that's my name…"

She tilts her head to the side, making her silver-blue hair swish. A bead of sweat rolls down my face.

"My...name? ...Don't know."

Lilly and the others gasp softly in surprise at her choppy sentence—it's the first time they've heard her say something besides my name. But at the same time, the girl lowers her head.

So she doesn't have a name, after all.

"Vouivre" is the name that people chose for her species. She needs something to go by as an individual.

"Bell, give her one."

"What, me?!"

"Yep, Welf's absolutely right. You found her and brought her home, so to speak. You're the one who saved her. You should take on a fatherly role and name her."

How...How did it come to this...?!

Welf and the goddess are the only ones who say anything. Lilly, Mikoto, and Haruhime have their mouths shut but their eyes silently say, "Go ahead."

Heart racing, I search the others at the table. If I didn't know better, I'd say Welf is enjoying this. Even the vouivre girl is watching me blankly.

So much responsibility...! *Why do I have to be the one to give this girl something that will affect the rest of her life?!*

I look into her amber eyes. My mind is already reeling, but her expression flips my brain into desperation mode.

Vouivre, dragon, girl, jewel, garnet, bluish silver, amber eyes...

I try listing every physical trait I can see—it's no use!!

Cold sweat runs down my back, and my eyes spin. "Hurry up," somebody says. How long have I been thinking about this...? My lips tremble.

"Wi...Wilusine?"

"Huh?" Everyone responds with confusion, and even the goddess tilts her head to the side. Maybe I tried a little too hard to come up with a striking name?

"If I may ask, Master Bell…Is that name based on a fairy in a hero's tale…?"

Well…crap.

Haruhime, who likes myths and legends about heroes as much as I do, saw right through me.

There is a story about a fairy with wings of light named Melusine. The story revolves around her falling in love with a hero who saved her life, as well as her efforts to blend in with people and try to live among them. She tells the hero to never peek while she's cleansing herself, but he eventually breaks that promise and winds up seeing her wings, exposing her true form…They become separated afterward but reunite to slay a dragon that threatens to destroy the hero's hometown.

I've liked Melusine's story since I was a kid, so combine that name with vouivre and you get…Wilusine.

Too easy?

"Not a bad name, especially considering it was Mr. Bell's idea. A bit grandiose, though."

"Yeah, and long. Stands out like a sore thumb."

"Hmmm. Okay then, why don't we call her Wiene? Sounds cute, don't you think?"

"Ohh, very nice suggestion, Lady Hestia. That one's more down-to-earth."

Lilly, Welf, the goddess, and Mikoto take turns criticizing the name I came up with. Nobody pays any attention to me shrinking in my chair.

"I-I think Wilusine is a wonderful name!" Haruhime rushes in, giving me a compliment, and Mikoto takes notice. *Great, older women are trying to comfort me…*This is so pitiful it hurts.

*But "Wiene"…*That might actually be better now that I think about it.

"Wiene…? Me…Wiene?"

"Y-yeah. What do you think?"

Still attached to my arm, the vouivre girl asks me with that same childlike innocence.

But I'm sure that look on her face is a smile.

The vouivre girl's—No, Wiene's lips spread into an unmistakably joyful expression that takes everyone's breath away. Even the goddess is transfixed.

There's a pure, almost naive, childlike happiness on the face of a surprisingly beautiful monster right beside me.

The very foundation of the man-and-monster relationship has just crumbled. This strange girl overcame the wall that should have separated us, and now we're completely taken with her.

"Bell, Bell."

Wiene lets go of my arm in her moment of happiness and rubs her face against my unarmored chest.

My arms move on their own to catch her, but I'm speechless.

Her warmth envelops me, stirring all sorts of emotions in my chest for an instant.

"…Ahem."

Our goddess has been watching us the whole time, faking a cough to get our attention. Then she clears her throat to bring everyone back into the moment.

"Let's start off on the right foot—nice to meet you, Wiene! I'm Hestia, Bell's goddess! You'll be living with us starting today. Try to get along, okay?"

She puffs out her chest and gives Wiene an energetic greeting.

Wiene glances up at the goddess from her perch in my lap as Lady Hestia reaches out to shake hands.

"…Bell's…goddess?"

The words fall out of her mouth as the two make eye contact—and she buries her face back in my chest.

She leaves the goddess hanging with her hand extended. Lady Hestia lets her arm drop, having learned that gaining Wiene's trust won't be that easy. Haruhime and I force a smile.

"…Anyway, how long are you going to hold her, Mr. Bell? Do you so enjoy a girl's touch, even if it's a monster's?"

"Huh?"

"Gah! She's right, Bell! Let go of her! Ogling is disgraceful, disgraceful!"

"I-I'm not ogling!"

And so begins Lilly and the goddess's tirade.

I quickly deny all their accusations, but nothing will convince them that it's Wiene who won't release *me*. Welf and Mikoto quietly chuckle at our pointless argument as Haruhime follows the conversation with her eyes.

But now that the anxious vibe is gone from the living room, I notice how soft Wiene's body is. There's nothing I can do to stop the pitiful groan from my throat as I blush furiously.

Sometime later.

I'm not sure when, but Wiene must've succumbed to exhaustion at some point during my argument with my offended goddess and fallen asleep in my arms.

Running around in the Dungeon without a friend in the world…I can't imagine how much stress and anxiety she's been dealing with. Already in a deep sleep with her arms wrapped around my body, she absolutely will not let go.

Everyone tried their hand at prying me loose, but Wiene's incredible strength—a dragon's strength—kept her locked in place, and she only hugged harder and made me scream in pain.

With no other alternative, I ended up spending the night with her. Our goddess and Lilly had a few choice things to say, like "I won't forgive any 'mistakes,' got it?" and "Mr. Bell, please don't forsake your humanity." I swear their eyes were as cold as ice as they issued warning after warning, though I vigorously nodded my assent to everything they said.

As I lay down on a living room sofa with Wiene on top of me, Haruhime was nice enough to bring us a thin blanket.

…*But in the end, everyone came in…*

They've all gathered in the living room, claiming spots on other sofas or on the floor under the dim magic-stone lamp.

My goddess was the first one to join us, a blanket in her arms and an expression that said she couldn't leave us to ourselves. It wasn't long before Lilly, Mikoto, Haruhime, and even Welf settled in for the night as well.

Do they not trust me at all...?

"......"

Welf is currently sitting against the wall, one knee up for balance. His eyes are closed, his greatsword across his lap.

It's the same with Mikoto. She might be lying on a futon with Haruhime, but her shortsword Chizan is within arm's reach on the floor beside her. Even Lilly has a firm grip on her bow gun.

I know why they're armed and who those weapons are for.

It's not that they don't trust me. They don't trust *her*...

Surrounded by a soft chorus of shallow breaths of uneasy sleep in the dim living room, I look down toward the girl atop my chest.

If it weren't for the jewel ominously twinkling on her forehead, she could pass for a completely defenseless sleeping beauty.

What is she, really...?

I ask myself that while contemplating the vouivre girl—a monster who's fallen asleep, wrapped in salamander wool, on top of a human.

It would be a lie if I say that the lines of dried blood on her bluish-white skin, peeking out from under the robe, and her unusual smell aren't unnerving. Visions of an uncertain future keep popping into my head, too.

My brain silently works until...my eyelids become too heavy to stay open.

It's been a busy day for me as well. I must've reached my limit. Sleep can't wait any longer.

—In any case, the first thing I want to do tomorrow is take a bath.

That's my last thought before slipping into unconsciousness.

"I want more information about Wiene."

The next morning...

Hestia made a declaration at the dining table during breakfast.

"We can't decide what to do from here on out without knowing more about her. Are there any others like her? What's happening in the Dungeon right now? That's what I want to know."

A drowsy Wiene still refused to let go of Bell, who was the only one unable to eat with the rest of the familia. Meanwhile, Hestia ordered her followers to collect as much information as possible.

"However, I need to make this clear: No tidbit of information is worth drawing unwanted attention. No one can know...Don't let anyone figure out there's a monster living with us."

The fact that a creature like Wiene existed at all was one thing, but the public would panic if word got out that an untamed monster was in the city. Lilly told everyone in no uncertain terms that Wiene must never be seen or mentioned at any time outside the manor.

"I'll do some investigating, too, so please focus on this, starting today."

"Guess that means Dungeon crawling is on hold for a while," Welf commented in response to Hestia's request.

"Indeed. Also, Mr. Bell, Miss Mikoto, and Miss Haruhime, please avoid talking to anyone you cannot trust beyond a shadow of a doubt."

""""Ah, yes...""""

Lilly issued a warning to Bell, Haruhime, and Mikoto, who all agreed with a heavy nod.

It wasn't that the trio couldn't keep a secret but more that they were terrible liars. The three of them sank back into their chairs, trying to look as small as possible. Hestia giggled to herself as she watched her followers banter before standing up from her chair.

"Just be careful, everybody. Well then, let's get to it."

Late-morning sunlight poured onto the streets of Orario.

The sky overhead was a clear blue as far as the eye could see. Average citizens went about their business, brushing shoulders with adventurers as they traveled along the main streets toward the Dungeon.

"What now? This 'important thing' you want to talk about better not be a new excuse for skipping work."

"I-I've been working really hard! I've turned over a new leaf, Hephaistos, believe me!!"

They were on the fourth floor of Babel Tower, inside *Hephaistos Familia*'s branch shop.

Hestia came to her part-time job at this high-end weapon shop today like always, but she had asked her friend Hephaistos for a word in private.

It just so happened that the Goddess of the Forge had come to the shop this morning for an inspection, and she agreed to hear the young goddess out.

"So? What is it? You better not pull me away from an important meeting for some nonsense."

The crimson-haired goddess led her counterpart to a consultation room in the back. Separated from the commotion of the sales floor by thick, soundproof walls, Hephaistos was certain they wouldn't be overheard. She crossed her arms and suspiciously raised an eyebrow at Hestia.

As this was the first time Hestia had set foot in this room, her head was on a swivel. She immediately went up to a beautiful longsword mounted on the side of a bookshelf and examined her reflection in the blade until her attention was drawn to Hephaistos's figure over her shoulder.

"Have you ever…heard of a monster that can speak?"

"What kind of question is that? Of course I haven't."

"Should've figured…"

Hephaistos looked more annoyed than anything as Hestia's shoulders sank.

Hestia's crimson apron, her work uniform, shifted as the young goddess slowly faced her friend.

"If, hypothetically, there were a monster that could speak…what would you do?"

"…More details—now."

Seeing the young goddess's unusual earnestness, Hephaistos narrowed her patchless left eye.

*   *   *

"A talking...monster..."

The Blue Pharmacy, situated off a backstreet between Northwest Main and West Main streets in Orario's seventh district, was also *Miach Familia*'s home, but the building didn't get much light. The little sunshine that did make it through the windows fell on three figures in the middle of a conversation: the god of the familia, Miach; the god Takemikazuchi; and Mikoto.

"This monster really speaks? Meaning it's fully aware of itself and its surroundings?"

"Yes...It spent last night in our home."

Takemikazuchi had a similar reaction to the news as that of a certain crimson-haired goddess in Babel Tower. Mikoto's voice was heavy as she explained the situation.

Mikoto had received permission to consult with any trustworthy deities, like Miach and Takemikazuchi. On the other hand, she was also not to share any information with mortals, no matter how trustworthy.

Ouka, Chigusa, and the rest of *Takemikazuchi Familia* had gone into the Dungeon while the members of *Miach Familia* were busy collecting ingredients to restock the shelves of the pharmacy. Mikoto used this chance to consult the two gods about the vouivre girl's existence.

"I thought your behavior last night was a little strange. So that's what happened..."

Miach could attest to *Hestia Familia*'s anxiety after witnessing their behavior the previous night once he had finished house-sitting for the day. Finally connecting the dots, he nodded.

"Lord Takemikazuchi, Lord Miach, do you know of any other similar incidents?"

"Can't say I do. A talking monster...That's news to me. And shocking, to be honest."

Mikoto had never seen Takemikazuchi so perturbed.

"Yes, even now I have a hard time believing it to be true...However," Miach said, "the mortal realm's 'Unknown' is so complex that even we can't predict it. The possibilities are limitless…Perhaps something is also happening in the Dungeon even as we speak."

Mikoto sat quietly and listened to the deity's warning, his aquamarine-blue hair shifting from side to side as he spoke.

Takemikazuchi observed Mikoto's reaction from his spot next to her and asked a question of his own.

"What is your view on the matter, Mikoto? How do you feel about this talking monster?"

"…I don't know."

She answered with honesty, weakly shaking her head.

"I understand that Wiene…Lady Wiene is different from other monsters, but…I am unsure how to treat her as of yet."

Her lips quivered as she went on to list specifics.

"I find myself constantly on guard, concerned that she might betray our trust…I stand vigilant, ready to act at a moment's notice."

"……"

"I cannot relax, no matter how hard I try. I am…afraid of her."

Mikoto's gaze fell to the floor as she struggled to string the words together.

Takemikazuchi fiddled with the loops of hair framing his face while he listened to her. Beside him, Miach watched Mikoto with an understanding gaze.

"Well, I'm sure anyone would react the same way…"

The deity reassured her that this response was only natural.

Mikoto didn't have anything to say. She sat in silence, staring at the floor.

Guild Headquarters, lobby.

Welf stepped into the spacious chamber of white marble, brushing against many other adventurers who were passing through before venturing into the Dungeon.

He was perfectly comfortable walking among them with his ears wide open. He'd learned during his time as a struggling young smith that small treasures could be found in the most mundane of conversations. This was nothing new. Due to his leveled-up Status, his hearing had become more sensitive than any lower-class adventurer's, and he used every bit of this ability to sift through the noise in search of information. It went without saying that he didn't approach any adventurer or Guild employee with inquiries to speed up the process.

With a black workman's jacket over his shoulders and a greatsword strapped to his back, Welf made his way to a corner of the lobby.

Several Guild employees were posting new information on a public bulletin board as a cluster of adventurers watched.

"—Oi, did ya hear? Another monster stealing equipment."

"I see. In the middle levels this time, too."

"Oh yeah, I heard some of the guys in Rivira got a little too worked up an' beat its ass half to death."

He heard every conversation among the adventurers. Scanning the bulletin board, Welf quickly spotted a sheet of paper.

It was a drawing of a monster holding a sword and wearing armor.

"...Nah, couldn't be."

But the attempt to laugh it off did nothing to ease the tension in his face.

"Well, well. Hey there, cutie...So how about it, little elf? Pour us a round of booze?"

"We'll listen to what's on your mind...Hee-hee-hee!"

Long, golden hair flowed out from beneath a hood. A female elf—Lilly disguised using her Cinder Ella skill—ignored the crude laughter of the men. She quickly made her way through an underground bar where the sun didn't reach.

Northwest Main Street, Adventurers Way.

A little distance away from the weapon and armor shops lining the street was a bar in need of a good cleaning. The wooden building itself had an emblem hanging over the front door, signifying it was a familia-owned establishment.

Familias that ran this type of business provided a venue for average citizens and those who wanted to remain anonymous to post quests and hosted information brokers, people willing to share what they knew for a price. With these transactions constantly taking place, it was also common for customers to exchange information among themselves.

Several familias like this one operated inside Orario's city walls.

Just as dirty as ever...

Lilly whispered to herself as she reminisced about her days as an outlaw and continued to ignore the catcalls and whistles coming from all around her. Barely standing 120 celch tall, she knew the beauty of her transformed face garnered a lot of attention.

The bar was dark and shabby. There were so many quests pinned to a bulletin board in the corner that its surface was hidden beneath the mass of paperwork. On the first floor, civilians could access the familia's services at their leisure, but this underground bar was only accessible from the stairwell located in the back of the building. From the dim magic-stone lamps to the shady characters gathered in the basement, everything about this place was suspicious.

An animal person missing his front teeth chuckled as he downed an unpleasant-looking beer. One Amazon wore so many rings around her fingers and neck that her tall frame sparkled in the dim light. A masked man was lurking in the back corner. Several customers sat on sofas or around small tables, all conversing in hushed voices.

If the Guild could be called the front, this was the back. People with something to hide frequented these bars rather than the Guild. Reliable or not, information spread through these hubs like wildfire. At the same time, Lilly understood that carelessness in a place like this often resulted in losing every valuable on your person.

Under no circumstances should Bell ever set foot in a place like this.

"One Alb Spring Water."

Clunk! The barstool clattered as Lilly took a seat and ordered a drink from the human bartender.

Ice water procured from the sacred peaks of the Alb Mountains—a popular nonalcoholic drink among elves. Lilly took a sip before addressing the bartender.

"Do you have any information about talking monsters?"

"…Nope, got nothin'."

The bartender didn't even blink as he accepted the payment and generous tip Lilly placed on the countertop. His message was clear: The information was valuable, and a pretty face wasn't going to jar it loose without paying full price.

Lilly had chosen this disguise as insurance. It was her way of ensuring no one would ever know *Hestia Familia* was seeking out information about talking monsters.

The bartender kept his eye on the "elf" as he silently wiped down glasses that didn't need cleaning. Lilly was one breath away from asking if he knew of any customers who might have more information when someone plopped into the seat next to her.

"I know something about these talking monsters. Not much, but something."

This newcomer, a wheat-skinned chienthrope, wore lightweight battle gear and knee-high boots.

She must have been eavesdropping, because her doglike ears were perked up and a grin was stretched across her face.

Lilly frowned.

"Mud Hound Madl."

"Oh? You know my nickname? That's surprising, since people usually forget about me with all the really famous adventurers out there…But yeah, I hate that name. What were the gods thinking, calling me that? Bit cruel, don't you think…?"

The girl looked surprised when Lilly mentioned her title and started blabbing away as if the two were friends meeting for drinks. Crossing her lithe legs beneath the counter, she ordered her own drink. "Barkeep, Honey Beer!" Then she whispered her allegiance: "*Hermes Familia.*"

"So then, you were saying?"

"Weeeell, um, Lady Luck hasn't been kind to me these days…Not too sure I can pay for this beer."

With a smile and a wink, the newcomer made a circle with her thumb and forefinger.

Lilly's beautiful elvish face twitched. Clicking her tongue, she pulled a small bag of coins out from her robe and forcefully placed it on the counter between them.

The chienthrope happily wagged her tail and started chattering enthusiastically.

"Well, like I said, it isn't much. Stories about people hearing words randomly in the Dungeon have been circulating for a while now. Rumor has it a few adventurers have even heard whole sentences when no one else was nearby, and there was another story going around for a while about a beautiful singing voice deep in the Dungeon...Oh, one more thing. Other people are after that info as well."

"......"

"Everyone laughed off those rumors—everyone but these guys. They were serious. They put up requests for any news at all in bars all over Orario, too, not just here, and they're willing to pay. A lot."

The girl glanced at the bulletin board in the back corner for a moment.

"And who might these guys be?"

"About that, I'm stumped...*I'd like to know, myself.*"

The newcomer suddenly became a bit more aggressive as she went on to explain that she had posted her own requests for information on this group.

Squinting with a faint grin on her lips, the chienthrope leaned in to get a better look under Lilly's hood.

"New around here...? What's your affiliation? You seem kinda *dirty* for an elf."

Lilly silently cursed to herself as the dog-person's face came uncomfortably close, animal nose sniffing the air in front of her face. Her current companion had the same "scent" as she once had.

There was no doubt in Lilly's mind that this woman was a thief. Not some disgruntled child like her former self, but the real deal.

Madl's work as a deliveryman for her familia, combined with her activities in this darker part of society, granted her access to a great deal of information.

It was highly likely she was pursuing information about talking monsters as well. Lilly's search for the same information had gotten her attention, and now Lilly was her top suspect.

However, Lilly didn't share Bell and Mikoto's trust in *Hermes Familia*. Perhaps the two of them hadn't lived in Orario long enough to notice, but that familia's constant stance of neutrality was extremely fishy.

Hermes Familia could easily turn from friend to foe if it fit their needs. Fifteen years in Orario's gutter had taught Lilly as much.

No real information of value…but knowing there are others asking about talking monsters is good enough for now.

The time had come for her to move on. Without another word, she stood up from her stool.

"What? Leaving already? But there's so much I wanted to talk about."

Ignoring the cheerful voice behind her, Lilly left the bar.

However…

…She's tailing me.

She noticed a presence following her through every twist and turn of the backstreets from the moment she stepped out the back door of the bar.

It was just one person, and Lilly was 99 percent sure it was the same thief. In a worst-case scenario, she didn't stand a chance against an upper-class adventurer.

Cinder Ella and items were her only option. Lilly took unusually large strides, walking onto a dimly lit path and extracting from her robe a pouch connected to a string—a Malboro stink bomb.

She'd used similar tactics many times back when she was living the shadowy life of an outlaw.

Knowing that this opponent would take some time to deal with made her cringe—although this was nothing compared to being chased by the battle-hardened elf from that insane bar—Lilly dove into the dark alleyway.

Bright sunlight is shining down from directly overhead.

There isn't even a cloud in the sky. The summer sun hanging over

Orario makes it almost too hot outside. Warm enough that I roll up my sleeves, anyway.

Bright sunlight and a clear blue sky—the vouivre girl can't tear her eyes away.

With the goddess and everyone else out, it's up to me and Haruhime to house-sit the manor.

Having arrived here at night, Wiene hadn't seen the sun yet. She had been saying the same thing since she noticed where all the light was coming from this morning:

She wanted to go out.

"What is...that?"

We've brought her into the courtyard in the middle of our home, Hearthstone Manor.

Maybe it's because the Dungeon doesn't have a sun, but Wiene is fascinated.

Haruhime turns to the inquisitive girl and walks up to her from behind.

"We call it...the sun."

"The sun..."

Wiene gazes up at the brilliant sky as she echoes Haruhime with a smile.

Without any sunlight to speak of, the Dungeon is rather cold. Of course, there are a few exceptions, like in places with fire-breathing monsters and floors with active volcanoes.

But I'm sure most monsters don't know what it's like to feel sunshine on your skin.

"...It's warm."

Wiene's eyes light up as she watches the sky and she laughs.

Her expression is so innocent, and I think her amber eyes are tearing up.

I get lost in the moment, staring at her profile from behind, when she suddenly turns toward me, tossing her long silver-blue hair.

"The surface is beautiful."

I can't think of her as a monster anymore.

Her naive, innocent smile is as bright as the sun.

*   *   *

It may be our job to hold down the fort while the others are out, but that actually means Haruhime and I are tasked with looking after Wiene.

Whatever we do, we can't let her leave the manor. She knows nothing about the outside world, so we have to keep her entertained in here.

"Bell…it's very hot. Is it okay to take this off?"

"N-no, you mustn't, Lady Wiene!!"

"Y-yes, you must put up with it."

"Ugh…" she mumbles, pulling at the salamander-wool robe's collar around her neck like she would give anything to remove it. Haruhime and I panic a little but somehow manage to persuade her. This is a relief, considering Wiene is completely naked underneath.

I asked for Haruhime's help to get Wiene cleaned up after the goddess and everyone else left this morning. It was a real struggle because the girl doesn't completely trust Haruhime yet, but she did manage to wash off a lot of the dried blood and dirt.

Haruhime also tried to put proper clothes on her, but…that didn't end well.

That's the only thing that she's outright refused. Maybe she's scared?

In any case, Wiene was having none of it, so we at least convinced her to put back on the salamander-wool robe from yesterday.

Even if you call her a monster, she's still a girl…I just hope she can let her guard down around Haruhime and the others…

The robe still provides ample glimpses of her lithe legs and cleavage, so I have to be careful where I look…Not to mention she has no sense of shame whatsoever.

Haruhime, dressed in the maid outfit she always wears around the manor, and I do our best to keep up, but Wiene pulls us along at her own pace.

"Bell, what is this?"

"That's a magic-stone lamp. They make light like the ones in the Dungeon…"

"What about that?"

Wiene doesn't want to go back inside. Her leg made a complete recovery overnight, and now she's giddily skipping along out under the sun.

Since we're surrounded by four walls in here, I doubt anyone will catch a glimpse of her. For someone like Wiene who has no place she belongs, whether on the surface or in the Dungeon, this is her only safe haven.

Peering with curiosity into the walkways along the courtyard, Wiene makes new discoveries at every turn. Her cheeks glowing a light pink, she grabs hold of my arm every so often.

"Lady Wiene, would you like to partake in a meal? You didn't have anything to eat this morning."

"…A meal?"

"Um, it's another word for food…Wiene, you haven't eaten anything since yesterday, right? I'll eat, too, so how about it?"

"…Okay."

Wiene looks up at me with concern, not completely sure what Haruhime was suggesting. I softly smile at her, and she slowly nods.

Haruhime retrieves a basket from the passageway, and the three of us take a seat on the grass.

"…Yum…"

"D-do you really think so?!"

"Yes…"

"That is a rice ball, handmade by Lady Mikoto! Would you like to try this fruit?!"

Haruhime seems thrilled, her fox ears standing straight up and her tail wagging back and forth almost as if she were presenting her own cooking. Meanwhile, Wiene quietly nibbles on the food in front of her.

The vouivre glances over at Haruhime's beaming face.

I know that bugbears eat the honey cloud fruits on the eighteenth floor—and many monsters go after trap items as well—so it seems reasonable to assume monsters can eat our food, too. If not, we'd have to go to a pantry to get food for her, and Haruhime seems as relieved as I am to discover that isn't the case.

She reaches out to pat Wiene on the head while the vouivre girl is busy gobbling down fruit. Wiene dodges her hand with a *wiff* and pulls away.

Haruhime's shoulders droop, and Wiene leans closer to me.

"Ha-ha-ha…"

Seems like Wiene is still a bit wary of her.

But she did let the other girl gently wipe down her body, so I think there's a little bit of trust between them.

The next thing to capture Wiene's attention is Haruhime's ren-art fox tail. She's watching it very closely, mimicking its movements with her body. Haruhime catches on, sweeping her tail side to side and making up a game as they go along.

You'd almost think they were sisters…

Haruhime was scared stiff at the sight of her yesterday, but now she's trying to bond with Wiene.

Her laudable efforts to accept this girl—a monster—make me so, so happy.

Then again, perhaps only Haruhime, who survived a great deal of hardship herself, is capable of this kindness.

"Bell, do you have any poshun?"

"You mean potions? I have a few in my leg holster back in my room; I can go…"

"Do you know…it has a good smell? Smells just like…the fruit there."

Wiene is talking quite a bit.

Maybe it's because of the warm sunlight or just that she was really frightened before, but she's using more words than yesterday. Smiling and giggling like this, she's speaking a lot more freely and fluently, or so it seems to me.

No—it's not just me.

Ignoring her earlier reticence, it's amazing how fast Wiene is picking up words and expressions—acquiring language. As I review our conversations, I'm sure of it.

But I don't think she's learning, exactly…What is it, then?

She looks like a girl…but she's a monster.

I answer her questions with a forced smile, but there are a lot of unsolved mysteries.

She has a good grasp of grammar and bears a strong resemblance to us. There's not much difference between her and other people. However, her bluish-white skin and scales clearly indicate she is a monster.

The red jewel embedded in her forehead sparkles in the sunlight.

"Bell, Bell."

Then, as she giggles and playfully tugs at my arm…

…she tries to change her grip, sliding her hand across my skin—and the sharp claws on her fingertips carve into my arm.

"!"

I have no battle cloth or armor for protection, and my rolled-up sleeves do nothing to protect me as three long streaks appear on my forearm.

Turning red immediately, the gouges her claws leave behind start leaking drops of blood. Blades of grass beside me turn red.

"Huh…?"

"M-Master Bell?!"

I freeze in place as Wiene stares at her own bloody hand, shock in her eyes. Haruhime screams when she catches a glimpse of my injured arm.

"I shall bring the first-aid kit!" she yells, jumping to her feet once she sees the bleeding won't stop and rushing back into the manor.

"Ah, n-no…Bell, does it hurt?"

Wiene reaches toward me, amber eyes trembling, before coming to a sudden halt.

She abruptly pulls back her hand—and the claws that drew blood.

Moving back and forth between my pained eyes and bleeding arm, Wiene's gaze then falls onto her own fingers. Her face suddenly contorts.

"I…no…so sorry, Bell…!"

A river of tears flows down her cheeks. I can hear shock and sadness in her unsteady voice.

Then she withdraws her trembling hands and holds them tight against her chest.

She wants physical contact but can't touch me.

She can't reach out because she'll hurt me again.

"Sorry, sorry…!"

More apologies.

She's afraid of her own hand, that it can hurt people so easily. She's afraid of herself.

Watching her go through this is too painful.

"……!"

I can only watch so many tears roll down her cheeks before my hands move on their own.

Surprise flashes across her face as my injured right arm reaches out, and my hand clasps the claws covered in my blood.

Her claws dig into the palm of my hand and open new wounds, but I pay them no heed.

"It's all right."

I smile at her like I did when we met.

Paying no attention to the pain, I tighten my grip.

"—Bell!!"

Overcome with emotion, Wiene shouts my name and dives into my chest, wrapping her arms around me.

Burying her face in my neck, hot tears dampen my skin.

She's really…just a kid.

Afraid of being hurt and hurting others, she seeks warmth and kindness like a lost child.

That's the only thing I can think of as I listen to the soft whimpers beneath my ear.

I wrap my blood-free left arm around her slender body and softly run my fingers through her silver-blue hair. Her shoulders quiver, and I swear her eyes are closed with pleasure.

She presses her nose against my neck like a cat wanting attention.

Overtaken by a sudden warmth, I gently pat her on the back of the head.

"—?"

I gently rub her back until she calms down, and suddenly I feel like we're *being watched*.

Being rather sensitive to this feeling for various reasons, I quickly look toward the source—a single bird sitting on top of the roof.

An owl...?

Several questions come to mind as I inspect the vertical patterns in its white feathers.

Aren't owls nocturnal? And why would there be an owl in the city in the first place?

The owl, far removed from the nearest forest, regards me with what I'm positive is a twinkle in its eye.

It suddenly spreads its wings and takes off before I can get a better look.

"......"

The owl disappears into the heavens, leaving me close-mouthed and confused.

It was just a bird, and yet I can't shake the feeling I was being *watched*.

All this thinking causes me to tighten my grip on Wiene—as I sense another observer right away.

Twitching in surprise, I look around to see—

"......Awww."

Haruhime is standing nearby, holding a first-aid kit in her arms.

For some reason, she almost seems jealous at seeing Wiene tucked comfortably in my embrace.

"......"

"......"

"Bell, Bell!"

Wiene's happy voice in my ears, I break out into a sweat when I see Haruhime's tail swishing back and forth.

The sun descends behind the city wall as night falls.

Our goddess, Welf, and everyone else is home by the time the sky completely darkens.

"I'm hooome."

"Welcome back, Goddess. Oh, hey, everyone. So, um…how'd it go?"

"Horrible. Couldn't find any leads at all."

"Many things happened to Lilly, but it was impossible to obtain any direct information concerning talking monsters…"

"Lord Miach and Lord Takemikazuchi as well…They know nothing about this matter."

Lady Hestia drifts through the front door, tired after a long day at her part-time job. Welf follows her in, scratching his head. For some reason, Lilly looks even more tired than the goddess. Mikoto avoids my question altogether…No one seems satisfied with their day as they step into the passageway.

I know we only started gathering information today, and we'll need an amazing amount of luck to strike gold on day one, but judging by their expressions, this could actually take a while.

I mull over that thought as the three of us who had stayed home today go to greet everyone.

"So, how was your day?" Welf asks.

Everyone else is looking at the girl hiding behind my back, Wiene.

She's gripping my shirt, extra careful to not extend her claws. Haruhime walks up beside the trembling vouivre girl with a smile on her face and bends over at the waist before whispering, "Why not try doing it yourself?"

She nods, and ripples run down her silver-blue hair.

"…W-welcome back."

She steps out of her hiding place just enough to expose half her face. Wiene's quiet voice fills the hall.

The goddess, Welf, Lilly, and Mikoto watch in shock as Wiene quickly jumps out from behind me and hides behind Haruhime.

Haruhime and I exchange glances and light smiles.

"She certainly…got used to you."

While Lilly and Mikoto continue standing in stunned silence, Welf breaks the ice, though he isn't sure what expression to wear.

He's right. Wiene is finally opening up to Haruhime. Her blue frame is pressed against the renart's back, forehead between her shoulder blades. Meanwhile, Haruhime is gently patting her on the head with her golden fox tail.

It must tickle, because Wiene is twitching like she's fighting back a giggle. Haruhime glances over her shoulder and smiles along with her.

Lilly still hasn't recovered from the shock of a greeting from a monster. She's standing there with her mouth hanging open. My goddess is next to her, arms crossed over her chest and grumbling.

"Well, well, Haruhime. You've got the makings of a great mother. No doubt at all."

Maybe she's still sore about being rejected point-blank last night?

"It's delicious…! Mikoto is amazing!"

"Th-thank you…"

Everyone has gathered in the dining room after changing clothes.

The first thing Wiene says after taking a bite of dinner causes Mikoto a great deal of turmoil.

A wide array of food, including meat and fish, covers the table in front of us. Tonight's menu isn't too intricate, everything lightly cooked and seasoned only with salt. Thick slices of ham have been cut into small pieces for convenience. There's a plate topped with whole grilled fish and bowls of vegetable soup. The only trace of Mikoto's Far Eastern traditional cuisine on the table tonight is a dish of sweetened fried eggs. Apparently, Wiene approves.

"Haruhime said so. Mikoto is amazing. Makes good food."

"N-no, there is so much I can do to improve. I'm vegetarian after all, and…!"

Mikoto is flustered at Wiene's glowing praise—well, just embarrassed, really.

Not sure what to do with herself, Mikoto sways her black ponytail from side to side as her face reddens.

I realize we're not feeding an animal at a zoo here, but…Wiene's voice is louder than usual. Maybe the tasty meal is exciting her? "Ahn!" She opens her mouth and waits with pure bliss for Haruhime to feed her a thick chunk of steaming-hot fried eggs.

Even the garnet jewel on her forehead is twinkling along with her amber eyes.

"Uh, wah...I've spent all this time wondering how to approach her. How laughable..." The vouivre girl's innocent smile seems to have disarmed Mikoto, who's hanging her head low.

"Miss Mikoto, that is a monster. Please go easy on yourself."

"Why so uptight, Supporter? Keeping an open mind and mending bridges is very important at times like this...and that's why I'm going to do that with Wiene right now."

"Please do not compete with Miss Haruhime! How can deities act so carefree?!" Lilly issues another warning, but the goddess waltzes over toward Wiene like it's a day at the beach. "Mark Lilly's words, this is a dangerous time for our familia!" Lilly raises her voice further still, but to no avail.

Haruhime smiles at Mikoto and invites her over; the goddess is hell-bent on bonding with our houseguest, and Lilly is equally determined to stop her. Wiene is in the middle of all the fireworks.

"Is it okay for them to get attached? Not worried about Li'l E but... is this a good idea?"

"Um, are you...nervous around Wiene, Welf?"

"I'd rather avoid her, to tell the truth."

The goddess asked me to give up my seat next to Wiene, so I've left the women's conversation behind to sit down beside Welf as he eats.

Having taken refuge, I ask for Welf's opinion, but he forces an awkward smile and shrugs.

"Still, it must be nice to escape for a bit. She hasn't left your side for two days, right? Don't tell me you're feeling lonely now that she has other friends?"

"W-Welf!"

I know he's just teasing, but I still snap. At the same time, I can tell I'm blushing, so I don't blame him.

I've figured out that no matter how startled or scared Wiene is initially, she becomes friendly when she knows that you mean her no harm.

The scene unfolding around the table is proof enough. It's all thanks to Haruhime assuring Wiene everything is okay, and now she's talking with everyone without fear.

I don't know how long she was alone, but I think she's trying to put that frightening solitude behind her by becoming friends with us—with people.

Our noisy dinner continues with the men and women on different sides of the table. Wiene is happily and contently eating alongside everyone with an indelible smile.

"Lilly, Lilly."

"L-let go of Lilly! Why would you want to hold her like this?!"

After our lively meal comes to an end and the dishes are put away, we move to the living room.

Wiene suddenly takes an interest in Lilly for some reason and wraps her arms around her. Much smaller than the vouivre girl, the prum disappears into her embrace.

"Aww, she likes you, Supporter."

"And whose fault is that?!"

Lilly has made her stance toward Wiene very clear, but the girl must've been entertained by their hilarious argument earlier and let her guard down. A vein pops out on Lilly's forehead, her face turning crimson in frustration as she glares at the goddess from Wiene's arms. Thoroughly enjoying the moment, Lady Hestia strokes Wiene's long silver-blue hair.

"A-and she really stinks! Lilly noticed it before, but our 'monster friend' has a definite smell to her!"

Lilly yells once she breaks free of Wiene's embrace.

The vouivre girl mournfully watches her go as Mikoto and Haruhime nod at each other.

"Yes, that is true…"

"I wiped her down with a moist towel this morning, but…"

Wiene hasn't had a proper scrub since coming out of the Dungeon yesterday. She's been wearing the same salamander-wool robe, too. It's been absorbing all her sweat over the past two days, so it probably smells worse than she does…Then again, it's not as if I can talk. Being glued to her all this time, I haven't taken a shower, either.

As I suddenly become self-conscious of my own stench, our goddess's eyes light up as though a magic-stone lamp came on inside her head. "All right, then!" she says with a smile.

"Why don't we all take a bath together?"

The smell of cypress trees wafted in the air as white steam rose to the ceiling.

"Ooo…This is…bath?"

"Yes, it is. It feels nice to soak in the bathtub."

Haruhime smiled at the completely naked Wiene while holding a thin towel over her plump breasts with one hand.

A spa-like bath was located on the third floor of the manor. The women of *Hestia Familia* left their clothes in the changing room and let the warm steam wash over their healthy, vibrant skin.

"It's been a long time since all of us shared a bath," Mikoto casually remarked, the skin covering her arms and legs smooth enough to make women jealous.

"Schedules for venturing into the Dungeon and my part-time job don't really line up, do they?" Hestia responded, her shapely bosom jiggling as she spoke.

Both the girl and the goddess let down their long black hair with blissful anticipation.

"Using this bath one or two at a time is the very definition of luxury…More people using it at once saves money. Lilly thinks we should do this more often."

The cypress floorboards creaked under their bare feet as the women made their way inside the bathing room and Lilly offered her opinion on the financial benefits of the arrangement.

This Far Eastern–style bath had been installed at Mikoto's request. The lavish design and spacious interior impressed even Haruhime, who hailed from a royal family and had spent years with *Ishtar Familia*. The tub was large enough to easily accommodate ten people at once. With steam constantly rising from its softly rippling surface, there was nothing more enticing to behold. A steady stream of fresh hot water flowed out of the nozzle in the back corner, softly echoing in the bathroom. The wooden floor and ceiling framed the view of Orario's nightscape beyond the window. If it weren't for the white noise from outside, the ambience would be perfect.

Wiene stared intently at her own reflection dancing on the surface of the hot water.

"Lady Wiene? Let's wash up before entering the bath."

Haruhime, who had always carried herself with purity and grace while being groomed as a prostitute, procured water from a bath with a bucket before pouring it over herself and guiding Wiene away from the shallow pool.

Hestia and the other girls followed suit and began washing their bodies.

"Bell's not with us. Why?"

"Mr. Bell is a boy! It's common sense!"

"Boys and girls have their differences, Wiene. That goes for monsters and deities, too."

Wiene had looked around the room as if something were missing. Lilly offered a retort, and Hestia provided an additional explanation while washing her arms. The vouivre girl had invited the boy to join them to the point of pestering. "Please no…" The boy turned her down every time, desperately trying to come up with an excuse as his face burned red.

"Lady Wiene, please hold still."

"Th-the scales…"

Instructing Wiene to sit down on a bathing stool, Haruhime knelt behind the girl and began washing her hair while Mikoto scrubbed her body from the front.

The girl's bluish-white complexion stood out even more in the steam-filled bathing room. The two girls were in awe of the monster's smooth, shimmering skin. However, the scales clustered around her shoulders and lower back were a constant reminder that this girl was not a normal person but a type of dragon. These scales presented a serious challenge for Mikoto because their sharp, sturdy points tore the washcloth to shreds whenever it passed over a patch. Determined to complete her mission, Mikoto held Wiene's limbs and carefully avoided the scales as she covered the girl's body in a soapy lather.

"That tickles!" giggled Wiene. She occasionally squirmed under Mikoto's and Haruhime's hands running over her skin and through her hair.

"You have beautiful hair, Lady Wiene."

"I do?"

"Yes. It's like a stream of pure spring water."

Wiene's face lit up when she heard Haruhime's compliment behind her.

The renart—her long golden hair, fox ears, and tail all dripping wet—carefully handled the vouivre girl's silver-blue hair as if washing silk.

"Shall we rinse?" said Haruhime, and she emptied a bucket of water over the girl's head a moment later.

All the dirt and grime flowed off her skin along with the suds. A now clean Wiene shook off before leaning backward into Haruhime.

A soft *plop* filled the room when the girl's head met Haruhime's curvy chest.

"Lady Wiene?"

"…E-hee-hee!"

The vouivre smiled up at Haruhime from her resting place on her chest.

Meeting the girl's gaze, the renart smiled down at her like an older sister.

Mikoto couldn't help but smile, too, her eyes narrowing as she watched from beside them.

"She's taken quite a liking to you, Miss Haruhime…Perhaps you might have the talent to become a tamer as well?"

"It's because Haruhime would make a good mother…Completely different from you, Supporter."

"Why drag Lilly into this competition?!"

The prum and the goddess watched the affectionate pair's

interaction from a short distance away. Once their brief argument died down, they followed the other girls into the bath.

Small waves crisscrossed the surface as everyone got settled, piping-hot water lapping against their shoulders. Mikoto's sigh of pleasure was closely followed by several more.

"Feels good..."

"Yesss, it's because your muscles have worked so hard all day and now they can finally relax."

The words slipped from Wiene's mouth as the warm water embraced her body. Hestia, also very much enjoying the bath, looked up at the ceiling and explained to the vouivre girl.

Several bathers had tied their long hair above their heads, but all their faces were relaxed and at peace.

"......"

"Lady Lilly, is something troubling you?"

At about the time that everyone's skin had taken on a pink sheen...

Mikoto tilted her head and inquired as to why Lilly was brooding quietly by herself.

"...There are too many well-endowed ladies in this familia."

Lilly's chestnut-colored eyes were focused on Mikoto—specifically, her torso.

Her gaze shifted across the various figures of her peers, somewhat obscured beneath the surface of the clear water, and her goddess's enormous breasts. Lilly sank deeper into the bath and blew frustrated bubbles in the water.

There was no point in comparing herself to the deity dubbed "Loli Big Boobs," but she definitely ranked lower than Haruhime and Mikoto in terms of breast size, too. Leaving out the young prum, the average size and shape of *Hestia Familia*'s feminine curves was almost intimidating—and the biggest shock came from Mikoto, who normally kept herself literally under wraps. The up close and personal view was a bitter pill to swallow.

Mind racing, Lilly turned her attention to Wiene and was filled with a sense of relief that she wasn't at the bottom of the hierarchy. However, that relief was instantly followed by a twinge of self-loathing for thinking such a thing. *Splash!* Her head disappeared beneath the surface of the water.

"—Being with Bell is better."

One heartbeat later.

Wiene sprang to her feet, her light-blue skin tinted pink by the hot water.

Lilly and the other girls were caught off guard by the vouivre girl's swift movements and were late to react. With the speed and dexterity of her dragon lineage, the girl climbed out of the bath in the blink of an eye.

"—No, don't get out!!"

"Please wait, Lady Wiene!!"

"Sh-she must be stopped!!"

"E-everyone?!"

The bathing room descended into an uproar as Lilly, Haruhime, and Hestia raced after the stark-naked monster girl. Mikoto called out after them, a moment too late.

Lilly led the charge of mostly naked women, carrying washcloths to cover what they could, into the passageway in pursuit of Wiene, but to no avail.

"GAH!" A boy's startled yelp reverberated through the manor.

…After the dust settled, everyone finished bathing, then changed into pajamas and went to the living room.

All of us are looking at Welf and Wiene sitting on the floor in the middle of the room.

"Okay, hold out your right hand."

The vouivre girl cautiously sticks out her hand—and Welf goes to work on her claws.

He's brought a few tools in here from his workshop, including a grinding stone. Except this time he isn't sharpening a blade but blunting keen edges.

His skills as a smith are on display as his steady hands move with purpose. Dragon claws are extremely valuable drop items sharp enough to inflict life-threatening wounds on upper-class adventurers as is. As carefully as possible, Welf removes each spear point with ease.

Thanks to him, no one has to be afraid of her claws.

"All right, that should do it."

Welf releases his grip on the girl's light-blue wrist.

Wiene's eyes go wide as she gazes at her perfectly rounded fingernails. Her lips curl into a smile.

"Thanks, Welf!"

"...Don't sweat it."

A few moments pass before Welf acknowledges her appreciation with his own smile.

Wiene jumps to her feet and rushes to my side.

Eyes brimming with a mixture of hope and fear, she reaches out to me.

First to my left hand, then my arm, and finally my chest.

Her new "fingernails" are so smooth that they don't even snag on my shirt, let alone pierce my skin.

Tears of happiness glisten in her amber eyes as she realizes her hand isn't covered in blood.

"Bell...Not hurt?"

"No, not at all."

She starts tearing up in earnest, smiling from ear to ear.

Wiene reaches for me with both hands. Her palms clap against my cheeks, rubbing back and forth like she's playing with a dog.

"E-hee-hee!" She giggles and smiles brighter than the sun. Her fingers sliding across my skin tickle my cheeks and neck, but I grin and bear it.

"You mustn't touch others this much, especially faces! And what are you smiling for, Mr. Bell?!"

"I-I'm not exactly enjoying..."

Lilly's glaring daggers at us from across the room.

I'm just trying to keep Wiene happy by going along with her game, so why am I suddenly on the receiving end of a lecture?

"...Does Lilly...hate Bell?"

"Huh…? Th-that was sudden."

The prum's obvious irritation and angry tone prompted Wiene to ask that question.

Lilly's face goes blank, so the vouivre asks again:

"Hate?"

"L-Lilly…Lilly, um…!"

Her chestnut eyes anxiously quiver as words leave her.

Cheeks turning red, her eyes jump between Wiene and me.

Her mouth is moving, but no sounds are coming out. Wiene's shoulders droop, her expression clouding—then Haruhime suddenly leans forward.

"I love Master Bell!"

Her face pops into my line of sight from behind my seat on the floor, and she makes an ardent declaration.

The sight of Haruhime's flushed cheeks catches Lilly and Wiene by surprise as my heart skips a beat.

Welf stops picking up his tools, stands, and turns toward us.

"I'm pretty fond of the guy myself."

"Of course I love him, too!!"

"Ho-ho…I as well."

The goddess and Mikoto chime in.

Lilly looks around the room as everyone gathers near us. She must've decided that it was pointless to go against the grain and yells at the ceiling:

"—Argh, fine! Lilly does, too!! Lilly loves Mr. Bell!"

The magic-stone lamps on the ceiling shake, their light wavering.

Hearing over and over that I'm loved…My cheeks are burning up. I can't help but smile with my goddess and friends.

"I love you guys, too."

I put the warmth of our familia into every word.

Suddenly, Wiene puts both her hands on my chest.

"Everyone loves Bell…Everyone loves one another."

She squeezes her eyes shut as another expression of joy blooms like a flower on her face.

"Warm…"

In that moment, with everyone here, it feels like we all fit together. The air is free of tension, and Wiene dives into my chest.

Wrapping her arms around my shoulders, she presses her ear against my heart as if hoping to hear it beat.

One look at the giddy happiness on her face is enough to melt all our hearts before we know it.

I put my hand against her silver-blue hair and look up.

The scene in the living room is reflected in the glass window.

Humans, demi-humans, a goddess, and a monster.

All of us have our differences, be it skin color or race or all matter of things. But here we all are, together around one girl.

The picture of a warm family.

After *Hestia Familia* spent some time with the monster girl, the members decided to call it a night and returned to their rooms one by one.

The magic-stone lamps on each floor of the manor turned dark.

"Please tell me, Lady Haruhime. What are your thoughts on Lady Wiene…?"

"I feel much the same way as Master Bell. I do not want to abandon her. It may, however, be empathy getting the best of me…"

Haruhime and Mikoto lay on adjacent futons in a dark room.

As they lay on their sides, green and violet eyes met as they spoke.

"I view myself as a courtesan…Separated from Miss Mikoto and the others, perhaps I see my former self in her. My own selfishness may be blinding me…"

"That is not so, Lady Haruhime. You are still the same generous person you were back in those days."

Haruhime had donated food to the impoverished shrine where Mikoto and her friends lived many years ago, even before she knew their names. Reflecting on the memories of those days brought a smile to Mikoto's face.

Her face hidden in shadow, Haruhime smiled back.

"What are your thoughts on her, Miss Mikoto?"

"It pains me to admit...but I have yet to reach a definite conclusion," Mikoto said. "However...I feel that Lady Wiene's smile is the same as our own. If possible, I would like to build a lasting bond with her...Like our familia."

"...Thank you, Mikoto."

Mikoto and Haruhime slowly closed their eyes beneath the narrow streaks of moonlight between the curtains over the window.

Just like when they would take naps together at the shrine in their childhood, they leaned in close enough to feel each other breathe as they drifted to sleep.

"Lady Hestia knows...The gods and goddesses know something about the Dungeon."

Inside the dim and mostly empty living room...

A lone magic-stone lamp cast a faint light on the room from its spot on the wall. Welf had almost finished cleaning up after disarming the monster girl when Lilly broke the silence.

"That was also the case when the Black Goliath appeared. They are hiding the truth about the Dungeon...or *something* inside it...from the people."

"Probably."

"Despite that, the existence of that monster surprises them."

Lilly sat in a chair, swinging her short legs back and forth as she spoke. Welf had his back to her, responding with the occasional grunt or a word or two to show he was listening.

"An Irregular incarnate, even to the gods...We have a problem on our hands, but it may be much more trouble than it's worth."

"You accepted that risk when Bell brought her back here. What's the point in moaning about it now?"

"Lilly did not 'accept.' She gave up...Mr. Bell likes people too much to see reason."

The prum, who simultaneously supported both the familia and Bell, continued her conversation with the young man.

"If her presence here puts our familia in danger…When that time comes…"

"You'll chase her out and leave her to her fate?"

"…If necessary."

Welf raised his head and turned to Lilly upon hearing her thoughts on the matter.

Lilly's concern for her ally's future was so strong that she was willing to become hated in order to protect it.

"Take a look in the mirror. Determined people don't make that expression."

"……"

Lilly's face contorted. Distress filled her downcast eyes.

Without lifting her gaze, she strung words together and squeezed them from her throat.

"Following our emotions will lead to disaster…If all of us become attached to her, we will surely regret it."

"……"

"It can't go on like this forever. It's impossible for tonight to repeat itself for the rest of our lives…"

Because that girl was a monster.

Lilly's voice faded to a whisper. This time, Welf didn't have anything to say.

"Well then, why don't the three of us sleep together tonight? Just family!"

"Just family?"

"Huh? Goddess…?!"

They were in Bell's room, third floor of the manor.

The room itself was mostly devoid of identifiable features, save for the closet that had been refurbished into a storage unit for equipment such as mended armor and other items for adventuring. Hestia was standing in the open doorway, a pillow tucked beneath her arm.

Wiene flat-out refused to sleep anywhere other than at Bell's side, and Hestia arrived on the scene to fulfill her divine duty. She practically forced her way into the room so she could keep an eye on the two.

No one else knew she was there.

"First things first…Wiene, you must now call me 'Mama' and Bell 'Papa.'"

"Mama, Papa…?"

"Goddess, what are you teaching her?!"

Hestia coached Wiene and gently stroked the girl's hair while Bell yelped in despair.

The vouivre girl inquisitively tilted her head as the deity, shorter than herself, reached up to lovingly pet her head.

"Bell, at times like this, you must obey the mortal realm's rules about how families behave. We have an image to uphold."

"What image? I've never heard anything about this!!"

Bell's astonishment did nothing to curb Hestia's enthusiasm. A crisp smile on her face, she gave him an energetic thumbs-up.

"But…but my room only has one bed! So it's not possible!"

"What do you mean, Bell? You slept with Wiene snuggled up next to you last night, yes? So you can do that with her but not with me?"

"Th-that's not what I…! You're a goddess! Sleeping next to you would be…!"

"We slept on the sofa back in the room under the church, remember?"

"Huh? We did?!"

She didn't sleepwalk her way on top of me?! Bell raked through his memory in search of answers.

Hestia turned to Wiene and gave her a friendly smile as the boy clutched his head in both hands a short distance away.

"Is it okay with you, Wiene?"

"…Okay."

Bell's only hope of escape had vanished. The three of them climbed into the single bed and lay down.

"Is…isn't this a bit cramped?"

"Hee-hee, I think you mean 'cozy.'"

"It's very…warm."

Bell's face turned bright red; he knew that they were close enough to touch each other with the slightest turn. Meanwhile, Hestia's smile widened as Wiene settled into the bed.

The vouivre lay between human and deity, all three of them on their backs. While it would have been more efficient for Hestia to sleep in the middle based on their height, Wiene looked so comfortable that neither of them had the heart to move her.

Every magic-stone lamp in the room was extinguished; the sound of rustling sheets filled the space. Bell's anxiety prevented him from moving at all while Hestia and Wiene jostled for bed space. The sound of light breathing began to fill the air as the clock on the wall ticked on.

With all the lights off, sleep descended upon the manor.

"…?"

Bell was somewhere between slumber and consciousness when movement beside him caused him to open his eyes.

He saw Wiene facing him, her body huddled up close.

She was holding onto Bell's right arm as she had done many times before.

"Can't sleep?"

"No…I'm fine."

Two voices whispered in the dark room. Her amber eyes closed to a sliver.

The garnet jewel emitted a faint light as her blue-silver hair slid down, exposing the bluish-white skin at the nape of Wiene's neck above her pajamas' collar. She smiled up at him from the pillow.

Bell quickly averted his eyes. "ZZZ…" Hestia snored and rolled over at the same time. Bell paused when he saw that the goddess had turned her back to them and adjusted his shoulders to face Wiene.

The vouivre girl donned a calm expression and snuggled in closer.

"…Wiene, where did you come from?"

Bell couldn't help but ask as she pressed her body against his like a sleepy child.

The girl from a different world finally trusted him. The question that had been eating at Bell this whole time slipped out before he knew it.

"I don't know."

"Do you have friends? …Are there any monsters that don't attack you, Wiene?"

"I don't know that, either…"

The girl claimed ignorance no matter what he asked and looked away. Then she mumbled that her earliest memory was of being alone in the Dungeon.

"But."

Wiene lifted her face up from Bell's chest.

"I have dreams."

"Dreams…?"

"Yes. Attacking Bell…people like Bell."

The boy's eyes went wide in surprise.

"Slashing people I don't know, biting them, tearing them apart…"

In an area filled with rocks and boulders, amid intricate passageways.

Baring fangs at drawn swords, sharp claws ripping through anything in their way.

Loud screams of those who avoided the fangs; ramming horns through the backs of those who ran away in a panic.

"Everything turns red…Scary dreams."

The sight of her hands, claws dripping with fresh blood.

Wiene described it all, how these dreams would play out whenever she closed her eyes.

"I'm always angry in the dreams…always get colder and colder."

"Huh…?"

"Lots of people, just like Bell…protect someone from me."

As Bell had protected Wiene from Lilly and the rest of the familia when they first met, the people in her dreams did the same, she explained.

There was one, possibly an elf, who embraced her badly injured partner and used his own body as a shield.

Another, a dwarf maybe, who blocked the passageway by himself, fighting against a whole wave of monsters at once to allow the rest of his party to escape.

Another, and another, and another…Listening to her fragmented stories, a picture began forming in Bell's mind.

Wiene curled up next to him, making herself as small as possible as her long eyelashes trembled.

"I see those people, and I feel cold."

"……"

"Like there's a hole in my chest letting everything flow out, until I feel empty…But those people were beautiful."

People supporting, protecting, and loving one another.

Sights normally overlooked, such as allies overcoming their fears to save each other, were suddenly so much clearer.

"What happens next is always the same. I become red, and everything goes dark."

That was how the dreams always ended.

A cutting flash of silver and a body going cold. Limbs that wouldn't move anymore. Bleeding that wouldn't stop.

Lying on the stone floor, staring at the ceiling as vision blurred into nothingness.

"I cry for help…but no one ever comes."

No amount of screaming or begging convinced any of her kind in the area to come to her aid.

Their battle cries filling her ears, they continued to attack the people.

Clouds of ash choked the air before everything turned dark.

"Very scary and lonely dreams."

The visions always ended without her receiving a helping hand.

"……"

Bell kept his mouth closed, listening to her story from start to finish.

Were those really dreams?

Or were they Wiene's—?

Bell's train of thought had reached that point when the vouivre girl buried her face in his chest once again.

"But I'm not scared anymore."

Because Bell was here.

Her muffled voice was tranquil as she wrapped her arms around the boy.

Wiene was smiling.

She yearned for his comfortable heat. Bell didn't say anything and accepted her embrace.

However, he gently reached out and stroked her hair.

"......"

Hestia, her back to Bell and Wiene, slowly opened her eyes.

Mulling over what she just heard, she gazed out the window at the night sky.

After a time, she heard the telltale breaths of two sleeping figures.

Hestia rolled over once again and, after hesitating a few times, wrapped her arms around the vouivre girl from behind.

A bluish darkness covered the sky.

Countless twinkling stars filled the night. Ash-colored clouds partially hid the moon from view as the heavens cast light and shadow on Orario.

Business was booming in the bars along the main boulevards and street corners. A small group of humanoid figures distanced themselves from the liveliest and noisiest area, the Shopping District and the Pleasure Quarter, to gather in an alleyway close to the city wall's East Gate in Orario's Eastern Block.

The wall's imposing shadow overhead, they met where the alleyway intersected a cul-de-sac.

Several adventurers sat atop a pile of wooden boxes and barrels that had been left outside. A god stood among them, although this particular deity was mostly preoccupied with adjusting the feather in his hat.

"Lord Hermes, Laurier and the others have returned."

The clouds high above drifted away from the moon as a beautiful woman sporting short aqua-blue hair appeared in the alleyway.

The white cape over her shoulders seemed to cut through the darkness. As soon as the words left her mouth, three demi-humans wearing traveler's robes appeared behind her.

Hearing the report of his follower, Asfi Al Andromeda, Hermes wore a delicate smile as he glanced toward her silver glasses and stood up from his barrel.

"Good work on your long journey, Laurier and company! I've been waiting."

Hermes thanked the three for their hard work as a young elf woman and two animal people, male and female, lowered their hoods. "So, how did it go?"

"Sir…We tracked the illicit sales taking place around the city and identified the merchant organization pulling the strings."

"You did? Well done."

Hermes nodded, seemingly satisfied with the elf Laurier's news.

Orario, possessing the world's only Dungeon—the sole source of magic stones—had to keep constant tabs on the black market. The Guild controlled all legal rights to magic stones and their related products, but that didn't stop people from smuggling them through the checkpoints and into other countries, where they would be sold to the highest bidder. While the Guild and the familias collaborating with them did everything in their power to eliminate these crimes, the truth was Orario had grown too large to prevent them from happening.

Therefore, it had fallen to *Hermes Familia* to investigate the various black market operations and shutter the organizations behind them. They traveled outside the city at the behest of the Guild to investigate where the products were being smuggled. This was one of the reasons that *Hermes Familia*, which nominally worked as a delivery service, could pass through various checkpoints at will. With Perseus's magic items at their disposal, the Guild placed a great deal of trust in the mid-ranking familia—even if they weren't completely honest about their members' Levels.

A letter had arrived informing Hermes that one of his investigation teams would be returning from their mission tonight, and he went to greet them in person.

"Every detail has been recorded here…Also, there is one more thing to report."

Laurier handed her god a rolled-up piece of paper, and as she continued, her pure-white complexion took on an ominous pallor.

"Just as you mentioned before our departure…*The sale of monsters* has been confirmed."

"...And the buyer?"

"Our inquiry led us to infiltrate an estate belonging to Elurian royalty...Further investigation revealed the possibility that nobility residing in other countries may also be involved."

The elf fought back a wave of nausea as memories of what she had witnessed flooded her mind. She pressed a hand to her throat to maintain composure and keep from vomiting.

"Monsters were chained to one another in underground holding cells. We were unable to ascertain whether or not they had been tamed. However, they were violated...N-no, it was worse than that. It was treatment that I did not believe people were capable of inflicting."

As Laurier adjusted her choice of words, the elf's golden hair swayed, and her pointed ears anxiously twitched.

"They were on death's door by the time we arrived...One asked us with its last breath—'*deliver this to my comrades*'..."

One of the animal people behind the elf stepped forward and held out an item wrapped in cloth.

Hermes pulled back the covering to reveal a heavily scarred monster horn—a drop item.

The deity narrowed his orange eyes.

The message and the horrid condition of the horn left the surrounding members of *Hermes Familia*, including Asfi, speechless.

The two animal people in traveler's cloaks remained silent, their lips pursed into thin lines. The elf, on the other hand, could no longer keep her boiling emotions at bay.

"—It spoke to me and asked for help! A monster!! It used words no different from ours, with tears rolling down its cheeks!!"

Her breathing became ragged.

Her right eye opened wide before she shielded it with her hand. She was on the verge of a breakdown.

A shudder ran through the young elf, who always strove to uphold pure ideals. It was no hyperbole to say that she was experiencing a crisis. Her beautiful eyes blurred behind tears as she laid bare the pent-up emotions inside her for her god and all to see.

"What was that?! Why did it look at me like that...?! ...What should I—I...!!"

Laurier was distraught.

Not saying a word, Hermes stepped up to her and took the elf's hand.

"Everything you saw, everything you witnessed is now my burden to bear. Don't let it trouble you any longer. Leave it to me."

Hermes pressed her hand against his chest so she could feel his heartbeat.

The calming rhythm coursed through the palm of her hand; her breathing returned to normal.

The trembling elf stared up at her god and saw his usual light-hearted smile. Then he removed his feathered hat before placing it on her head.

"That goes for the two of you as well," he said with a smile and patted the animal people on their shoulders. He then left the downtrodden trio in the capable hands of his other followers.

Trusting them to take care of things, he sent all of them home.

"...So what would you have us do, Lord Hermes?"

Once her allies had disappeared into the night, Asfi spoke to her god with thinly veiled agitation at his condescending behavior.

Sensing her half-lidded glare, the deity looked up into the sky in silence before turning to another of his followers who was still in the alley.

"Lulune, you said you found a suspicious child?"

"Yeah, I did, Lord Hermes. Some elf brat I've never seen before was asking around about 'talking monsters.' I tried to trail her but... she practically broke my nose with a stink bomb and got away." The wheat-skinned chienthrope massaged her nose as if she were still feeling the effects. "Sorry," she apologized through her cupped hands.

Hermes glanced at her while she spoke but quickly returned his gaze to the night sky—or at least to the visible sliver of it directly above the alleyway.

"The client's request is absolute. All we can do is keep gathering information..."

Hermes's words hung in the air.

"Haaagh, geez," he whispered under his breath. "Well Ouranos, you certainly gave us one hell of a job…"

The deity's sharp eyes gazed into the moonlight. A long moment passed before he unrolled the parchment scroll in his hands and gave it a once-over.

It was a list of all the merchant organizations connected with this smuggling ring, as well as who had bought and sold monsters.

Tracing the route all the way back to Orario, he noticed the name of one specific familia:

Ikelos Familia.

Chains rattled from deep in the darkness.

Rage-filled roars—and sometimes pained, mournful whimpers—accompanied the metallic clanging.

Hair-raising howls of agony echoed through the dark abyss.

"You let the vouivre cargo get away?"

As if its owner was completely unperturbed by the noise, an irritated voice cut through the air.

It belonged to a man with black hair.

He wore goggles made from smoky quartz, though the tinted lenses were unable to completely mask the glare of the red eyes behind them. He was rather tall, and his dirty battle cloth was open at the top, revealing well-toned neck and shoulder muscles. A large combat knife long enough to rival most shortswords hung from his waist.

He had situated himself atop the black bars of an empty cage, legs carelessly crossed, and the tone and quality of his voice suggested he was prone to violence.

"We had it cornered on the nineteenth floor but lost track of it… S-sorry, Dix."

"You realize what we could've had? Those freaks in charge of Eluria would've paid a fortune to get their filthy hands on a live one."

The goggled man, Dix, didn't even bother looking at the four adventurers below him while he spoke. The men and women hunched over in disappointment as he raised his head toward the ceiling.

The stone canopy was shrouded in darkness, giving the room an oppressive atmosphere. A few magic-stone lamps illuminated a great many black cages, as well as the faces of the numerous demi-humans walking among them. The incessant howls and clanging chains all came from inside those cages.

The man wearing goggles spat at the adventurers' feet before standing.

"If only we could find their nest…It's somewhere in the Colossal Tree Labyrinth for sure, so we can't be far."

Grabbing a red spear propped against the wall, the man approached one of the cages in the densely packed array.

The spear's blade was an odd shape, curved and incredibly sharp. Rather than lethal efficiency, this weapon had been designed with the pain of its victims in mind.

"And none of these bastards'll say a stinking thing…damn it all!"

The red blade flashed between the bars of the cage. A dark shadow flailed inside, howling as the spear plunged into its flesh.

The weak, almost pleading whimpering turned to high-pitched screams and ear-splitting squeals. Chains rattled as a crimson fluid splattered across the floor.

The man's face was devoid of emotion as he watched the dark shadow writhe in pain before pulling back the spear.

"Then again, a female vouivre, eh…Now that's a treasure I'd like to get my mitts on."

Tapping the weapon's shaft against his shoulder, the man narrowed his eyes behind the goggles.

"The nineteenth floor, you say? Tell me the details."

"Ah, s-sure…Rivira's adventurers were on a quest to hunt some firebirds when we found it. The place was crawling with them."

A disturbed adventurer responded to the man fidgeting with the blood-covered spear.

"There was some elf rambling about a monster that talked to her, but nothing else. No one took her seriously. I bet the vouivre is still in the Dungeon…if the other monsters didn't do her in already."

The man in the goggles listened to his underling deliver the difficult news. He considered the matter for a moment and then opened his mouth.

"So a bunch of people raised a fuss, yet no one claimed the kill… Could be that some idiot is trying to hide the monster."

The man's lips curled into a smile before the stunned adventurers, but immediately after, he burst into laughter.

"From what I hear, the vouivre's got one hell of a pretty face, yeah? Wouldn't surprise me if some adventurer got carried away and did something insane." With a grin, he added, "Monster fetishes are a thing, after all."

Knowing how adventurers think, no one would pass up the chance to brag about slaying a talking vouivre. Stories about the strange monster should be spreading through Orario like wildfire. The man explained his theory.

"Of course, other monsters could've finished it off, the way you said. And there's still a chance it's wandering around down there. I'll go have a look myself…Also, find out who took part in Rivira's quest—all of them."

Orders received, the adventurers gave him a curt nod before leaving as quickly as they could.

After watching them go out of the corner of his eye, the man in the goggles turned the other way.

"And there you have it…Lord Ikelos, may I rely on your cooperation once more?"

"—Hee-hee, is that how you ask your god for a favor, you arrogant little shit?"

Before the man in goggles was a lone god.

With eyes and hair of the same cerulean shade, the deity wore mostly black clothing over his dark-brown skin. A fake smile was

© Suzuhito Yasuda

etched upon his graceful features, which served as proof of his divinity.

The deity, who resembled a young man, had said nothing during the previous exchange so he could better enjoy the spectacle. He sat atop a stone pedestal, legs crossed.

"Gods can see right through our lies. I'd like you to check out any suspicious individuals I happen to find."

"That sounds absolutely mind-numbing…I'm a god, and you're sending me on an errand?"

The deity—Ikelos—sneered, eliciting a low chuckle from Dix.

"I think you'll find a way to not be too bored, no?"

"…Guess I got no choice, then."

After speaking to his follower, Ikelos put on a grin peculiar to gods starving for "entertainment."

"You better make me laugh this time as well, Dix."

"By your will, My Lord."

Two shadows stretched far into the darkness under the magic-stone lamplight.

Amid the smell of stone and the constant bestial roars echoing in their ears, god and man shared the same thin smile, as though they were reflections of each other.

CHAPTER 3
THE WORLD AND REALITY
AND MONSTERS

"There's a big difference between hearing about it and seeing it with my own eyes. It's a real shock."

Lady Hephaistos says this as she scratches at the patch covering her right eye while inspecting Wiene.

Hearthstone Manor's living room is bathed in morning light. Three deities have come to our home: Lord Takemikazuchi, Lord Miach, and Lady Hephaistos. Their stunned gazes are focused on the vouivre girl hiding behind my back.

"A monster that doesn't attack people…and is capable of communicating."

"This could rewrite our understanding of the mortal world, perhaps even change what we once considered to be common sense."

"I don't think we can neatly sweep this under a rug by just calling it 'Irregular'…"

The gods don troubled expressions as we, *Hestia Familia*, observe from the sidelines.

"So none of you have any experience with this, I take it?" Lady Hestia takes a step closer to her friends and asks one more time, but Lady Hephaistos just shakes her head from side to side.

To disturb even the gods…Wiene's very existence must be extraordinary.

"If anyone were to have any information…wouldn't it be the Guild, I wonder?"

Their conversation continues until Lady Hephaistos's suggestion sends chills up everyone's spines.

Even I react after she brings up the Guild.

"…You may be right. There is a possibility they know more than we do now."

"But do be warned, going to the Guild for information is dangerous."

The Guild acts like the governing body of Orario in addition to its role in managing all Dungeon-related activity. Chances are good that they're more knowledgeable about the current condition of the Dungeon than our lone familia. On the other hand, there's a good chance they'll withhold proprietary knowledge. Low-ranking employees like Eina and others don't know about a lot of things—for example, the top-secret information about our fight with the Black Goliath.

But then again, we'd be in a bad spot if they find out about Wiene. Our familia would obviously be in an incredibly dangerous position if word gets out that we're harboring a monster. Especially Wiene, the epitome of Irregulars. In the worst-case scenario, she could be taken away for experimentation or who knows what…

With all these frightening ideas running through my head, I can't help but agree with Lord Miach and Lord Takemikazuchi's assessment that it's too risky to consult the Guild. My goddess crosses her arms, a sour look on her face.

In the end, Lady Hephaistos says she can't make any promises, but she'll look into this herself and inform us if she comes across anything important.

"As for what we do from here…I'd like for Bell and the others to take a trip to the Dungeon."

After the other deities leave, our goddess faces us as she broaches the topic.

"It's painfully obvious that there's a limit to how much we can learn on the surface. The only option now is to expand our investigation into the Dungeon."

Six days have passed since I met Wiene.

Reviewing all we've learned over those days, the goddess asks us to return to the spot on the nineteenth floor where I found Wiene and search for clues.

"As Lilly mentioned before, we're not the only ones investigating talking monsters. The situation could change at any moment…If we want to make a move, the sooner the better."

"…Yeah. We gotta go."

Mikoto and Haruhime tense up when Lilly reminds them of her first day searching around the city. Welf voices his agreement.

We're just standing around right now. At this rate, the situation might get away from us.

Exchanging nods, we decide to expand our search into the Dungeon.

"Sorry about this, everyone…I want to know what's happening, too. I'm counting on you all."

The goddess looks at all of us in turn.

Remembering the shock of Lady Hephaistos and the other deities after our goddess's earnest intent, I realize all over again that we're entering unknown territory, where even the gods don't know what's happening. My skin is crawling.

"Bell…"

"…It's all right. I'll be back before you know it."

Wiene anxiously glances up at me. I say the usual reassuring words and do my best to smile.

"It's been a while since just the three of us roamed the Dungeon."

"That's because we haven't been shorthanded recently."

I walk out the manor's front gate with Welf, greatsword over his shoulder, and Lilly, backpack strapped behind her.

The ones heading to the Dungeon are Lilly, Welf, and myself. Mikoto and Haruhime are staying behind to take care of Wiene and look after our home.

It's our original three-man cell. How nostalgic. I share a smile with my two friends who've fought alongside me since before they joined my familia.

"Bear in mind that our destination is the nineteenth floor…Honestly, Lilly is concerned about the three of us going on our own. The journey to and from the site plus our investigation might take well over one day."

"Good point. I don't want to be away from home any longer than we have to be."

"Yeah…True…"

Lilly voices her concerns as we head to our home's closest city avenue, Southwest Main Street.

We made it down to the eighteenth floor the other day, but that was as a five-member party. Not to mention Mikoto and Welf had the benefit of Haruhime's Level Boost.

Having traveled to the safe point a few times already, we're quite familiar with the Dungeon layout as well as how to deal with the monsters that spawn on the intervening floors. Getting down there as a three-man party shouldn't be too much of a problem. The only worry is that it might take us a fair bit of time to do it.

Without Mikoto and Haruhime, it's only natural that the danger increases—and relying too heavily on Welf's magic swords and Lilly's stink bombs, which both have a limited number of uses, would be a pretty terrible plan—so we'll have to be more careful and slow down.

And a sappier reason is that I don't want to be away from home for a long time, since we left Wiene and the others there.

Though before I met everybody, I used to go into the Dungeon alone all the time, so I'm fortunate to have these worries at all, but...

As a side note, whenever I visit Rivira, I often hear about solo specialist upper-class adventurers who regularly travel to and from the safe point floor all alone, especially those who are Level 3 like me.

In my case, though, I have an overwhelming lack of experience... and the middle levels—a place one enters fully prepared to die—had given me a complicated kind of trauma. At the very least, I don't particularly want to go any farther into there.

"Aghh..."

I know Welf and I have leveled-up since our first attempts to venture so far down, but we can't let our guard down. Not to mention that we want to get to the nineteenth floor as quickly as possible.

I take in the vast blue sky overhead and try to come up with a good idea...and then the face of a certain adventurer pops into my mind.

Of course *she* could...

"Is there something on my face?"

"Ah, n-no!"

We've come to the always busy West Main Street.

I purposely try to avoid meeting a pair of sky-blue eyes, instead peering at the constant flow of horse-drawn carriages and adventurers passing by.

"Is something wrong, Bell? You've been glancing at Lyu ever since you got here."

"N-no, nothing's wrong…"

We're in front of The Benevolent Mistress.

Syr made lunch for me again today, so I'm swinging by to collect it.

She prepares a meal for me every day, including days we don't go into the Dungeon. On those days she feeds it to the other staff members and asks for feedback…or so I hear. Humbly giving my thanks, I receive the lunch basket from her, but she points out that my gaze keeps wandering toward the elf woman.

It seems my thoughts are showing in my behavior.

Basically, *Is it possible to ask Lyu for help on this trip…?* Or something like that.

Having a former adventurer with amazing skills like hers in our party would all but guarantee us reaching our destination in no time.

But asking her to come just because it would be convenient for us…? I think that's pushing it a bit too far. We couldn't have won the War Game without her, and she's come to our rescue so many times that taking advantage of her like this would be rude.

I force a smile for Syr and Lyu, trying to gloss things over, but…

"Mr. Bell, we have nothing to lose, so please ask Miss Lyu to assist us."

"Huh? Wait a sec—Lilly?"

"We cannot afford to be picky about our methods. We have no choice but to make this request."

…However, Lilly tugs at the back of my shirt and whispers her thoughts.

She's right. It's already pretty late in the morning, so I bet other people like Ouka or Daphne have already led their parties into the Dungeon. It's too late to ask them to accompany us, but still…

I turn around in an effort to dissuade her as quietly as possible, but I give up as soon as Lilly brings up Wiene. There's nothing I can say.

Still indecisive, I face Lyu and Syr again before trying to negotiate.

"...You are attempting to reach the safe point?"

"Y-yes...Is that...too much to ask...after all?"

Leaving out our true destination on the nineteenth floor, I claim that we're trying to reach Rivira instead.

At Lyu's response, my voice and body both get smaller as I watch her standing still, holding one of the bar's trays.

"Bell, why do you want to go all the way there?"

"W-well, you see, there's something we have to do today, kind of like a quest..."

Syr tilts her head, displaying her confusion as I try to sound as convincing as possible...but her expression never changes, and her sky-blue eyes unblinkingly stare at me. I can't meet her gaze, so I let mine wander.

I feel guilty for hiding something in the face of such sincerity.

Lilly and Welf sigh at my suspicious behavior, or rather my inability to lie.

"...Mr. Cranell, I must apologize, but I have much work to attend to at the moment..."

Those were the exact words that I expected, the inevitable rejection—when out of the blue...

"Bell Cranell!"

An assertive voice comes up from behind me.

All of us spin around to find a beautiful, wild woman with one hand resting on her curvy waist.

"A-Aisha?"

My eyes land on Aisha Belka, who's wearing clothing fit for a dancer.

Formerly a high-ranking member of *Ishtar Familia*, she's a second-tier adventurer and a passionate Amazon. She was also one of Haruhime's few allies when she was forced to work as a prostitute.

She has beautiful, long legs; tanned bronze skin, as displayed by her exposed stomach; and most of all, an intense allure emanating from her entire body. Every man on the street is craning his neck for a better look at her.

"Wh-what are you doing here…?"

"Wanted to check up on that scrawny fox and maybe see your face, so I dropped by your home, only to hear that you left for the Dungeon. I was gonna head back without any more fuss, but here you are. Aren't I lucky?"

As Aisha draws closer, her reply sounds convincing.

This isn't the first time that she's paid us a visit to see if Haruhime is doing okay. Welf and Lilly have interacted with her on occasion as well.

Today didn't go as she planned, but she happened to bump into us in the end.

"If you don't mind my asking, what are you all doing hanging out outside a bar?"

Aisha looks back and forth between our groups and asks a question of her own after I quickly introduce her to Lyu and Syr.

I hesitate a little, but then I explain the situation without saying much about Lyu.

"Oh? So you need an escort? I'll take you up on that."

"Huh?!"

"You're just going down to the safe point and coming right back up, yes? Piece of cake."

Everyone is stunned by Aisha's response, including Welf and Lilly—and so are Syr and Lyu.

"A-are you sure…?"

"It's a quest like any other. As long as there's a reward, I got no reason to say no. Plus, I've always wanted to try heading into the Dungeon with you."

The first part was very matter-of-fact, but she said the second bit with a bewitching smile while crossing her arms.

Her clothes are so revealing they could easily be mistaken for underwear, and she's pushing up her ample cleavage, on par with Lady Hestia's. I know Aisha's considerably sultry demeanor has set my cheeks on fire.

…I'm aware that I have trouble interacting with this quintessential Amazon.

Her bold personality is part of it, but the constant sight of her vibrant dark skin along with her provocative cleavage makes me blush furiously. Meanwhile, Lilly's glare and Syr's wide grin are really scaring me.

Sweat drips from my forehead…but honestly, having a second-tier adventurer like her come with us would be a great help. That way, I wouldn't have to drag Lyu into this.

Aisha narrows her eyes the moment that thought crosses my mind.

"But just warning you—I ain't cheap."

"Eek…?!"

Her arms slither around my shoulders like a snake and pull me in close.

I'm terrified even before I feel Aisha's soft body pressed up against mine. Mostly because she's licking her lips right in front of my face.

The scene startles Lilly and Syr, while Welf lets out an exasperated sigh.

Even Lyu, who hasn't said a word, frowns.

"Wh-what's the reward…?!"

"Oh, you remember, right? *Since the last time I missed out on my chance to indulge.*"

Nightmarish memories of being hunted in the Pleasure Quarter flash before my eyes. Aisha's musky perfume and wheat-colored skin bring back the terror I endured that night.

At the carnivorous smile on her lips, all the blood drains from my face, turning me pale as a ghost—

"—Hands off him."

Like a sword flashing by, a wooden tray tears through the air with terrifying speed.

Aisha sidesteps the vertical slash at the last possible moment.

Finally free, I shift my trembling eyes in the direction of the tray-bearer. A cold stare the likes of which I've never seen before is emanating from Lyu's sky-blue eyes.

"Stand back, Amazon. I will not allow you to perform obscene acts on him."

The Amazon warrior isn't fazed by the arctic glare. Instead, she looks excited for a fight, lips curling upward.

"Oh? What's this? Sayin' you got dibs on this male?"

"...Do not misunderstand me. He has already been engaged to his promised partner."

What is she saying?!

"Well, isn't that interesting? I was planning on entrusting him to a little sister of mine."

"Please refrain from saying such ridiculous nonsense. You will only cause trouble for Mr. Cranell."

"Fine, I get it, I get it. We'll have our taste first, and then you and that friend of yours can start off by holding his hands like a bunch of elves."

"I refuse to trust him to someone of such poor character. I advise you and your sister to withdraw."

A fierce argument unfolds right in front of my widened eyes.

Aisha glares down at Lyu with her height advantage, but the elf isn't backing down. I can almost see sparks flying right now. Facts and hypotheticals fly between the two women and—I have no idea what's going on.

...The fastidious elves might have about as much trouble seeing eye to eye with the uninhibited Amazons as they do with dwarves, if their relationship isn't actually worse.

Thinking this, I start sweating bullets as Lyu's menacing eyes meet Aisha's provocative grin.

"Syr, my apologies. I will be absent for half the day. Please inform Mama Mia."

"L-Lyu?"

"This woman is dangerous and cannot be left to her own devices. I will participate in this quest to protect Mr. Cranell's chastity. I shall return by evening. You have my word."

Ch-chastity...?

Lyu didn't take her eyes off Aisha as she spoke. Even Syr is bewildered.

She's absolutely serious about protecting me from Aisha's "evil influence"...

Either she puts this amount of effort into everything she does, or a strong sense of loyalty and courage is motivating her. This is no joke.

"...Well, it appears we've happened to acquire two valuable allies for this journey, and that is a good thing."

"...Must be tough being a famous adventurer, with people keeping an eye on you all the time..."

Lyu is standing between Aisha and me like a knight. I blankly stare at the two of them as Lilly's and Welf's comments reach my ears.

But I think it was the pity in Welf's voice that stung the most.

With Lyu's and Aisha's pledged support, Syr saw us off as we made our way toward the Dungeon.

They were nice enough to adjust to our tight schedule, and rather than going to retrieve their own equipment, the two of them bought weapons and armor at the assorted shops on the way to Babel Tower to save time.

Then, with the assistance of two second-tier adventurers in our temporary party, we breezed through the upper levels in no time flat.

"HAAAAAAAA!!"

Her voice rips through the air with a ferocity worthy of the large weapon in her grip, and she lays waste to several hellhounds in one attack.

We've made it to the rocky cave-like halls of the fourteenth floor. Aisha looks right in her element, grinning from ear to ear as the attacker in our formation. She makes quick work of any monsters in our path.

She purchased an unusually large greatsword at a weapon shop before we entered the Dungeon. It's much sharper and heavier than her usual wooden sword, but she still swings it around like a feather.

No monsters can get close. Her handiwork is eliciting some complaints from our longsword user, Welf.

Aisha was momentarily free after the destruction of *Ishtar Familia*, but she's already undergone Conversion.

As for where she belongs now, I once asked her when she was visiting Haruhime, but…

"That's a secret."

She laughed and dropped the subject.

I'm sure I could find out by perusing the public records on file at the Guild…

"…Lady Aisha? Have you reached Level Four?"

"Sure have, eagle eyes!"

Lilly's ranged support was completely unnecessary with our overwhelmingly powerful front line, so her naturally superior vision allowed her to pick up on some telltale signs and led her to ask. Aisha affirms it without a second thought.

She went from Level 3 to Level 4. In other words, a level-up—reaching a higher plane.

I got the same impression as Lilly when her move turned out to be so much faster than when we fought, but…I can't hide my surprise after hearing it for myself. Aisha looks my way for a moment before charging into another pack of monsters and tearing them to shreds.

"It's because I had to deal with some rough things. I shut myself up in the Dungeon for a while to toughen up a bit."

Apparently, she's been on more than a few of her own adventures since our battle in the Pleasure Quarter.

She was already at the very peak of Level 3 adventurers back when she led the Berbera. It's already been a month since that fight, so the prospect of her leveling up isn't actually that strange.

I can feel it when Aisha grins back at me with lust for battle: *She's moved up.*

Combining ground-shattering kicks with slashes of her greatsword, she smashes in the heads of monster after monster. She flows through the battlefield like a lethal, bladed torrent that leaves gruesome fragments in its wake.

The loose fabric of her revealing outfit shifts along with her hair as the Amazon's momentum guides her away from spurts of blood. Not a drop touches her during the dance of death.

"Antianeira…I see. So this is her."

Lyu whispers Aisha's title to herself from her spot a few steps back from the front line. At almost the same moment, the Dungeon wall cracks open behind the Amazon. I don't even have time to count the creatures pouring out before Lyu cuts them all down with her two shortswords in the blink of an eye.

"Heh, not bad."

"You, too."

Aisha pays Lyu a genuine compliment after watching her wipe out the horde.

Instead of purchasing weapons on our way here, Lyu bought a battle cloth resembling traveler's garb. Combining it with her hooded robe, she's hiding her identity as usual. Dressing the same way she did during the War Game would only attract unwanted attention, so she's settled into a plain outfit. The only weapons she has on her are the two shortswords she apparently carries at all times.

Aisha might have caught on to who she is.

But she doesn't say anything.

She must've considered it a minor detail in light of the current battle and only hacks her way through the waves of monsters alongside the hooded warrior from the War Game.

"—KIIIH!!"

"!"

The devastating power of our front line blazes a path through the Dungeon.

Welf and I, who are on standby in the middle ranks, suddenly come under attack from monsters emerging from an adjacent passageway.

It's a swarm of rabbit monsters, al-miraj. Welf engages the first wave, slicing down several with a swing of his greatsword. I'm slow to react beside him, and they launch a flood of nature weapons—stone tomahawks—right at me.

I knock each of the incoming tomahawks away with the Hestia Knife and Ushiwakamaru-Nishiki. The disarmed al-miraj give in to their monster instincts and charge directly at us, the horns on their heads leading the way.

Weaving in and out of their attacks, I block one head-on, knock it off balance, and line up the counterstrike—

"—!"

My body slows down just before making contact.

"Bell!"

"Mr. Bell!"

Something about seeing my reflection in its big red eyes causes me to hesitate.

In fact, I've come to a complete stop. Welf's and Lilly's yells ring in my ears as the al-miraj's red irises narrow. It jumps directly for my breastplate.

It hits me dead center, and the impact knocks me off balance.

Crap—!

Landing flat on my back, more al-miraj converge on me.

This is ba—!

Just as I try to raise a blade that will never make it in time—a wind passes over me.

"KIH—?!"

A hooded robe flutters; four monsters succumb to flashes of silver light.

More accurately, they crumble into ash moments later, their magic stones shattered.

The shadow that saved my life makes quick work of the remaining monsters.

"...Th-thanks, Lyu."

Dropping back from the front lines, Lyu wiped out all the enemies in an instant.

She offers me her hand, which I take, staggering to my feet.

"Seriously, that was pathetic. What a letdown, Bell Cranell."

The battle over, Aisha walks up to us, tapping the blunt edge of her greatsword against her shoulder with extreme disappointment.

After all, I'm Level 3, and a middle-level monster just got the best of me. It *is* a letdown.

The censuring look in her eyes says, *You are a man who defeated me in battle.*

There's no way I can respond after that embarrassment.

"Mr. Cranell, that was not like you."

Lyu watches me from beneath her hood as she approaches.

"Has something happened?"

"……"

Her tone is soft, as if trying to protect my feelings, but all I can do is stare at the floor.

Spending so much time with Wiene has affected me more than I thought.

Will other monsters we encounter start talking, the way she did?

Are they all capable of the same thoughts and feelings that we are? Can they all cry?

I haven't done anything since we came into the Dungeon, letting everyone else deal with the monsters.

This has never happened before.

Welf and Lilly silently watch me with knowing expressions.

I can't keep going like this…

It won't end well.

I have to flip the switch. This is just wasting Lyu's and Aisha's time.

I tell myself that over and over while looking at my clenched fist.

The party presses forward again after I say a quick apology.

But even so…

I can't get Wiene's face out of my head, and there's no silencing the doubt in my heart.

Bell's party arrived at the eighteenth floor.

Thanks in large part to the exploits of Lyu and Aisha—and to the fact that other adventurers had already exterminated the floor boss on the seventeenth floor, Goliath—it took them only three hours.

They passed beneath the "afternoon" light shining down from the crystals far above. The brightest of them all was a mum-shaped formation that grew out from the ceiling's center like an upside-down blossom. The adventurers formed a loose line as they journeyed toward Rivira, the settlement that had been built on a rocky island in the middle of the lake on the west side of the floor.

As always, it was bustling with upper-class adventurers looking to rest and restock in the relay town.

"—So when are the boys coming back?"

"How should Lilly know? Boys will be boys, and there are things that only they can attend to, yes?"

Aisha spoke up amid the tents filled with weapons and items for sale and sparkling crystals lining the street.

She turned around at a particularly large crystal column at a corner. Lilly casually answered while adjusting the straps of her bulging backpack, as the Amazon glanced at the heavily armored adventurers walking by.

Only Lilly, Aisha, and Lyu were at the street corner.

"You played me good. Never thought the two of them would leave you behind and head off on their own."

Bell and Welf had excused themselves by saying, "We'll sell off some drop items and be right back," and left the group.

The girls hadn't caught a single glimpse of the pair since then.

"You said you had business on this floor? Are we not allowed to know?"

"Miss Aisha, what are you talking about? Lilly doesn't understand."

Refusing to give in, Lilly kept up the facade with a satisfied smile.

"Cheeky runt," Aisha muttered through a mirthless grin.

Beside them, a long sigh escaped Lyu's hood.

"Should we have said something to Lyu and Aisha before we left...?"

"You know as well as I do we can't have them with us while we look around. Let Li'l E handle it."

Welf and I walk shoulder to shoulder through the labyrinth of trees.

Lyu and Aisha got us to the safe point, but we came down to the nineteenth floor, the Colossal Tree Labyrinth, on our own. The two of us set foot onto the floor where I met Wiene.

"Don't forget, those two are adventurers, too. They agreed to this 'quest,' so there's no need to tell them anything else."

Adventurers need to understand only what their mission is and how to carry it out—nothing more, nothing less. Unnecessary details just get in the way. Welf flashes a grin as he explains this unwritten rule among adventurers.

I still feel bad for leaving Lyu and Aisha in the dark...but it's just as Welf says. Our top priority is keeping Wiene a secret. We had no choice but to split up.

Somehow, I manage to smile back and change my focus to the task at hand.

"I know we just got here and all...but this level is completely different from what we've seen so far."

On high alert, Welf makes his passing comment as we head through the particularly wide passageway.

Tree bark covers every bit of the Dungeon walls here, making it look and feel as though we're exploring the inside of the giant tree. As it occurs to me that the route is as complex as a mess of intertwining branches itself, we spot a narrow path at least ten meders above our heads. A long series of bumpy tree roots come together there, forming a staircase. There's something around every turn that goes to show the nineteenth floor is much bigger than I thought.

I'm used to bright spots on the ceiling providing light, but not here. Instead, the darkness is kept at bay by bioluminescent moss growing thickly along the ceiling, walls, and floor, sparkling like stars in a night sky. Their beautiful blue radiance is so fascinating that I have to remind myself I'm in the Dungeon.

Welf is right: This floor is completely different from any other area we've explored.

I'm used to the many crystals and various biomes of the Under

Resort, but the true meaning of the word *uncharted* is striking me anew.

"I bet *Miach Familia*'s going to start sending us down here on quests a lot more from now on."

"Ah-ha-ha…"

All the plants in here have distinctive smells, including some sweet, flowerlike aromas with potential to beguile adventurers.

There's a far greater variety of flora in the Colossal Tree Labyrinth than just trees and moss. White flowers are blooming from the crease where wall meets ceiling overhead. A cluster of giant mushrooms comes into view after we round a corner. A lot of these are the main ingredients for potions and other items. It's amazing. We could take some back with us right now.

Strangely colored grasses in various shades, a wall covered in thorny vines, small golden flowers that blossom where the path forks, blue liquid dripping from the ceiling to form a puddle on the floor…There are so many rarities around us that chemists would love to get their hands on. The things they wish for literally grow on trees down here.

"Bell, I'll lead the way. This is a good chance for me to get some excelia."

Still as alert as ever, Welf has been nice enough to keep talking to me like we're chatting back at home.

I'm sure he's trying to keep my spirits high, since I can't put up a decent fight right now.

Having never been here before, both of us are really on edge. We're beyond the safe point of the eighteenth floor. Many people call the thirteenth floor the "First Line" because it's the start of the Cave Labyrinth. Even though it's still part of the middle levels, you'd be better off considering everything beyond as a completely different world.

Not only do adventurers have to contend with the fearsome potential of bugbears and mad beetles and the ranged attacks of gun libellulas and firebirds, but monsters in this area are particularly good at inflicting Status effects. Having a large supply of antidotes helps, but possessing the Advanced Ability Immunity is considered to be the key to clearing floors in the Colossal Tree Labyrinth.

The middle levels end at the twenty-third floor. Advancing to the twenty-fourth floor requires a Status above Level 2 as well as a party you can trust...I wonder if our two-man cell, with me at Level 3 and Welf at Level 2, is strong enough for the nineteenth floor. If we don't take everything head-on and avoid battle as much as possible, I think we should do okay.

Lilly equipped me with a dagger-size Crozzo Magic Sword and a couple of Malboro stink bombs in case things get dicey.

I think the main source of my anxiety is that we're not used to this floor yet.

"Tsk...mad beetles and gun libellulas."

"They're blocking the way forward...Let's go!"

A swarm of mad beetles blocks our advance while a few of the dragonfly monsters known as gun libellulas zip around through the air. Welf's black robe flies out behind him as he charges toward the group of insect monsters, our first encounter on the nineteenth floor.

He's wearing Lilly's Goliath Robe over his usual workman's jacket.

It's a protective item capable of repelling everything from monster claws to flames. Lilly insisted Welf take it with him when she found out we'd be moving ahead as a two-man cell.

Its performance is great in the Colossal Tree Labyrinth. Not only does it repel the mad beetles' hooked pincers, but it even deflects the ranged attacks from the gun libellulas' spear-like abdomens.

With hardly a scratch on him thanks to the robe, Welf drives into the mad beetles with a complicated expression.

...I can't afford to hesitate!

I clench my fist while watching Welf make headway against the swarm.

If I become a burden, we'll end up in a situation we can't recover from. Welf can fight alone for only so long before his equipment and items can't take any more.

Silencing my unresolved doubts, I launch several Firebolts in quick succession and shoot down the gun libellula flying above us, sweeping the skies clean.

The Hestia Knife pulses with violet light, as if responding to the latest Status I received from my goddess. I drive the blade into every creature that comes into range, and their dying cries fill the passageway as Welf and I advance.

Then, a short while after deviating from the main path leading to the next floor…

"We getting close?"

"Yes…I found Wiene around here."

Careful not to let my guard down, I've been checking the simple map stuffed into a pouch on my belt over and over, holding it up to the light to confirm where we are until I recognize our position.

We're in a tree-lined path where many passageways meet. The ceiling is high overhead, and there's a large hill in the distance covered in tree roots. From here, it almost looks like the base of a mountain.

I'd bet that's how Wiene hurt her leg, falling down that hill.

"Didn't see anything all that useful on the way here…"

"Wish I knew what 'useful' meant…" Welf adds with a sigh as we make our way toward the steep incline.

We come to a stop in front of a lone tree surrounded by thick underbrush.

It's the place where Wiene hid after hurting her leg—and the place we first met.

…*Should've known it wouldn't be that easy.*

No matter how many leaves we push aside, no clues present themselves.

I check our location again; we're on the west side of the map. There's a pantry farther west. It's a good distance away, but if Wiene came from that direction and fell down the slope, that would mean she was born somewhere over there.

*We might need to press even farther in…*Just as that thought crosses my mind—

…*An adventurer?*

—a humanoid figure appears from another passageway.

A hooded robe shrouds their tall frame. The person must be wearing chest armor, because their torso is much thicker than their lower body. Their height is about the same as Welf's. While I can't really tell their race or gender thanks to the cloak, for some reason, I get the impression they're female.

The hooded figure seems to be searching for something, their head turning this way and that.

Following the same path that Welf and I took, the stranger approaches.

Welf and I, having chosen a suspicious place to stop, exchange abrupt glances and immediately pretend like we've been collecting raw ingredients for an item.

After a bit, we stand up. For the moment, we head back the way we came, passing by the hooded figure moving in the opposite direction.

"—You…smell like my kind."

In that instant…

…a penetratingly cold voice enters my ear as the robed figure's head swivels toward us as we pass.

Shiver.

Chills running up our spines, Welf and I leap backward.

Every fiber of my being screams at me to put some distance between us, and my body quickly responds.

Feet firmly planted on the ground, the figure slowly turns in our direction, shoulders squared.

"…What was that?"

The words that brushed my ears in that moment were clumsily formed; however, the pressure emanating from the figure increased tenfold.

Welf whispers to himself in shock beside me while my heart races.

"……"

The stranger has fixed an unmoving stare on us.

Within the depths of the hood, the narrow silhouette of a feminine face appears.

But those blue eyes, zeroing in on Welf and me like those of a bird of prey, call to mind the ocean or perhaps the sky.

"The ones who kidnapped my comrades—was it you?"

"—?!"

They exude bloodlust beyond reason.

It's incredibly ferocious, like that of an animal.

Like that of a monster.

An aura that mere people could never hope to replicate: an instinctual urge to kill.

Those blue irises under the hood shift—becoming vertical slits.

—No way.

The pronunciation of a child, a hostile gaze, and, most of all, an extreme case of déjà vu—Wiene's face flashes through my mind.

Welf and I struggle against our shock while speculating about the true identity of the stranger.

"...No, it can't be. You don't smell like blood."

We're frozen in place. But as soon as the wave of hostility hits us, the figure's high-bridged nose twitches slightly. The killing aura suddenly vanishes.

The slit pupils return to normal. Now the beautiful eyes reflect calm rationality while studying us.

"Perhaps you are the ones that Fels mentioned?"

"Fels...?"

"What the hell are you talking about?!"

I can only mumble in confusion as Welf pushes through his own disorientation to deliver an angry shout.

I can't discern what the stranger's statement is supposed to mean, but they said what sounded like a person's name.

There's something beguiling about the crystal-clear tone and rhythm of that voice. Regardless, I'm totally lost.

Being this speechless isn't just pathetic; it's painful. I can't even think. This turn of events has shocked me so badly that my throat has gone bone dry.

"……"

The mysterious person—no, "she" stays silent.

This is awkward. Monsters are howling somewhere off in the distance, but my ears hardly register the sound. It's like we're in our own little bubble deep in the Dungeon.

There are about five meders between us. She's facing this way with her back to the hill and not budging.

Time grinds to a complete stop. After what feels like an eternity, she opens her mouth to speak again.

"I have a question for you two. Can we all coexist?"

"Wha…"

What does that have to do with anything? Her question came from so far out of the blue that words abandon us.

"Do you think we can hold each other's hands?"

"What are you…?"

"Your kind kills us. And we kill your kind in turn…Is this our destiny? Is it impossible for us to understand each other?"

The questions continue unabated, but there's a common thread through all of them: a refusal to give up hope.

The blue eyes peering out from underneath the hood are half-lidded and weary.

"I…want to bathe in the sunlight. Instead of this closed, dark hell, I want to spread my wings in the world of light."

She looks toward the ceiling, the hem of the robe swishing around her feet.

Her hood shifts just enough for me to catch a glimpse of her face. Like Wiene's, it's stunningly human.

"There's something…different about you two…Maybe I can hope, just a little."

After that, she crouches low—and then she flies off.

""!!""

Still facing forward, she arcs through the air away from us.

Even an adventurer blessed with a Status couldn't possibly imitate this. Light as a bird, she clears the hill in the blink of an eye and is gone a moment later.

Welf and I are in shock…Only then do we notice that several golden feathers have fallen from beneath her robe. They slowly spiral to the floor where she once stood.

"You gotta be kidding me…There's no way…She's…"

Welf whispers in spite of himself as though lost in a daydream.

Standing motionless next to him, I can't agree more.

"The same as…Wiene…"

I can't give voice to anything more than that.

After our shocking meeting.

Welf and I stand there for a short while, but it isn't long before a herd of monsters finds us. We haven't had a chance to collect our thoughts, but we need to start moving again.

We face the monsters and shake them off before retracing our steps back to the main route that will lead us out. Both of us agree that we're too dazed to collect any more information. The truth is, during the attack, things got a little dicey thanks to my inability to focus.

"……"

"……"

Neither of us speaks on the way back.

We still haven't been able to get over the shock of what happened. We're afraid to bring it up—like if we talk now, it'll shatter some weird equilibrium.

With stony faces, we travel through the labyrinth.

"……"

One way or another, we manage to break past every monster we encounter and reach the passageway connecting to the eighteenth floor.

A party of five adventurers appears on the path in front of us. A male human wearing goggles and carrying a peculiar red spear catches my eye.

It's not particularly strange to see our fellow adventurers, though something in my memory is pulling at me. Then I suddenly realize:

The four demi-humans behind the goggled adventurer are the same men and women who chased after Wiene, and the ones who I had managed to slip by with my acting.

I hide my face as quickly as I can. Welf must've noticed something was up, because he subtly changes his path, shielding me from their line of sight.

Then, once we pass each other, I get a strange sense that the man wearing goggles is watching me.

"……"

Moving as little as possible, I glance at them out of the corner of my eye. Sure enough, all of them are staring at us.

"*Hestia Familia*…Little Rookie, eh?"

"Yeah…that's him, all right. That punk was recruited for Rivira's quest!"

"Was he now?" said the goggled man with a sneer as the boy disappeared up the tunnel leading to the eighteenth floor.

"What do you think he was doing, sneaking around down here with hardly anyone else with him?"

"…Yo, Dix, you can't mean…?"

"Yeah, something's off. It's time for our god to get serious and do some probing, don't you think?"

After returning to the safe point in one piece, we rendezvous with Lilly and the others.

Aisha starts complaining about us going off on our own, but when we don't respond, she notices our odd behavior and decides to not criticize us any further. Lyu also remains silent, not asking any questions, either.

While I feel guilty about what we did, I'm too rattled to be concerned about it right now. We head for the surface right away.

"Don't worry about a reward. Let's leave it as a favor you owe me," Aisha says with a smile before parting ways with us.

I doubt she'd ever admit to it, but I'm really grateful for her thoughtfulness.

"Mr. Cranell, please consult me should you find yourself in any hardship. I am not very capable, but I will do what I can."

With those considerate words, Lyu returns to her workplace.

"......"

I wind my way through the city streets alone.

As soon as we exit Babel Tower, I go off on my own without Lilly or Welf.

Sometimes I need to be by myself to get my thoughts in order.

It's still early evening. The sun might be on its way down in the west, but the sky above me is still mostly blue. Bringing Lyu and Aisha along turned our fact-finding mission into a day trip.

My feet take me around the city, away from the main street crowd and noise.

"Ohhh? Is it my lucky day or what? Hey there, Little Rookie."

"......?"

After idly walking about, just as I start thinking about finally heading home, I hear it.

Along my route back to Hearthstone Manor, on Southwest Main Street, a certain deity calls out to me.

I don't recognize him...It's probably the first time we've spoken.

He has deep-blue eyes and hair, as well as darkly tanned skin. He's of average height, and his clothes are mostly black. I think about how he reminds me of a god—or more precisely, has a god's frivolous smile on his face—and he sociably approaches.

After he calls me by my title, I come to a stop and readjust my posture.

"Um...Is there something I can do for you?"

"Hee-hee, no need to be so guarded—though I guess that's impossible, huh? We gods do warrant caution, after all, right?"

Ever since I received my first level-up, unfamiliar deities have made passes at me, and if not a pass then something else. Anyway, since then, the number of messes I've gotten into in this town has increased dramatically. I can't even count how many at this point.

It's rude, but I slouch slightly in reluctance while the god laughs again. "Hee-hee! The name's Ikelos. Good meeting you."

"Lord…Ikelos? So, what do you need from—?"

"Just listen. Those arrogant kids of mine are pushing me around at the moment."

After instructing me to listen, he starts listing complaints about his followers while continuously circling around me, sometimes peering at my face, other times patting my shoulder like we've known each other forever. Lord Ikelos's behavior has gone past excessive friendliness to just mockery, leaving me absolutely bewildered.

Confronted with this incomprehensible conversation, I suddenly recall Lady Hestia's advice: *If some weird god seems like they're going to catch you, hurry up and run away!* I start wondering whether it would be better to forgo etiquette in a situation like this while sweat rolls down my face and—

"Know anything about a talking vouivre?"

"……………"

Lord Ikelos comes up from behind me and whispers those words without any warning. It feels like something has my heart in a death grip.

"I hear she's got a daaamn fine face…Came from the nineteenth floor apparently. Maaan, I'd love to get just one look."

He's trying to get information out of me, I realize.

Lord Ikelos's syrupy voice fills my ears, along with the sound of my rapidly increasing pulse.

It feels like every vein in my body is quivering, and my palms get clammy.

Unable to answer, I sluggishly turn to face him as though all my joints have rusted over.

His lips quirk upward, a little too close for comfort.

Those dark-blue eyes sharpen as if they can see into my heart.

"Sooo if you happen to know—"

"Bell."

A new voice interrupts while I stand like a frozen statue.

This newcomer cuts off Lord Ikelos in midsentence.

"L-Lord Hermes...?"

"Well, well. What a coincidence, meeting you here."

Lord Ikelos and I turn toward the speaker: Lord Hermes sporting his usual feathered hat and dandy's smile.

He raises a hand at us as he walks closer.

"Bell, you can go now."

"Huh...?"

"A deity is giving you trouble, right? I don't need the whole story to notice that."

Lord Hermes chuckles at my stunned silence before shifting his attention away from me.

As though we had changed places, he casts a sideways glance at the ever-grinning Lord Ikelos.

"Besides, Ikelos and I need to have a little chat."

Running his finger along the brim of his hat, Hermes puts on a thin smile.

"Move along, Bell."

"S-sorry...Excuse me."

At Lord Hermes's insistence, I don't even say a proper farewell as I turn my back to them.

I quicken my pace without so much as a glance in Lord Ikelos's direction.

"What gives, Hermes? Couldn't you see I was in the middle of talking with the Little Rookie?"

"Well, I just couldn't stand to watch a god sink his poisonous fangs into such a sweet child, now could I?"

"Hee-hee, what a terrible thing to say."

Hermes and Ikelos exchanged quips without making direct eye contact after Bell left.

The two then left the main avenue and exited into a small plaza furnished with a water fountain, as though they had planned this all along. There wasn't a single person around, making their conversation feel like a clandestine meeting.

"I paid your home a visit, only to find it empty...It took quite a bit of effort to track you down."

"Ah, my bad, my bad. The place just didn't feel like home anymore, so I guess I moved."

"It might be a good idea to give the Guild a heads-up when you do that, Ikelos."

Hermes and Ikelos conversed smoothly. Both seemed to know a great deal about the other, hinting at a long relationship.

At any rate, both gods appeared more interested in probing each other for information rather than catching up on old times.

"So? What's this 'chat' we need to have, Hermes?"

"Oh, nothing major. There's something I want to ask you...A little bird told me that *Ikelos Familia* was involved in an Orario smuggling ring."

"Hey, hey, where'd you hear that? How can you be sure it's legit?"

"Let me see...I think it was Elurian royalty?"

"...Hee-hee. A 'little' bird, you say? You've been venturing out pretty far to dig up dirt on this."

Ikelos seemed to quickly realize Hermes's information was too good. His grin deepened.

"Am I a suspect, Hermes?"

"As much as it pains me to investigate an old friend from our days back in the heavenly realm...Ikelos, in the past your familia was on the list of candidates aiming to join the Evils."

"Ugh, how many times do I have to tell you those charges were bullshit? At the very least, I never claimed to be an evil god."

Agitated by the accusation, Ikelos deftly denied it and evaded his question.

All the while, Hermes kept a constant eye on him from beneath the brim of his hat, his characteristic smile still on his lips.

"I also have some interesting news."

"Oh? Do tell."

"Monsters, normal and *otherwise*, are being taken out of Orario and sold around the world. It's almost like someone's interested in spreading chaos."

It was at that very moment…

Ikelos's dark-blue eyes opened wide as Hermes struck straight to the heart of the matter. The edges of his mouth seemed about to split open with his grin.

"Hee! Hee-hee-hee-hee-hee-hee-hee…!! Are you saying that's what I want, Hermes? That I have the dream of beasts—to strew nightmares across the mortal realm?! Now that's interesting!!"

Ikelos burst into laughter as if the idea thrilled him to no end.

Hermes stayed quiet, watching the other god clutch his stomach in the throes of mirth.

Once the echoes had faded into the darkening sky, Ikelos straightened with a smile on his face.

"Sorry to say it, but that's got nothing to do with me. I didn't give those orders. My brats are the ones going wild."

Ikelos laid it out plain and simple, uninterested in hiding anything.

"I gotta tell you, though, there's way fewer idiots in my familia these days; just a lot more arrogant wise guys. They don't show the divine any respect whatsoever. Use me to run some stupid errands."

"……"

"But…everything they do is ridiculous crap. It's hilarious."

Only a deity who was desperately trying to contain their bliss would show a smile like his.

From a god's perspective, it was men's folly that made them interesting—that made a front-row seat to the show so enticing.

"It's the god's responsibility to rein in his familia."

"You can't seriously believe that, Hermes. The brats may be able to put up with hardship, but they can't resist pleasure. Are we gods not the same? I can relate, painfully so. And that's why," Ikelos continued, "as long as they keep me entertained, I won't get in their way."

Ikelos leaned in close to Hermes's face and declared his opinion point-blank.

"You can smash my head in if you like. Give me a one-way trip back to the upper world. But that's not gonna stop my brats now, will it? It might give 'em a little trouble, but it's only a matter of time before they sign up with someone else."

"I figured."

"Ehh, have a look for yourself. Use all the little brats of yours hiding around here to give me and mine a once-over. I couldn't care less. Have at it. More interesting that way."

At the risk of ruining himself and his followers—perhaps even looking forward to the demise of his own familia—Ikelos let those words hang in the air.

Thin smile still on his face, the god left the small plaza.

Hermes watched him go and sighed as soon as Ikelos was out of sight.

"My, my. Nothing nastier than a god desperate for some entertainment."

"Look who's talking."

Hermes's followers heckled their god from their hiding places around him.

The last rays of sunlight that still reached over the city wall illuminated *Hestia Familia*'s home.

Four people were currently inside while Bell's party was out gathering information: Mikoto, Haruhime, Wiene, and the goddess Hestia. After asking Hephaistos for the day off earlier in the morning, the deity awaited Bell's return along with her followers.

Each of the women stayed busy.

Hestia spent the day poring over her collection of books in search of information about everything from monsters to Orario's history.

Meanwhile, Mikoto patrolled the passageways, ever vigilant.

Taking care of Wiene fell to Haruhime.

"Haruhime, found you!"

"Hee-hee, indeed you have."

Wiene dived into a shadow cast by one of the inner walls and wrapped her arms around Haruhime in her maid's attire.

The two were playing hide-and-seek. It was one of the games that Bell and Haruhime had taught Wiene when the two of them were in charge of looking after her.

Today, after making Wiene promise to never go outside and only play in the inner garden, the two girls took turns.

"Now you're 'it,' Haruhime!"

"Yes. I am going to count now."

"Ooone, twooo," Haruhime called as she turned to face the wall of the inner garden.

Wiene quietly snuck away, running with a grin on her face.

Robe swaying at her feet, she looked for a suitable hiding place.

...I wonder when Bell will come home.

Right as she was about to crouch behind a planter full of flowers...

Wiene's expression clouded over as thoughts of the absent Bell crossed her mind.

He had always been right by her side, until now. Haruhime was with her, as usual, but it just wasn't the same without him.

That twinge of loneliness was making her anxious.

In a dark world where everyone and everything tried to hurt her, that boy's smile had become the beacon of light that saved her from isolation.

Like a child yearning for a parent's warmth, the young vouivre girl couldn't help but long for him.

"......"

Wiene glanced up to the third floor of the manor before her gaze fell on the renart, who was still facing the wall.

After a moment's hesitation, she decided to break her promise and leave the inner garden.

The urge to visit Bell's room on the third floor drew her through the passageways like a magnet.

She found her way to an unlocked door. *Creak.* The hinges groaned as Wiene pushed it open and cautiously peeked inside.

The room's owner nowhere to be found, the girl quietly made her way toward the pile of folded blankets on top of his bed.

Wrapping one around her shoulders, she slowly rubbed her cheek against it.

"Bell's...smell..."

Taking in as much as she could with one long whiff, Wiene buried her face in the sheets.

She curled up into a ball as her mind filled with memories of the boy who had always slept right next to her.

"...?"

Without warning—

People approached along the hallway.

Four in all.

Proceeding from the other end of the long passageway, their footsteps entered the room right next door, one not in use.

Thinking it a little strange, Wiene felt her heart skip a beat, believing she'd get a lecture if discovered. She held her breath in an effort to escape detection—

"Another monster, not just Wiene?"

—Voices from the other room reached her ears.

Amber eyes went wide.

Silver-blue hair rustled.

Ears, sharper and longer that an elf's, twitched back and forth. They originally allowed her to detect intruders from far away in the vast Dungeon, but now they allowed her to pick up the details of the discussion on the other side of the wall.

Wiene soundlessly sat up in bed before she realized what she was doing.

She quietly placed her ear to the wall.

"Are you sure, Welf?"

"Absolutely. It was at the same place Bell met Wiene on the nineteenth floor..."

Welf nodded. His face stayed eerily still despite Hestia's surprise.

Welf and Lilly had come directly home after Bell went off on his own. Hestia and Mikoto had convinced them to meet secretly on the third floor.

To make sure Wiene—and Haruhime, who had grown close to her—didn't overhear.

"We talked. It said that we 'smelled like her kind'…It was probably talking about Wiene."

"Another being similar to Lady Wiene…I never thought there could be more…"

Mikoto couldn't hide her shock as Welf went into detail about their encounter. As she fell silent, so did Lilly next to her

"…Welf, what was your impression of it?" Hestia asked.

"At the very least, it seemed to be more experienced than Wiene. Its pronunciation was a bit odd, but it hid itself with a robe, pretended to be an adventurer…That, and I think it knew something."

A small noise escaped Hestia's throat at Welf's answer. Mikoto gulped as well.

The atmosphere suddenly became much heavier. Lilly, who had been silent up to that point, opened her mouth to speak.

"Lilly thinks we should stop harboring Miss Wiene."

"!!"

All eyes turned to Lilly.

The first one to recover was Mikoto.

"Lady Lilly, what are you saying?!"

"Lilly will be blunt. We are on the cusp of a very serious situation. An Irregular that not even the gods can comprehend, other groups on the prowl for information about talking monsters…Now that we've discovered other monsters able to speak, we can no longer afford to wait."

Her point was that these Irregulars were at the heart of a major disturbance, and they were getting sucked in.

Using information she had gathered at different bars and other hubs over the past week, Lilly painted an objective picture of the situation.

"However, if we stop protecting her...then what will happen to Lady Wiene? Should we abandon her, she'll...!"

"...It may be difficult, but there's a chance for her outside the city wall. She's a vouivre. Familias outside Orario and monsters living on the surface would pose little threat to her."

Born in the middle levels, she hailed from the most powerful type of monsters: dragons.

Lilly maintained a neutral expression and explained that the vouivre girl's potential strength would be all the protection she needed.

"She can live out her life hidden in the Deep Forest Seoro."

"Lady Lilly...!!"

Mikoto, ever loyal to her friend Haruhime, raised her eyebrows in anger.

Lilly watched her ally's impassioned plea coldly.

"Then tell me this: What will happen if that girl stays here?"

"!"

"Is it possible to keep her hidden from everyone indefinitely just as things are now? Once certain things are set in motion, the situation won't allow the status quo to continue. At present, *Hermes Familia* is actively moving at someone's or *something's* request."

Lilly was so devoid of emotion that her face reminded Mikoto of traditional masks from her homeland in the Far East.

"Will people believe that this completely unrestrained monster has been tamed? Not likely. Our familia has no officially recognized tamers registered with the Guild. What's worse, anyone who sees her beauty will suspect something *else* is taking place."

"......"

"Should other deities catch wind of the situation, they will surely descend on us like wolves to watch the slaughter. Our familia is on thin ice as it is. Should this come to pass, Lilly anticipates nothing but more difficulty paying off our debts."

She explained with an uncharacteristically long lecture—still in a deadpan, matter-of-fact tone.

The overwhelming force of her argument left Mikoto with nothing to say in response.

Neither Hestia nor Welf had anything to add, standing with their mouths closed in the oppressive atmosphere. It was just as Lilly said. Right now, they were trapped in a maze with no exit.

"The girl is, in a figurative sense, a bomb. Even if all is fine now, there is no doubt she will put our familia in danger sooner or later… Mr. Bell is too kindhearted to see reason. It is up to us to make the decision to protect him, even if he hates us for it."

Lilly lowered her head. She had to hide her contorting face from her allies and will her voice to remain steady as she formed her next words.

"She cannot stay with us…She is…a monster."

The prum weighed the familia's future against the girl and stated her conclusion in no uncertain terms.

Her declaration reached the other side of the wall.

"…It's still too early to think that way, Supporter. You should calm down."

"…Lilly is…sorry."

Hestia stepped in to mitigate the situation.

She first turned to Lilly, who was speaking out of concern for the familia and Bell's safety.

The prum fell to her knees and squeezed out an apology. Welf and Mikoto stood quietly, tight-lipped.

"…?"

Among the motionless group, the first one to notice was Mikoto.

A sound coming from the next room—something moving.

The room's suffocating atmosphere made it difficult for her to connect the dots, almost fatally so.

Tap, tap, tap. Thumping in quick succession. As soon as it clicked, she rushed to the door and jumped into the passageway.

Frantically scanning the hall, she couldn't see anyone.

Welf and the others followed her, just as shocked.

"It couldn't be…"

Heart racing and nerves wound tight—Mikoto realized she wasn't in peak condition.

Despite activating her Skill many times, its hampered range couldn't detect anything in their vicinity.

"Haah…haah…"

Wiene ran.

She dashed through the corridor, down the stairs, out the door.

I…I…!

The words she had overheard during the secret meeting.

—It is up to us to make the decision to protect him.

—She cannot stay with us.

—She is…a monster.

The prum girl's voice haunted her like a curse, stabbing at her heart.

Despite being a monster, she also possessed a heart sensitive to pain. Each syllable of Lilly's words cut deep into her, just like those terrifying swords through her skin.

I can't be together with everyone…? I can't be…with Bell?

Her beautiful silver-blue hair fluttered behind her. The garnet jewel on her forehead pulsed as if screaming into the sky.

Translucent tears fell from her amber eyes.

Bell. Bell! Where's Bell?

She wanted him to say it.

That it wasn't true.

She longed to hear those words just one more time.

"It'll be okay."

She yearned to see his flustered but kind smile, to feel his arms around her. She wanted him to hold her and run his fingers through her hair.

To deny it all.

Please…!

Wiene desperately searched for the boy through teary eyes.

That one desire to see him drove her to flee from the only haven she'd ever known.

Frightened by the presence of people at every turn, she doubled back many times through the backstreets and hid her face beneath her robe's hood.

She rushed headlong into the unknown on a frantic search for the bright smile that had burned its way into her memory.

"Wiene's not here?!" yelled Bell the moment he heard.

It was just before dusk. The boy's mind had been racing nonstop since his encounter with the god Ikelos. After he hurried home, his fears had come to fruition, as if to mock him.

Every member of the familia had convened in the front passage-way, ready to depart at a moment's notice.

Bell froze like a statue. Haruhime threw herself into a deep bow in apology.

"I have no excuse! It was because she left my sight...!"

"I've searched with my Skill, but I'm not getting anything..."

Tears flowed down Haruhime's cheeks. Mikoto stood next to her, downtrodden and frowning.

Her Skill, Yatano Black Crow, allowed her to sense nearby monsters that she had encountered before—but Wiene was not in the manor.

At the news that the ace in the hole provided by Mikoto's Status was no use, Bell could feel the blood draining from his face.

All thoughts of Ikelos were gone from his mind.

"......!"

After explaining their secret meeting that had ended abruptly only a few minutes earlier, Lilly gritted her teeth and clenched her small hand into a fist.

"—We'll search!! Mikoto, come with me!!" Bell took off without missing a beat.

"Yes!" Mikoto set off after him as she responded.

"We're coming, too!"

"I-I as well!"

"She can't have gotten far! Spread out and find her!"

Welf's, Haruhime's, and Hestia's voices echoed through the entrance. Lilly, however, was out the door without a word.

Leaving their home completely empty, all of *Hestia Familia* charged out into the night to pursue the vouivre girl.

Nightlife had completely enveloped the city.

After twilight descended, the streets grew more crowded every moment. Adventurers back from the Dungeon and everyday citizens looking to relax after a hard day's work made their way to the bars.

With the evening rush well under way, each establishment had its doors wide open to invite customers inside. The aroma of meat grilling over charcoal and pungent brandy wafted out onto the streets as bards delighted the masses with beautiful melodies from their harps and lively flute performances.

It was a feast of entertainment for the nose and ears.

Even the quieter corners of the city were coming to life.

"……!"

Wiene watched it all from beneath her hood as she navigated one such street.

For her, seeing so many new things alongside the sheer number of humans and demi-humans in the area was overwhelming. Yet curiosity was the furthest thing from her mind. The music from behind unseen corners, the constant horse-carriage traffic, even the innocent laughter of children playing tag in the street sent shots of adrenaline through her veins. The street's stone surface was cold beneath her bare feet.

Hiding herself entirely with the robe, she was in constant fear that any one of these people would pull a sword on her at any time. She stayed out of sight, keeping to the edge of the streets.

Bell...

Amber eyes sifted through the crowd from deep within her hood, searching for the boy's white hair.

Compared to the main thoroughfares, this street was rather narrow. Her gaze first passed over the throng, then went to the alleyways, and finally shifted all the way to the residential area at the end.

Then, as she was scanning her immediate vicinity…

…she saw it happen.

—*Ah.*

A horse-drawn cart came to a stop in front of the store at the corner. She saw something sway as the horse's whinny filled her ears.

A tall pile of boxes was about to collapse like a house of toy blocks.

One of the restraints must have come loose; she couldn't tell. But that didn't change the fact that the load was going to fall. One of the children playing in the street, a completely unaware chienthrope, was directly in its path.

Wiene's eyes flared open.

The others around her who noticed watched with bated breath, many about to shout a warning.

Several wooden boxes were about to come down on top of the boy.

—*Hurt.*

That would surely bring him pain.

A lot of pain.

Enough to make the child cry. Just like what all those claws and blades had done to her.

No sooner had that thought passed through her mind than her body moved.

"!"

Thud! Wiene kicked off the ground and shot toward the boy like an arrow.

She rushed to the youth's side so quickly she could have teleported to the spot.

When she saw the expression of horror on the boy's face as he became suddenly aware of his precarious situation, she saw herself in front of the firebird's raging flames. Memories of the boy who had saved her flashed before her eyes.

—I have to help.

That thought set off a chain reaction.

Wiene's body changed.

Something *grew* from her back.

Disturbing fleshy sounds erupted from beneath her robe, and her light-blue skin ripped open along with it—and a wing extended.

"—Huh?"

A deafening crash drowned out the child's whisper as the boxes came tumbling down.

Several of them broke open as they struck the stone pavement.

Once the splintering echoes filling the street had faded, frightened demi-human onlookers who hadn't budged began to yell, drawing even more attention.

The broken cartons and their contents lay strewn all over the street. Beer bottles and other trash rolled through the scene as the crowd spotted a child huddled in fear beneath a figure expanding like a predator's widening maw.

Large enough to swallow a man whole.

A single wing, with a light-blue frame and ash-gray skin.

The distinctive wing of the king of monsters—a dragon.

The street that had been bustling just moments ago fell silent.

"……"

Wiene held her wing in a protective arc and looked down at her feet.

The boy didn't have a scratch thanks to her shield. Immense relief flooded through her veins as she made eye contact with the scared child and moved her lips.

"Are you all right?"

However…

"Uu—waaAAAAAAAAAAAAAAAAAAAAAAAAAAAAAAAAAAAA!"

Wiene's voice was lost in the boy's scream.

All the terrified boy could see were piercing amber eyes and a monstrous wing that did not belong on a person's body.

© Suzuhito Yasuc

The panicked demi-human child jumped to his feet and ran, leaving Wiene in stunned confusion.

"Mo—"

"A MONSTERRRRRRRRRRRRRRRR!"

Shrieks tore through the air one after the other.

The child's scream was the spark that ignited the chaos in the quiet street.

Like the retreating tide, the throng tried to put as much distance between Wiene and themselves as possible. Even the horse still attached to the cart took off at full speed. Human mothers pulled their children away; a young werewolf shielded his unconscious lover with his body. A pudgy prum merchant fell to the ground in shock.

A cacophony of footfalls accompanied a chorus of rising screams. The onlookers were on the verge of panic.

The twilit street corner became engulfed in a vortex of terror.

Wiene, at a complete loss for words, stood at the center of this massive semicircle of people.

"A harpy—no, a siren!"

"What's it doing here?!"

The nearby lower-class adventurers drew their weapons, flashing silver.

Wiene gasped and recoiled in fear at the sharp metal surrounding her while the eyes trained on her filled with anger and fear.

The last rays of red sunlight illuminated the mysterious monster wearing a torn robe.

The only parts of the monster's face visible to the bystanders were the two sharp amber eyes lurking in the darkness beneath its hood and her jewel's crimson, bloody glow. Without knowing what she was, they saw only a horrifying three-eyed monster.

The crowd's terror escalated to hate and disgust directed at the cornered one-winged monster.

"M-monster!!"

An instant later, an elf woman threw a stone.

"Ah!"

It hit Wiene square in the head, and the hood did nothing to stop the blow.

That was the trigger.

The panic and fury reached a crescendo. Enraged bystanders picked up projectiles at their feet and flung them at her.

The monster trembled in fright as a rain of stones and rocks descended upon her.

"Begone, monster!!"

"This is our home!"

"Go back to your filthy Dungeon!"

Missiles arced through the air as the ones pelting the small monster laced their words with hatred.

"The hell are you doing? Stop!" "Don't make it angry!" Despite being lower class, the adventurers in the crowd knew what winged monsters could do and desperately tried to intervene. However, the mob couldn't be stopped. An avalanche of angry insults poured onto the monster that dared to set foot in their territory. Hatred flooded toward their age-old enemy.

"Ooph…"

"Whoa. Damn."

Elsewhere, a few deities noticed the commotion.

Climbing nearby buildings for a better view, they watched the scene unfold.

One grimaced, while another was concerned for his safety. The last grinned while taking in the spectacle.

A miniature version of the eternal struggle between men and monsters of the mortal realm was playing out right before their eyes.

"O-ow…That hurts!"

The besieged monster's soft cry went unheard among the mob's relentless shouting.

Although her newly sprouted wing could protect her from the stones, it could do nothing to shield her from the intense loathing.

Her heart wept, and the incessant vitriol of their words gouged deep into her soul.

Tears surfaced in her eyes as she shrank in on herself.

"B-Beeeell…!"

"A monster, here?!"

"Yeah, just a few blocks over!"

The instant he heard those words…

Bell launched himself off the stone pavement and tore through the streets.

"Sir Bell!"

He and Mikoto had been searching as a team up to that point, but he soon left her behind.

Wind whistled by his ears, and his eyes teared up. "*Faster!!*" he yelled at himself, driving his legs as hard as he could.

Wiene!!

As nightfall quickly descended over the city streets, Bell's heart pounded behind his ribs; blood burned in his veins.

He sprinted through the streets, following the directions he had heard, as well as the increasing commotion, toward the girl's location.

Then—

"!!"

There she was, protecting herself from a hail of stones with a large wing he had never seen before.

In Orario's seventh district, on a corner of the west-northwest edge of the city far from Central Park, Wiene was alone, trapped in the center of a storm of antipathy strong enough to intimidate even the boy himself.

"Master Bell!"

"Bell!"

Haruhime and Hestia arrived at the scene at almost the same moment, closely followed by Welf and a winded Mikoto. They stood still for only a few heartbeats.

As for Bell, the sight of tears falling from beneath her hood set his spirit alight.

—*She's crying.*

—*Wiene is crying for help!*

He charged forward.

"Hold up, Bell!"

Welf called out to the boy weaving his way through the mob.

Bell was planning on protecting the monster—in front of this crowd, in front of deities.

There would be no going back if he made it to her. He would become just as hated and feared as the fantastical girl.

Even so, he didn't heed his allies' pleas.

He wouldn't stop. He couldn't abandon her.

Bell closed in, just a few steps away from the tearful Wiene.

However…

A shadow made it through the mob just before the boy.

"?!"

Paying no heed to the stones, the small, robed figure rushed to Wiene's side.

It was a beautiful young elf, long golden hair running down her back.

No one had expected to see a child-size demi-human burst onto the scene, and the crowd stayed their hands in surprise. Now that there were no painful stones raining down on them, the mysterious 120-celch-tall figure used the reprieve to grab Wiene's hand.

Members of *Hestia Familia* were just as shocked as the rest of the crowd to see her guide the monster toward an adjacent alleyway. Bell was no different, eyes going wide as the elf girl met his gaze—with chestnut-colored eyes. Everything clicked.

—*Lilly!*

She had disguised herself with her magic skill, Cinder Ella.

The prum's agility allowed her to reach the vouivre girl before anyone else.

As she dragged the flabbergasted girl behind her, the veiled Lilly yelled directly at Bell:

"To the underground room!!"

Leaving him with that message, Lilly and Wiene disappeared into the alley's dark shadows.

Bell, who had cleared the mob, had an epiphany while the crowd was having a fit trying to process what just happened.

Now I get it!

Remembering where they were, Bell understood the true meaning of Lilly's message.

He sent Hestia a look over his shoulder, and she confirmed her understanding with a strong nod.

"That's what she meant…!" Welf said with a smile as he worked it out, too.

"Let's get going!"

"A-and where are we going to?"

Lilly had purposely omitted key pieces of information from her message to prevent others from finding their rendezvous point, which meant Haruhime was in the dark.

Bell and the others left the confused throng behind, departing the scene as quickly as possible.

"To our hidden home!"

The sun has completely set, and now a pale-blue moon hovers above the city in the night sky.

I can tell that much from the silver light filtering between cracks in the rubble.

I take my eyes off the shoddy ceiling and look around at the goddess, Welf, and everyone else gathered here in the narrow underground room.

We're in *Hestia Familia*'s former home, a chamber hidden under a church.

We came to this secret underground area per Lilly's instructions when she had Wiene in tow.

The church itself was destroyed by *Apollo Familia* during the lead-up to the War Game, and we were forced to move…but compared to the wreckage upstairs, the basement still resembles what it once was.

"That was some good thinking, Supporter, using this room as a hiding place."

"Lilly heard about it from Mr. Welf, when he came back here to retrieve a drop item..."

Welf and I came back here a while ago to retrieve the money and drop items, like Goliath's Hide, that were still in here. It's a good thing we didn't bother putting the debris back over the entrance when we left, because the path came in handy. Thoughts of that day flit through my mind as I listen to the hushed conversation of Lilly and the goddess.

There's no way anyone could live here, but it's more than good enough to serve as a meeting place in an emergency. There's a pile of rubble directly overhead, so I guess this is now our hidden base.

I wonder what's going on outside...I bet the Guild has gotten involved by now.

But we decided to stay here until the dust settles.

"*Sob, hic...sob...!*"

Soft weeping echoes throughout the underground room.

The source is Wiene, who is currently latched onto me.

Her new wing is folded up on top of her back, but it's still big enough to cover half her body.

Apparently, it sprouted when she tried to protect an unfamiliar child.

The atmosphere is heavy. Everyone—from Lilly and Welf leaning against the wall to Mikoto and Haruhime lingering in the corner and the goddess sitting on the dusty bed—looks sullen. Wiene and I sit in the middle on the floor.

...The reality of our situation has been made all too clear today.

Wiene's nature as a monster.

As well as what Lilly and the goddess had warned us about.

The aura of animosity around monsters and men, the overwhelming hatred.

People can't let monsters exist.

Their fangs, their claws, and the wings that grant them flight, all inspire fear and make people want to avoid them at all costs.

On the other hand, that reaction originates from a time when the surface races could do little to resist their invasions during the Ancient Times—a latent fear that holds to this day.

Monsters are the enemy.

That undeniable truth has struck all of us hard today.

"Um…Bell."

Wiene looks up at me as everyone else stares at the floor.

Small hands gripping my shirt, her light-blue cheeks streaked with tears, the girl struggles to string words together with trembling lips.

"Can I…not be with Bell?"

I can hear her clinging to faint hope in her voice.

But I can't say anything.

I want to say it'll be okay.

I've said those few words so many times—only now they won't come out.

The truth is too much. Wiene looks at the pathetic expression on my face, her own contorting in sadness.

All I can do is hold her.

On the verge of tears myself, I hold her tiny body as close as I can.

People and monsters aren't meant to coexist.

One look at the ominous dragon wing on her back tells me as much.

The curtain of night fell, shrouding the city in darkness.

Deep in a back alley, far from the noisy main streets…

All was quiet around the ruins of a church that had collapsed on itself. A goddess's statue, reduced to pieces in front of the rubble, lay peacefully silent.

An owl peered at the debris, its silhouette illuminated by the tranquil moonlight.

Vertical patterns ran through its white feathers. Alight on an iron guardrail on the roof of a nearby building, it curled its talons around the top rung.

Just as one of its eyes gleamed in the night, it spread its wings and descended from its perch.

Crossing beneath the ocean of stars that dotted the night sky, the bird suddenly descended and latched onto an outstretched arm—its master's.

"So it was no use after all..."

A black-robed figure standing atop another roof retrieved the owl—its familiar—while muttering quietly to itself.

Its gloves were covered with intricate designs. A blue crystal embedded among them glowed with the same light as the owl's eye.

A long sigh sounded beneath the dark fabric that completely concealed its wearer's true identity.

"I admit I had hope for them...but that day is still too far off."

The owl closed both of its eyes as if sympathizing with its master's words.

The black shadow stared off toward the north, where its familiar had flown in from, and spotted the church ruin.

"We cannot delay any longer."

Its gaze traveled toward the moon.

"The rest is up to you, Ouranos."

Then, it whispered to the white marble pillars of the Pantheon below its feet—Guild Headquarters.

CHAPTER 4
MISSiON

© Suzuhito Yasuda

"A winged monster?"

Freya repeated the news.

"Yes, My Lady. It is said to have appeared during the early evening hours."

"Ah. I thought the city seemed much noisier than usual…So that's what happened."

Freya seemed satisfied with the report of her boaz follower, Ottar.

Countless stars twinkled in the darkened sky. In the middle of the night, Freya sat in an ornate chair on the highest floor of Babel Tower. Ottar patiently waited at her side.

A glass of wine in one hand, she asked him a question:

"What is the damage to the city?"

"Beyond a few isolated bouts of panic, there has been none. Someone took the monster away before it attacked any citizens."

"Someone, you say…Any word from the Guild?"

"None, My Lady. As they are currently gathering information, it is highly unlikely they will contact us at this time."

Out of everything taking place in the city, Ottar made sure only the most important information reached his goddess's ears.

However, Freya wasn't the least bit interested in the rest of her follower's polite and concise report.

At least, not at the moment.

"Shall I order a search?"

"Well…that may be a good idea if the situation escalates, but don't bother for now. Should worse come to worst, we can pay Hermes a visit. I'm sure he is more up-to-date on these developments than we are."

Ah-choo! A sneeze sounded somewhere around the base of Babel, but it was impossible for Freya and Ottar to hear it.

The Goddess of Beauty sat back in her chair, substantial breasts shifting beneath her revealing black nightgown.

"If this is the last we hear of it, then that's all it amounts to. The Guild will contact us if something happens. That will mean they have work for us to do."

Freya Familia's assault and complete eradication of *Ishtar Familia* had resulted in a penalty from the Guild. Now Freya had no choice but to listen to the powerful organization's demands for a little while longer.

While it was well within her ability to reject the penalty by force, it was necessary to maintain the image that the Guild was in control of Orario. Jealous goddesses weren't shy about voicing their opinions. Besides, dealing with a perturbed Loki, who was her uneasy ally, was more trouble than it was worth.

Freya wasn't about to let anyone hold her back, but she also had no interest in becoming an arrogant ruler like Ishtar.

"They may use us again, so please bear with it."

"By your will, My Lady."

Offering a gentle apology to her followers, who would be pressed into service should the Guild call, the goddess smiled.

Then she swirled the wine before bringing the glass to her lips.

"I wonder if this will be entertaining."

She whispered under her breath, a trace of expectation in her voice.

"A humanoid...monster...?"

Aiz asked for clarification after hearing the news.

"Yep, yep! Word has it that it showed up in the western block."

"Not a large-category monster...?"

"Doesn't sound like it. The few lower-class adventurers who saw it called it a harpy or a siren. Probably doesn't have anything to do with what happened during the Monsterphilia, though."

The Amazonian twins Tiona and Tione took turns answering Aiz's questions while the blond human girl tilted her head in confusion.

Chirping birds sang outside the windows bathed in morning light. Aiz's friends told her what had happened the previous night as they strolled through the narrow hallways of *Loki Familia*'s home.

Apparently, it was all the lower-rank adventurers in the familia were talking about.

"I heard there was panic in the streets last night. Guild employees are all over the place asking people what went down."

"…Does Finn know?"

"Of course. He's asking anyone who's free to join the investigation. I think he has his own theory."

Aiz turned to Tione after hearing what Tiona had to say.

"Hmm." The human girl raised her eyes to the ceiling.

Their general had given the order despite their familia having little connection to the incident itself. That meant his love of the city and its citizens was strong enough that he was compelled to get involved.

Most likely, it upset him to know that a monster was lurking somewhere in the city, terrorizing the townspeople.

As an adventurer who called Orario home, Aiz took this news to heart.

"What should we do if we find this monster?"

"Finn said that capturing it alive would be best, but…"

The younger Amazon paused, interlocking her fingers behind her head. Tione finished her sentence.

"If it's endangering lives—kill it on the spot."

Long blond hair flowing down her back, Aiz reached for the hilt of the saber hanging from her waist.

"Understood."

She nodded.

The Guild was in utter chaos.

Reports had come in that an unidentified winged monster had suddenly appeared in Orario's seventh district and attempted to attack a young boy the previous night. Citizens flooded the Guild in droves, demanding to know what had caused such a lapse in security. Some employees fielded questions on the front lines while others worked tirelessly to gather detailed information.

Their first priority was to discover how a monster had been allowed out of the Dungeon and into the city. Not to mention that a certain adventurer had reported seeing a barbarian in an underground tunnel close to an orphanage in Daedalus Street just days prior.

After everything that had happened at the Monsterphilia, their dignity as a governing body was on the line.

What in the world was going on? Guild employees had to find an answer.

"Ughhh. I just pulled an all-nighter, too!!"

"We're in a state of emergency. There's no point in complaining."

The half-elf Eina Tulle was among the Guild employees putting in serious overtime.

Along with her friend and tearful coworker, Misha Frot, she was constantly on the move.

Relaying information from the reception counter to the head offices and visiting the scene of the disturbance to interview witnesses were just the tip of the iceberg. Work piled up faster than it could be completed. All the while, grinning deities got their kicks from the pandemonium and even went as far as providing false tips to make the show more interesting. The Guild employees were forced to authenticate each one before pursuing any leads.

"But, but, but…it just showed up out of nowhere. All the tamed monsters are still in their cages, right?"

"Yes. *Ganesha Familia* has confirmed that all monsters are accounted for."

Misha posed her question, practically bouncing around behind the half-elf as the two traveled through one of the Guild's back passageways. Eina answered with a nod.

The Guild kept strict tabs on all tamers living in Orario, but *Ganesha Familia* was the only organization allowed to keep live monsters in the city to help with training for the Monsterphilia.

They also conducted many experiments on captive monsters and tested theories inside the walls of their expansive home in the name of "improving efficiency in the Dungeon."

"Don't forget that all tamed monsters are fitted with tracking plates. They'd know the instant one of them escaped."

These plates were magic items designed to attach to a monster's body, no matter its shape, and constantly broadcast its location to a receiver. A broken plate would immediately set off the receiver's alarm, alerting *Ganesha Familia* to the situation. If one of their captives escaped, the familia would be the first to know.

The creature sighted in the seventh district was said to resemble a human with wings. Witnesses described it as a harpy or siren.

None of them mentioned seeing a tracking plate on its body.

What bothers me is the reports saying the monster was wearing a robe...If it was trying to hide itself, that means it's self-aware...

That thought made Eina's blood run cold.

She rubbed her upper arms while the two continued their conversation.

"Tulle."

"Chief? Is something wrong?"

Eina and Misha stepped into the front office and were halfway to their desks when their animal-person boss spoke up.

The slender chienthrope man wore glasses similar to Eina's, along with a troubled expression...though perhaps "apologetic" would be a more apt term. He gave her another assignment.

"The boss wants to speak with you. It's urgent, so go to his office right away."

"Eh...?"

Eina froze on the spot.

"Oh no..." whispered Misha in a hollow voice and forced a weak smile.

—*Did I...do something wrong?*

Eina pushed her glasses back up her nose, dread in her veins.

"...Excuse me, sir."

After ascending to the top floor of Guild Headquarters, Eina knocked on an oak door.

"Get in here," came a grouchy command from inside. Grasping both handles of the double doors, Eina pulled them open and went inside.

The first thing she saw in the spacious room was a massive book-case that covered an entire wall. Then her eyes fell to the ornate rug on the floor. Everything in this room, from the antique jars and paintings on the walls to the velvet upholstered sofa and alabaster magic-stone lamps, was of the highest quality. Deities residing in Orario were known for their love of luxury, but even they might feel a little underdressed in this chamber.

Eina made a quick bow before walking to the middle of the room. Struggling to keep her nerves under control, she approached the one in charge.

He was sitting in an elegantly designed chair, partially hidden behind the mountains of paperwork on his desk.

"You're late, Eina Tulle."

Looking up from his half-finished document, the man glared at Eina with green eyes.

His pointed ears identified him as an elf. However, the rest of his form lacked the beauty and refinement of his kin.

His suit, much higher quality than the average Guild employee's, was under immense pressure to contain his gut. Saying that he had a spare tire for a belly would be an understatement, as his overall fig-ure was difficult to describe. One receptionist had ironically referred to his stout build as orc-like, but she wasn't far off the mark. All his limbs were short and pudgy, and he had an impressively flabby set of jowls.

With high-quality garments adorning his body, he resembled a merchant basking in a lifetime of riches.

This was the head of the Guild, Royman Mardeel.

As the one with the right to make the final call on the Guild's deci-sions, he had direct control over Orario's day-to-day affairs.

"Do you realize how much time has passed since I summoned you? You must think very highly of yourself to keep a man like me waiting."

"My apologies…"

Despite his tirade, Eina chose to remain humble rather than retaliate.

Elves were known for their long life spans, and Royman was no different, having served at the Guild for over a century. His lifestyle had changed to one of extravagance and debauchery once he reached his current position, resulting in his obese figure.

His nickname was "the Guild's Pig."

Every other elf in Orario despised him, preferring to pretend he didn't exist.

They saw him as a shameless glutton who had forgotten the pride of his race. His lust for money, plus his burgeoning waistline, had triggered his fall from grace and prompted harsh criticism.

Being so thoroughly despised and yet so powerful, not even his inborn elfish respect for kin could prevent his arrogance. Only before the gods and goddesses of Orario did he ever show humility.

And Eina was only a half-elf.

She had a feeling thoughts of her "impurity" were crossing his mind at this very moment.

Well, I knew this would happen from the moment he summoned me, but…

Eina wasn't fond of Royman.

She was sure Guild employees who didn't have issues with him were in the minority.

But the fact remained that, no matter how much he spoiled himself, he held authority.

Working at the Guild for over 100 years wasn't just for show. While his lavish tastes might have rubbed some people the wrong way, he made many contributions to the Guild on the whole.

If he hadn't, those around him—especially the Guild's "true leader"—would never have granted him permission to rise so far in the first place.

He must be exhausted…

Everything that bothered her about him, all the complaints eating away at her even now, could be attributed to the stress of being at the mercy of the deities' every whim…Thinking about it in those terms made it possible to sympathize with him.

Eina repeated that to herself over and over, clinging to her faith that everyone was good deep down. She maintained perfect posture in his presence.

"Hmph, so you're the one using her feminine wiles to ensnare adventurers. Oh yes, I know. You used that body of yours to sweet-talk your way into the laps of two upper-class adventurers, the ones making money for our city. Your promiscuity is causing the rest of us a lot of problems."

Royman's eyes traced the curves firmly held in place by her suit, and Eina felt naked under his intense stare. She wanted to flinch, but she suppressed the knee-jerk reaction and held her ground.

This was an attempt to get under her skin.

In his case, it wasn't so much sexual harassment as an insult. She could put up with that.

"…That's a misunderstanding, sir. Nothing that you have insinuated has taken place."

"Shut your mouth! Use what little elvish blood you have to feel proper shame."

Royman didn't appreciate being contradicted about the incident a few days ago involving the dwarf Dormul and the elf Luvis, and his face flushed red as he growled.

Eina swallowed a sigh—and Royman's eyes flashed, glaring at her.

"But worst of all, you've been keeping information about Bell Cranell from us, haven't you?"

Ah…

He didn't miss a thing.

Eina hadn't reported on Bell's Advanced Ability, Luck, or on his magic attack, Firebolt—the first of its kind that didn't require a trigger spell. The latter had already been revealed during the War Game, but it was his astounding rate of growth that had propelled the Guild to investigate. More than likely, Royman was trying to force her to divulge any information she had. To make matters worse, Eina had never submitted Bell's level-up model. This was a document detailing how he had leveled up and was, at that very moment, still buried deep within her desk. A scolding like this was inevitable, but it was too late to worry about it now.

She had, however, submitted reports along the guidelines set in place to protect adventurers under her counsel like Bell and their familias…Royman must have thought she'd left a few things out after seeing the reports.

Once again, Eina had to prevent her shoulders from flinching under the pressure of Royman's astute observation.

"You're deliberately withholding information to keep him from becoming some god's new toy, aren't you?"

"N-no, it's not like that…!"

"Do not lie to me! You've sided with adventurers ever since the day you got here, have you not? As his adviser, failing to divulge the secret to Bell Cranell's growth is costing us far more than you can imagine!"

Slamming his fist onto the desk and grunting like a pig, Royman maintained his verbal assault. Eina could only try to bear the storm of criticism and wait for it to pass.

Royman did eventually calm down.

Forehead and saggy chin soaked with sweat, Royman took a deep breath.

"…As to why you're here."

Eina tensed again as the leader of the Guild wiped his face on a cloth and reached for something on his desk.

"See to it this reaches *Hestia Familia*…Give it to Bell Cranell."

"Eh?"

He thrust a sealed letter out to her from between two towering piles of paperwork.

Stunned, Eina reached for the document with trembling hands only after Royman's gaze became too intense to bear.

"Um, sir, what is…?"

Sealed with the Guild's official stamp, it appeared to be some sort of notification.

Perhaps a quest?

Royman spoke up, answering Eina's question before she could ask.

"I should tell you that it's no quest but a mission."

"!"

Eina's eyes widened in that moment.

"A secret one at that. *Hestia Familia* is the only group allowed to know, and no Guild personnel have clearance. Take extra care when you give it to him…I don't think I have to say it, but you are forbidden to pursue this matter any further."

A mission.

A direct order from the Guild that no one could refuse. All familias and adventurers residing in Orario were required to obey it.

What's more, this one was top secret. Eina couldn't understand why Bell, an adventurer under her counsel, would be tasked with something this important.

"You are his adviser. This is your job."

Royman delivering the order himself would attract too much attention, given his position.

He explained the situation as he reclined back in his chair before an astonished Eina.

"Give it to him, clear? I won't allow you to say no."

"S-sir, what is upper management thinking—?"

"An underling like you doesn't need to know. Now get out of here. I'm busy."

Royman spat out his retort.

Then he unleashed another verbal barrage, reminding Eina—so many times she couldn't get his voice out of her head—to make sure that the goddess Hestia also saw the mission. With nothing more to say, Royman demanded that she leave his office.

A secret mission…But why…?

Closing the doors behind her, Eina stood in the middle of the passageway.

Her emerald-green eyes quivered as she looked at the seal on the document in her hand.

Upper management's decision? But in that case, why would Royman see to it personally…? Was it his preference?

No. She shook her head once she reached that conclusion.

What if he was ordered to—?

—*It couldn't be.*

A gut feeling shook her to the very core.

The organization known as the Guild had a true "leader" that outranked upper management.

Something was happening behind closed doors.

Suddenly anxious, Eina felt her heart lurch in her chest.

We made it back home during the night.

Somehow, we managed to keep Wiene and her new wing out of sight along the way.

Night might be over, but there's nothing we can do to stave off the stifling gloom descending on the manor. Everyone—except for Lilly, who forced herself to go back out into the city to gather information—has stayed inside ever since we returned. We're lying low, staying as far away as possible from the commotion in the streets.

Except for one thing.

I've been summoned to Guild Headquarters. Just me.

"I'm sorry for asking you to come here on such short notice."

"I-it's fine."

We're in the consultation box.

Eina is standing right in front of me, and it takes every ounce of willpower I have to keep my body from shaking.

A messenger from the Guild arrived with the summons, complete with Eina's signature, at around noon. The letter said it was urgent, so I hurried to the Guild as fast as I could.

My nerves won't calm down.

Why'd it have to be today of all days?

Am I a suspect on their list for what happened last night?

Then again, Eina sent me the message. She's my adviser, so I doubt she'd be the one to contact me if that is what's happening.

Wiene did finally fall asleep after a long night before I left, but I'm still worried about her.

Neither Eina nor I take a seat in the soundproof room. She seems unusually stiff as we stand face-to-face.

"…This is for you."

"Huh?"

Suddenly even more nervous, I glance down at the sealed document in her outstretched hand.

"Miss Eina, what…?"

Not sure what to think, I take it from her. She pauses for a long moment before telling me.

"It's a secret mission. I was instructed to give it to you personally."

Well, that's…surprising.

A mission from the Guild? A secret one, at that?

It's a direct order from the top. Usually they involve taking care of an Irregular in the Dungeon or exterminating a particularly strong monster, or maybe dealing with something outside the city wall. Sure, *Hestia Familia* has been in the spotlight recently, but we barely qualify as average. Why would we be chosen for such a mission?

If something is so important that it needs to be done in secret, then wouldn't one of Orario's strongest familias or adventurers get the call…?

I look down at the paper in my hands in disbelief.

"May I…open it here?"

"Yes. But don't show it to me…I'm not allowed to know."

Our conversation is stilted and awkward.

I slowly pull back the seal as Eina watches, her mouth slightly agape.

Hands moving at the speed of molasses thanks to my nerves, I slowly unroll the piece of parchment.

"Each member of the familia, including the vouivre girl, is hereby ordered to proceed to the Dungeon's twentieth floor."

"……………"

Time freezes.

My body goes ice cold. I can't even feel my hands and feet anymore.

The simple Koine letters, those swashes of ink dancing across the page, almost triggered a panic attack.

"Please make sure Goddess Hestia sees this as well...Bell? What's wrong?"

I hear sounds, not words.

I can't even blink, reading the message over and over as I struggle to breathe. The letters keep going in and out of focus.

But how...? Since when—?

So many questions flare up in my head that none of them can finish before the next one begins.

"Vouivre girl." That's Wiene for sure. Someone knows that *Hestia Familia* is protecting her?

The Guild knows everything?

Is this a threat?

If that's true—

What's the point of this mission?

What is the Guild trying to do?

How can I figure this out with my brain going in every direction at once?

"Bell! Bell?!"

Eina calls my name again and again as I start coming back to myself.

Her voice pulls my gaze away from the parchment. I stare up at her, white as a ghost.

"Miss Eina, what does the Guild—?"

My throat stops moving; the words are stuck.

I can't ask.

I can't ask her what the Guild knows.

If they're friend or foe.

I don't know who I can trust anymore.

I can almost hear Eina's face twisting.

Is it possible that even she—?

—No, that can't be true!

I shake my head free of those thoughts before they get out of control.

This person would never investigate me. She's not watching my reaction looking for clues.

Eina is just an employee at the very bottom of the Guild's hierarchy.

She said it herself: She wasn't "allowed to know."

I can't let this situation make me doubt someone who's always been there for me.

That's it. This right here is—

A mission assigned by the Guild's higher-ups.

I gulp down the air in my throat.

A powerful force is at work, and we're about to get swept up in its wake.

"—Please, Bell, talk to me."

"!"

Eina takes a step closer as I struggle with our predicament.

I raise my head to meet her imploring, straightforward gaze.

"If something is troubling you, please tell me. You have my word I will not tell a soul. I can't just sit back and watch you be in pain."

Her eyes quiver as she bears her heart.

"Even if I fail as an adviser in the eyes of the Guild, I want to do everything I can to help adventurers like you."

My eyes are trembling, too.

"This is all I can do, to listen to what you have to say. So please—"

—Trust me.

Her plea cuts deep.

She doesn't know anything.

But if I tell her what's going on right now, if I give in to her kindness, then she'll get dragged into this mess, too. She'll be stuck in this dark quandary because of me.

I...I can't let that happen.

"—It's...nothing...Please don't worry."

It took everything I had to form those words.

Eina hunches over as if collapsing on the inside. She looks despondent.

I can't meet her eyes.

Even staring at the floor at her feet, I can tell she's looking away.

A barrier stands between us. I can almost hear it rising.

Leaving Eina behind, I make a quick exit from the box as if to flee.

"A mission…"

Resisting the invisible force pulling me back toward the Guild, I return home.

Not wasting any time, I go straight to the living room where everyone is waiting. Welf whispers to himself in disbelief with the parchment in his hands.

"So they know? Because of what happened yesterday?"

"It's too sudden for that. The vouivre girl…Miss Wiene kept her face and body well hidden, and yet they know what type of monster she is…The only explanation is that they've known for some time."

Wrinkles form on Welf's brow as he forces himself to remain calm while listening to Lilly's terse explanation. Mikoto and Haruhime are standing like statues off to the side. The goddess is reading the document herself right now, deep in thought and silent as the grave. Wiene isn't here.

No one in the room is sitting down.

As we exchange glances, I see I'm not the only one thrown for a loop.

"Lilly is more concerned about what this mission entails…"

She takes the document from our goddess and reads it herself.

I'm not used to seeing so much uncertainty on her face as her chestnut-colored eyes work their way across the page.

"Lilly can't understand what the Guild is trying to accomplish. This is not a warrant for our arrest, nor is it a demand to surrender Miss Wiene into their custody…Why send us to the Dungeon?"

In addition to the mission document decorated with a vine-like pattern, there's another sheet with detailed instructions.

Written in red ink, there's a big circle on a map of the twentieth floor. Our destination is in the deepest part of the floor, way off the main route.

It even tells us what time to leave:

Tonight at midnight, when it's darkest out.

"So the Guild doesn't intend to arrest us...?"

"For the time being, at least."

"We are to escort Lady Wiene back into the Dungeon...Whatever for?"

"Beats me. Maybe she's part of a plan to start something in the Dungeon...and we're making a delivery?"

Lilly answers Mikoto's question, prompting Haruhime and Welf to share their thoughts.

Welf takes the documents from Lilly while everyone is talking, his frown deepening by the second as he reads through the mission a second time.

"Can we even make it there? Us? Down to the twentieth floor? We're only going to get one crack at this."

"...Continuous use of Miss Haruhime's magic will provide us with the strength of two Level Threes, including Mr. Bell, and one Level Two. The twentieth floor is still in the Dungeon's middle levels, so our party should be okay—theoretically. The problem is our frightening lack of experience on that floor."

Adventurers usually take their time on each floor, learning the lay of the land and how to deal with monsters before pressing forward, for safety reasons.

But we have to skip all that and go straight to the heart of the twentieth floor, a place we've never been...One thing's for sure: We'll be venturing directly into the "unknown."

As Lilly pointed out in her answer to Welf's question, we have to endure the uncertainty and fear that accompany a new area, unfamiliar surroundings, and new monsters.

"…What's our course of action?"

After our discussion comes to a stop—

—Mikoto's voice fills the quiet living room.

"I don't think we have any choice but to go…"

"This is a mission. We don't have the right to refuse."

Welf and Lilly speak up, sounding weighed down by the circumstances.

The Guild, in charge of everything that happens in Orario, is aware of what we've been doing. That alone puts us between a rock and a hard place. If we try to resist—for example, make an attempt to flee the city—they'd shut us down before we could even get past the wall.

All they have to do to destroy *Hestia Familia* is tell the world that we've been harboring a monster in our home.

What's going to happen to Wiene…?

There's no point in guessing without knowing what the Guild is trying to accomplish. I understand that.

I know that we don't have a choice, just as Lilly pointed out.

It's just—I can't help but wonder what will happen if we do manage to pull this off…That's the one thing I can't stop worrying about.

Then again…I doubt the Guild would send us to the twentieth floor without knowing something that we don't.

There's the Dungeon, where Wiene was born.

And that monster, the one that called the vouivre girl "one of its kind."

I have no clue how this mission will play out.

But there's one thing I do know: It's entirely possible that the Guild knows something important about Wiene and has a plan for her.

Our path will become clear once we figure out what that is.

Adventurers…No, explorers?

At some point long ago in the Ancient Times, insanely brave people who ventured into the Dungeon, coming face-to-face with the "unknown," started being called adventurers.

Now we, too, are entering the Dungeon to make a new discovery. There's no choice but to follow in our forebears' footsteps.

"……"

All of us look to our goddess, Lady Hestia.

She hasn't said a word all this time. Returning our gazes, she slowly nods, telling us to go.

We nod, accepting her divine will. It's official. We'll do the mission.

"Everyone, I'm so sorry…This is all my fault."

After a few heavy moments…

Although I can't look at my friends, I apologize to them.

I know rescuing Wiene was the right decision. I won't let myself think otherwise. She's still hiding here, and I know in my heart protecting her was the right decision.

However, as a member of this familia, as their leader, I have to apologize.

They have to bear this weight on their shoulders now because of me. Lilly warned us this could happen, and she hit the nail right on the head.

I put everyone in danger.

That's exactly what a leader is supposed to avoid. I failed.

I guess I wasn't cut out for this position, after all.

It's that endless guilt that's preventing me from looking everyone in the eyes.

My trembling hands form fists on their own.

"Master Bell."

Just then…

Haruhime, who was standing close by, reaches out to hold my hand even though my eyes are still glued to the floor.

"I beg of you. Please do not regret coming to Lady Wiene's aid."

My head snaps up with a start. She's pleading to me with her eyes.

Taking my fist in both hands, she lifts it to chest height and squeezes.

"I would not be here today were it not for my rescue by you and Miss Mikoto—thanks to everyone, I am happy once again. Lady Wiene is no different. We rescued her, so that's why…!"

Her dazzling green eyes glisten with tears; her voice overflows with passion.

Her message is clear: Don't deny the good things that have happened, no matter how dire our situation is now.

I feel my eyes widening as the first tears fall from hers.

A few heartbeats pass until Haruhime realizes she's still holding my hand and jumps, blushing on the spot.

Lilly walks up behind Haruhime with a half-lidded glare and gives her fox tail a hard yank.

"Wha—!" she squeals.

"You've got nothing to apologize for."

I break out in a cold sweat as Haruhime disappears from my line of sight and Welf speaks up.

"This is what familias do, right? Support one another," he says. "Or have you already forgotten what I put you and Hestia through during Rakia's invasion?"

He shrugs, grinning at his own lighthearted comment.

"Stir up all the trouble you want. I've got no room to complain."

"Welf…"

I can't say another word. Suddenly, I see Mikoto smiling at me.

"We appear to be in the same boat."

She says this with the conviction of a Far Eastern warrior adhering to a strong sense of justice.

Her violet eyes soften in a tender expression, too. I meet her gaze for a few moments before glancing over at Lilly.

Haruhime is next to her, whimpering and stroking her tail. As for the prum, she's also wearing a relaxed smile.

"Lilly will go anywhere with you, Mr. Bell. She is, after all, your supporter."

The whole familia is smiling at me.

My trembling fists start to relax in the calming warmth.

"…Thanks."

Rather than apologize…

I tell them I'm grateful.

"……"

Hestia watched her familia's conversation from a step outside their circle, unable to contain the smile growing on her lips as their bonds strengthened right before her eyes.

It was short-lived, however. Her gaze once again fell onto the mission document.

Her eyes first skimmed the characters spelling out the order to go to the twentieth floor. Then they passed over the vine-like patterns that covered the page.

The shapes looked like a mere decoration at first glance, but they were much more.

The design was a second message hiding in plain sight, written in characters that Hestia knew very well—hieroglyphs.

COME TO THE FOURTH BLOCK OF THE CITY'S SEVENTH DISTRICT ONCE YOUR FAMILIA HAS GONE. NO HARM WILL COME TO YOU.

That was the divine scripture's message.

Hestia heard that when Bell received the parchment from Eina, she told him to make sure that his goddess saw the document as well.

One purpose of this mission was to separate her from her familia before making contact.

The goddess narrowed her blue eyes.

Could it be the one pulling the strings behind the scenes is...?

Hestia tensed as she reread the message that was intended for her alone.

I ascend a flight of stairs cast in red light by the setting sun.

Looking out the window, the sun has almost disappeared. The whole sky is burning crimson in the early evening twilight. As for me, I'm putting one foot in front of the other, ascending one step at a time.

We decided to accept tonight's mission after a long discussion, and everyone has gone their separate ways to prepare.

Lilly went into the city to replenish our stock of items for the middle levels. Welf collected all our armor and weapons before shutting himself up in his workshop to make sure everything is in peak condition. Mikoto and Haruhime were put in charge of preparing food and water for the journey and left a little while ago. Even the goddess said she had something to take care of and went out. With Welf in his shop, the only ones inside the manor are me...and Wiene.

I reach the third floor of our home and walk straight down the passageway.

Arriving outside my own door, I quietly push it open.

The girl with bluish-white skin is lying on my bed in the corner of the room.

She's still wearing the same robe as yesterday, and her cheeks are streaked with tears as she lies curled up into a little ball like a child.

It's just as Haruhime and Mikoto, who's been using her Skill non-stop, told me. She cried herself to sleep and hasn't set foot out of this room since.

Almost as if she's afraid of the outside world.

"......"

I walk up to the bed, careful not to make a sound.

Doing my best not to disturb her, I take a seat next to Wiene.

It's quiet in here. Time flows peacefully, uninterrupted by the noise and commotion outside, and she's far away from those who wish to hurt her. Only her quiet breathing reaches my ears.

Given that we're nearing summer, it's still warm during the evening hours. But I don't want to open a window. It would only disturb this space, interrupt our time together.

This might be my room, but her scent is mixing with mine.

It's been only one week, but so much has happened. Her smell triggers so many memories that I see flashes of them every time I close my eyes.

"......"

There were a lot of problems.

I'm pretty sure I cried out every day.

Even so, I wouldn't trade this past week for anything.

My lips curl into a smile of warm reminiscence.

I reach out with my left hand and gently stroke Wiene's hair.

The silver-blue strands are firm and yet smooth as silk.

It feels so foreign to me as I softly run my fingers through it, just as I have every day since we brought her here.

"…Ah, umm."

Her blue eyelashes flutter as her eyelids twitch.

Her amber irises slowly peek out from underneath. They flit around in a groggy daze until they find me. A smile blooms on her lips.

"Bell…"

"It's me…Sorry to wake you."

She lightly shakes her head at my apology, saying it's okay.

Her wing, folded up over the torn robe on her back, moves right along with it.

Keeping her head on the pillow, she takes my hand from her hair and places it on her cheek.

Her skin is chilly, like a crisp breeze.

Still not fully awake, the vouivre girl looks at me happily.

"Wiene, I have something important to tell you, so please listen."

"…Okay."

She slowly sits up.

We make eye contact, sitting side by side on top of the bedsheet.

Our shadows stretch across the room, two silhouettes facing each other.

"Tonight…?"

"Yes. Together with Haruhime."

I tell Wiene about the decision we made with the goddess.

Of course, I leave out a few details.

I explain to her that all of us are going to the place where she was born. That's the story.

"……"

"…You don't want to go?" I ask as she droops her head.

I can't blame her for reacting this way. I haven't told her anything about why we're going into the Dungeon. This has to come as a surprise.

The idea can't be easy for Wiene to swallow. After all, the Dungeon is filled with scary things that tried to kill her.

The problem now is how to convince her to go. I rack my brain for ideas, when—

"No, no…I'll go."

She didn't look up, but Wiene couldn't have made herself any clearer.

I'm still struggling with disbelief when she raises her head.

"Bell…Haruhime. Everyone is trying to help me, aren't they?"

My eyes go wide.

The red jewel in front of my eyes twinkles in the last of the sunlight.

"Everyone has always helped me before."

"Wiene…"

"It's scary…but not if Bell and everyone else is with me."

The last sliver of sun sinks behind Wiene's head, but I can tell her whole body is trembling.

The innocent, outlandish girl who only wants to be kind is putting on a brave face.

She's trusting us.

"Sorry for crying so much…Thank you for protecting me."

Teardrops threaten to spill forth from her glistening amber eyes, but still she smiles from ear to ear.

Then she leans forward a little before burying her face in my chest.

"I love…Bell."

…No matter what.

I must protect this girl.

No matter what is waiting for us, I will protect Wiene.

I won't let her be alone. I won't let her die.

I swear on my soul.

Now it's my turn to hold back tears. Keeping my tear ducts in check, I wrap my arms around her.

Making sure to include her trembling dragon wing, I pull her into a big hug.

I hear light sobs from under my chin.

The sun has set; the last of its rays coming in through the window cast my room in a golden red light.

"A humanoid monster…That's the one."

Dix adjusted his goggles; the corner of his mouth curled into a sneer.

"Don't remember anything about wings, though…The beast didn't have any when you guys saw it, did it?"

"That's right. Just arms and legs like a person. Then again, vouivres are supposed to have snake bodies with wings anyway…"

"True that…A beast is a beast whether it's got claws or wings."

Thump, thump. Dix tapped the shaft of his red spear against his shoulder while listening to his underlings.

They were in a dark room with no windows. Surrounded by the iron bars of cages, the men talked among themselves without fear of being overheard.

"But you know all this went down on the day that god of ours went to pay him a visit…Is this what they call a Blessing? Perhaps our Lord isn't as stupid as we thought."

The praise for their absent temperamental deity rang hollow.

Dix chuckled at the thought.

"You thinking what I'm thinking, Dix?"

"Yeah."

His mind was made up.

His red eyes narrowed behind the smoky quartz lenses of his goggles.

"Keep an eye on *Hestia Familia*."

Dusk fell over Orario before finally shifting to night.

The city was far from asleep. The exception was Central Park, which was filled with a tranquil silence.

Hardly a soul passed through the area directly beneath Babel Tower. Lights from restaurants and bars formed a ring around the park, but few sounds reached the base of the white tower.

It was near midnight. The clocks would mark the beginning of a new day at any moment.

Bell led his familia to Babel Tower's west entrance.

He, Welf, and Mikoto wore salamander-wool cloaks over their armor. Lilly and Haruhime were equipped with Goliath Robes. Lastly, Wiene donned salamander wool as well but also had a slightly customized backpack strapped to her shoulders. The backpack had a hole in the inside lining to hide Wiene's wing and disguise her as an ordinary supporter to any passersby.

The vouivre kept looking over her shoulder at this strange apparatus hanging off her back as she walked. The party of adventurers surrounding her carried all sorts of weapons, and they strode forward with purpose. Their arsenal included a large shield, spare weapons of every kind, and even magic swords. The party had never looked so complete, and it was all thanks to Welf's hard work.

Pre-mission nerves were beginning to set in. Haruhime, Mikoto, and Lilly looked particularly anxious.

"......"

"Something wrong, Bell?"

The party stood in front of Babel's open doors, partially illuminated by the light pouring out from inside, when Bell suddenly turned around.

Greatsword over his shoulder, Welf called out to him as the boy scanned their surroundings.

We're being watched...

And there was more than one observer.

Bell could feel their gazes originating from somewhere around the deserted park. They weren't all that close, but they were definitely there, spread out all over.

Either the Guild had dispatched people to keep watch on them, or—

Bell's stomach churned as that thought dredged up memories of Ikelos's unnerving smile in the back of his mind.

Turning around, his gaze fell on the girl hiding her true identity beneath a robe: Wiene.

"Bell…"

Anxious amber eyes peered up at him from deep underneath her hood.

Bell took several light breaths, the two staring at each other in silence.

Setting aside his own concerns, he smiled to put her at ease as much as possible.

"It's all right."

Placing his hand on top of her hood, Bell mentally prepared himself for what lay ahead.

"—It's time."

Snap. Lilly made the announcement as she closed the lid on her broken pocket watch.

All eyes gathered on Bell. He nodded.

"Goddess, we're going in."

"Right. Just make sure everyone comes back."

Hestia had wanted to see them off and came this far to do so. Bell said a quick good-bye.

The deity gazed at her followers, waiting for a moment before turning to Bell and opening her mouth to speak.

"Bell…"

"Yes, Goddess?"

"…No, it's nothing."

See you when you get back, Hestia conveyed with her eyes, tilting her head to the side. The boy nodded again before entering Babel.

Their mission had officially begun.

The party set off for the twentieth floor.

CHAPTER 5
HERETICS

© Suzuhito Yasuda

The white crystals covering the ceiling overhead go dark and bathe the entire floor in blackness.

Blue crystals scattered about the forest and ponds start to glow in their place, producing a "nightfall" completely different from the surface.

We're on the Dungeon's eighteenth floor, the Under Resort.

"Night" falls on the safe point the moment we arrive.

We traveled through the upper levels and middle levels at high speed while making sure to keep Wiene out of harm's way. I think we pulled it off only because we used magic and items like there was no tomorrow. Then again, part of it could be due to our familiarity with the floors down to the eighteenth and knowing the quickest routes. It also helped that Goliath wasn't there.

We went straight north from the southern tunnel to the seventeenth floor, heading directly toward the massive tree in the center.

Many magic-stone lamps sparkle from atop the island in the middle of the lake off to our left, but we ignore them. A quick stop in Rivira isn't part of the plan. We're going straight down to the twentieth.

A few isolated encounters with small groups of monsters are all the resistance we find. We breeze to the middle ground and find the gateway to the nineteenth floor among the roots of the Central Tree.

"Now for the hard part."

"Indeed. I passed through here once for the quest on the day we met Lady Wiene, but…"

Wiene inclines her head toward Welf and Mikoto's conversation.

We can't help but smile as we take our first and only planned rest.

I doubt we'll get a chance to catch our breath the rest of the way. Finding a secluded spot close to the entrance, we all try to replenish the energy we expended getting down here so quickly.

The enormous tree's roots surround us like a horseshoe, and we're hidden safely in a hollow in its trunk. Thankfully, no one is going into or coming out of the nineteenth floor, since it's "night" down here.

Because hellhounds are no longer a threat, Welf, Mikoto, and I remove our salamander-wool cloaks. I feel lighter already.

Not only that, the cool night breeze feels amazing.

"Lilly, about the stink bombs…"

"Yes, our supply is limited. Lilly would like to save as many as possible for our return journey. Of course, they're an option in an emergency, but…"

Lilly answers my question while dropping her backpack down on the grass.

Our party will be in even worse shape on the return trip, so saving as many Malboro stink bombs as possible makes sense. I also understand that it's impossible to avoid every battle.

Lilly's backpack is so full of weapons and items that it's practically bursting at the seams. The pieces of equipment that didn't fit inside clatter against one another as she riffles through the pack to make sure everything is in order. I watch her out of the corner of my eye, but the trip home is the last thing on my mind. It's the mission that's important right now.

"Sir Welf, how many magic swords are in our possession…?"

"Three. Li'l E, don't go wasting yours, all right?"

"Lilly knows already!"

Welf answers Mikoto's question before shooting a quick warning in Lilly's direction.

Our party brought along three Crozzo Magic Swords. Two of them are the size of daggers and are meant to help protect the rear of our formation. Welf has the third one, a much larger weapon strapped to his back alongside his greatsword. Welf makes magic swords in advance to help out during our regular trips to the Dungeon. This time, we brought every single one he had.

Without a magic user to balance our party, I hope we can compensate for our lack of firepower with these…

...But when push comes to shove...

It all comes down to an adventurer's strengths, what each of us can do.

Weapons and items lend us their power, that's all. We're going to need quick wits and teamwork to make it through the truly difficult situations.

The bowels of this merciless Dungeon are going to test our mettle as a party.

I don't know what's going to happen...but I can't forget where my trust belongs.

"We should probably get moving."

I talk to the group after about thirty minutes of rest.

As I down the last of the potion in my hand, we walk to the tunnel entrance as one.

Tree roots carpet the tunnel floor, forming a stairwell. A single moss-covered path reveals itself to us as soon as we reach the bottom. This is the Colossal Tree Labyrinth.

"Lady Haruhime, if you will."

"Y-yes!"

Haruhime begins casting at Mikoto's behest.

It's important that no one else sees her use sorcery. We split up to keep an eye on the path in front and behind as Haruhime's beautiful voice echoes around us.

"—*Uchide no Kozuchi.*"

Sorcery is a kind of magic that only renarts can use—this one allows Haruhime to trigger her Level Boost skill.

A hammer appears out of swirling magic energy, coming down on top of Welf at the head of our formation and enveloping him in light.

"Good to go!" Welf says as he pumps his fist; sparkles glisten around his body.

"So pretty...You're amazing, Haruhime!"

"N-not at all...This is the most I can do to contribute...!"

Wiene has never seen Haruhime's Magic before, and the spell's glow twinkles in her eyes.

Haruhime constantly casting Level Boost is our key to progressing deeper into the Colossal Tree Labyrinth. Being on the front lines, Welf must constantly engage monsters in combat. The stronger he is, the better our chances.

We've done some experimenting with *Uchide no Kozuchi* and learned it can last for fifteen minutes—as long as Haruhime puts enough Mind into it. After the spell runs its course, she'll have to cast it again. We need to be constantly aware of the remaining time and rely on Haruhime to maintain the effect.

"Drink a magic potion while you've got the chance," Welf insists. Haruhime responds immediately, saying, "Yes, right away!" *Uchide no Kozuchi* requires a lot of energy, so it's better to be on the safe side.

Bringing the vial to her lips, Haruhime downs half the potion.

"Good, now we should be all set—Huh? Hey, Li'l E? What are you doing?"

"Just in case."

Welf turns around to face us, raring to go, when he spots Lilly standing next to the Dungeon wall. *Scrape, scrape.*

Using one hand, she is sliding a small knife under the moss growing on its surface.

This plant—often called Lamp Moss—is the only source of light on this floor. Is she collecting some?

"Lady Lilly, are you...? Surely you aren't planning to sell that on the surface...?"

"Are you so concerned with our familia's finances that you must take measures even at times like this?"

"Of course not! Lilly knows there is a time and a place!!"

The combination of Mikoto's groan of disbelief and Haruhime's genuine surprise draws a snappish retort from Lilly, her face suddenly bright red.

Well, I've heard that Lamp Moss sells for about the same price as the crystals from the eighteenth floor, but...

I want to believe that Lilly has something else in mind.

"There's no pleasing some people...Lilly's finished. Let's go."

Gathering the Lamp Moss in a small pouch and pulling the drawstring shut, Lilly tucks it into her robe.

Welf and I nod to each other as she stands up. It's time to press on.

"Bell..."

"Miss Wiene, please stay in formation. You don't need to worry about Mr. Bell."

Lilly gives Wiene a sharp warning from a different part of our formation, though her voice is dampened by the moss and tree bark covering the walls around us.

Welf and I lead the formation, a simple column with no middle rank, where Lilly, Haruhime, and Wiene bring up the rear. Mikoto is at the tail end.

Normally, Mikoto would be occupying the middle, but this floor is filled with monsters we've never encountered before. Yatano Black Crow won't fully protect us from those monsters, so she's in the back to respond to ambushes as quickly as possible. That way, Lilly can immediately provide her with whatever weapon she needs. Although Mikoto prefers to fight with a katana, she's just as good with a bow and arrow. Her ability to adjust to any situation and any position has often proved invaluable.

Lilly and Haruhime serve as our middle ranks in the formation, providing support with fresh weapons and items as necessary and, of course, Haruhime's Level Boost. Despite nominally being the weakest among us, they are the party's core. With Wiene between them, I can't allow any attacks to get through.

As the only Level 3 adventurers, Welf and I have the most difficult job—engaging monsters head-on or breaking past them.

All this is to protect the one at the very center of our party: Wiene.

"...Bell."

"I know."

Welf whispers to me, the lights surrounding him catching the corner of my eye. I keep my gaze trained on the path and nod.

Several enemies are already lurking in the darkness ahead of us. I bet we've got only ten seconds or so before they show themselves, so I tighten my grip on the Hestia Knife and Ushiwakamaru-Nishiki.

...Focus on what's important. No matter what shows up, I will protect Wiene.

A quick glance over my shoulder and I make eye contact with her. Her anxiety is written all over her face.

—What if the monsters we encounter start talking just like her?

—What if they possess the same feelings we do and can shed tears just like us?

I tamp down those questions with the determination coursing through my mind. Those excuses that once held me back are gone.

My heart is set; my eyes are focused. I am determined.

Ready for battle, our party ventures deeper into the expansive wooden labyrinth.

Clouds passed in front of the moon high in the night sky.

Hestia looked up at the lines of gray clouds traveling across the heavens as she crossed the city streets. Her familia had just ventured into the Dungeon, their mission under way.

The date might have changed, but the few people still in the bars and restaurants along Northwest Main Street—Adventurers Way—were still loud enough to be heard. Hestia traveled among flickering pockets of light around the magic-stone lamps, catching bits and pieces of their conversations as she passed by.

"Fourth block of the seventh district." That was the address on the document that detailed her familia's mission and where she was supposed to wait.

In truth, the place she once called home, the "hidden room under the church," was in the same neighborhood.

Simply put, it was inside a poor residential area.

"……"

Hestia arrived at the location and examined her surroundings.

With no streetlamps, the clouds in the sky hampered what little moonlight reached the dim alleyway. Hardly a sound came from the houses that lined the narrow street, almost as if no one lived there. The only identification she could find was a sign that read FOURTH BLOCK nailed to a wooden stake at the corner.

Everything about this dark street gave her the sense that something was about to appear.

—And she was right.

"...I suppose it would be foolish to ask where you came from?"

A ripple passed through the darkness on the other side of the street as a figure silently entered her line of sight.

The mysterious, human-shaped shadow was swathed entirely in black.

The figure came to a stop about five meders away from Hestia, midnight-colored gloves creaking at its sides as the person flexed their fingers.

Hestia forced herself to smile at this person's unexpected arrival and slightly unnerving aura. The corners of her mouth curled upward.

"It is an honor to make your acquaintance, Goddess Hestia. Thank you for traveling all this way."

"The pleasure's all mine. So, mind telling me who you are?"

The black-robed figure's voice was so indistinctive that it was impossible to discern the gender of its owner.

Was the cloak that masked his or her identity a way to counter deities, who could see through the lies of those who lived in the mortal realm?

Hestia's eyes narrowed as she carefully observed this newcomer. There was nothing to suggest anything about their identity as she pressed for answers.

"You don't strike me as a Guild employee. So why would you drag me all the way out here—"

Hestia held up the mission document in one hand as she spoke, waving it from side to side before words suddenly left her.

She froze in stunned silence.

Divine eyes quivering, she peered deep into the darkness under the figure's hood.

"Are you really one of our children...a human? Something tells me you are..."

"...My, my. No disguise can truly fool a deity."

The robe shifted as if its wearer was laughing drily at Hestia's dumbfounded expression.

The hooded figure's leisurely demeanor was in stark contrast to the trembling goddess's forced calm.

"What in the world are you...?"

"I would be more than happy to answer that and any other questions you have. However..."

The hooded figure raised its gaze to a spot well behind Hestia, the top of a nearby building.

"...it's difficult to have a meaningful conversation *while being targeted*."

Hestia's eyes flew open. With those words, the hooded figure spread both arms slightly.

"I suggest a change of scenery."

Thick black fumes poured from the robe's sleeves a heartbeat later.

"—A smoke screen!"

Miach leaned in for a closer look.

He was on the roof of a building overlooking the fourth block of Orario's seventh district. At the handsome deity's side was an equally surprised chienthrope, Nahza, her longbow set and arrow nocked, who also watched in disbelief.

Hestia had requested their "protection" only a few hours earlier during the previous day's evening. The goddess came to Miach and his followers after her own children were assigned their mission. She told him that the same message had summoned her to that spot.

Since Hestia had personally come to his home on her own, Miach accepted her request. He told his followers that it was a mission from the Guild but kept the information about talking monsters a secret from them.

Nahza, Daphne, and Cassandra had taken up positions around the appointed meeting place and watched over Hestia from afar.

If the goddess ever appeared to be in danger, Nahza would use her Sniper skills to eliminate the threat. She had been standing by, ready to loose an arrow at the first hint of suspicious movement.

"...?!"

Nahza, eyes trembling, was stunned that the mysterious hooded figure was able to sense her.

The ever-expanding cloud obscured Hestia in a matter of moments and blocked the entire alley from view. Miach watched the smoke screen—no, the black fog—inundate the area from his perch on the roof.

He could also see the other deities who had answered Hestia's call for help—Hephaistos, and Takemikazuchi with his familia—dart out from their hiding places...However, the alley was empty by the time the haze lifted.

The hooded figure and Hestia were gone.

"Lord Miach!"

"...They saw right through our plan."

Miach donned a sour expression as Nahza raised her head toward him from her kneeling position on the rooftop.

With Hestia gone, regret overwhelmed him.

"O-ooooh! That was the ghost! The ghost, Daphne...!"

"Ghost? The heck is that?"

"A black shadow that patrols the halls of the Guild Headquarters in the dead of night...! The spirit of an adventurer killed by a monster long ago, unable to pass on...!!"

"Let me guess, another dream of yours? Like I'm going to believe that."

"N-no, it's nooot! I didn't dream it! My old adviser at the Guild, Misha, told me about it...!"

"Quiet down, you two!"

The bickering of *Miach Familia*'s new additions irritated Nahza, who was well within earshot.

Miach took a deep breath before issuing orders to his followers.

"We're going. Staying here any longer would be pointless. For starters, we need to meet up with Hephaistos and the others."

Nahza, Daphne, and Cassandra nodded before taking their leave.

Miach was about to join them, but he cast his gaze over the deserted alley once more and watched the last of the fog evaporate.

"Hestia…"

More clouds rolled in overhead, completely blocking the moon from view.

"GRAHHHHHH!!"

Welf roared as he brought his greatsword down on top of the mad beetle, cleaving it in two.

No sooner did the bug monster fall in a spray of blood than a new monster trampled the corpse to take its place in the front line.

It was a fierce battle.

Bell's party encountered a mob of particularly aggressive monsters in a room located along the main route through the nineteenth floor.

"YAAAAA!!"

"GAH!"

In addition to mad beetles, Welf sliced into waves of bugbears on the ground as several gun libellulas swarmed overhead.

A monster fell with each swing of his greatsword: instant kills.

There were no exceptions. Haruhime's Level Boost gave Welf Level 3 strength and speed, allowing him to send enemies flying with ease. His thick blade tore through their bodies with no room for resistance. Filling the dual role of attacker and wall, the High Smith single-handedly stopped the horde in its tracks.

"!!"

Meanwhile, Bell engaged the monsters at an even faster pace, leaving a trail of corpses behind him.

Arcs of violet and crimson light cut through the air and vanished. With movements surpassing those of a normal attacker, more on par with finishers, Bell fought side by side with Welf to reduce their enemies one by one.

After sending a bugbear flying with a single spinning kick, Bell unleashed an electrifying inferno into the air.

"Firebolt!"

The gun libellulas unfortunate enough to be directly in the spell's line of fire were incinerated on the spot. Others in the area of effect caught fire from the intense heat and crashed to the ground.

The surviving aerial enemies came around for another pass.

Bang! Bang! The monsters launched a volley of the metal projectiles that grew naturally inside their bodies.

Bell dodged the first round before using his Swift-Strike Magic to counterattack. Although he kept an eye on Welf's battle with the mad beetles and bugbears, Bell prioritized the dragonfly monsters because of their long-distance attacks.

Lilly, Haruhime, and Wiene crouched down in a tight circle behind Welf and Bell, who stood on the front line. Lilly's and Haruhime's Goliath Robes deflected every one of the missiles but did little to protect them from the impacts. Gritting their teeth, the two desperately held their ground to avoid getting knocked down.

Their party had never experienced simultaneous ground and air attacks of this magnitude on previous levels in the Dungeon.

Mikoto stood farther behind them, providing cover fire with a bow. Her main objective might have been to protect the supporters, but she also found time to assist Bell and Welf from the rear ranks.

…Wiene! They're going after her!

The metallic rounds descended on them like rain. However, it was easy to see that most were aimed in Wiene's direction.

Cold sweat rolled down Bell's face.

Monsters, not much different from Wiene, pursued her with the same murderous intention as people above. It wasn't just the howling bugbears that had her in their sights, but the mad beetles' and gun libellulas' insect-like, multifaceted eyes were clearly focused on the vouivre girl.

The gun libellulas launched another volley. Wiene's amber eyes trembled as she watched from beneath Haruhime's embrace the missiles intended to kill zip toward her.

Bell flipped through the air, landing in front of her like a knight to the rescue, and knocked down each of the projectiles with his knives.

"Miss Mikoto, how many are there?"

Assisting the front lines with her handheld bow gun, Lilly called out when she realized the enemy numbers weren't diminishing.

Mikoto responded with an equally panicked yell after puncturing a mad beetle's head with an arrow.

"Seventeen, no nineteen—it's still rising!!"

Now that Mikoto had fought these monsters, Yatano Black Crow told her that their relentless foes were about to receive reinforcements.

Sure enough, more of the creatures poured through the entrance on the other side of the room.

"Ngh...I'm using it!!"

Lilly watched as Bell and Welf took down monster after monster without making a dent before she reached to her belt and withdrew a golden dagger—a magic sword.

The two young men immediately jumped away as soon as her voice reached their ears. Her path clear, Lilly brought the blade straight down with all her might. A stream of energy burst from its tip.

The electrical blast cut a straight line across the battlefield toward the entrance on the opposite side of the room. Every fiend in its way burst into crackling flame, bringing the fight to a swift end.

A *boom* exploded within the room a second later as though the intense blast of energy had collided with a wall farther down the passageway.

"...!"

Crack! Not even a moment later—

The yellow blade shattered.

Several hours had passed since they set foot on the nineteenth floor. The monsters they'd encountered were so strong that the group had been forced to use the magic weapon several times just to keep going forward.

It had reached its limit. Golden shards fell from Lilly's grasp.

"It gave out…Guess we relied on it a bit too much."

"But just now…!"

"I know. We needed it…but it just wasn't strong enough."

Several emotions crossed Welf's face as he looked at the remains of his handiwork and stopped Lilly's counterargument by raising his hand.

While it was true that Crozzo Magic Swords were extremely powerful, the blades themselves were actually rather frail.

"This is my problem," Welf bluntly stated, caught between his skills as a magic-sword maker and his pride as a smith.

At any rate, the battle was finally over.

"Bell, is everyone okay?"

"Yep, I'm fine. Didn't get hurt."

"But currently there are only two of Welf's magic swords remaining…Lady Lilly, what is our location?"

"We have pressed past more than half of this area. The twentieth floor is close."

Wiene bounded up to Bell, her salamander-wool cloak flapping behind her like a flag on a windy day, with a big smile on her face. At the same time, Mikoto approached Lilly for an update on their location.

Pulling out a map of the floor, Lilly pointed to a spot about three-fourths of the way down the main route. One of their three magic swords was gone, and they had consumed far more potions and magic potions than expected. However, the rest of their weapons were still intact and in good working order. Leaving their item situation aside, the party remained on track.

The group paused for only a moment to share the update before moving on to their next task.

Lilly instructed everyone to gather the loot scattered about the battlefield.

"Again, please don't leave behind a single magic stone. Bad things will happen should a monster find and eat one. Take any drop items that will fit…As for the larger ones, we have no choice but to throw them into thicker grass."

"Y-yes."

"I'll help, too."

Lilly issued the orders to make sure that their secret mission remained a secret by covering their tracks. The fighters and Wiene helped the supporters finish the job before pressing forward.

"I'm just gonna put this out there. I know that the monsters here are stronger and there's a higher encounter rate, but...Bell and I didn't run into this many last time. Or is it just my imagination?"

"That's probably because there aren't as many other adventurers. More than likely, there's nothing else to distract the monsters from us."

Consecutive battles were unavoidable, but the numbers were staggering. Lilly tried to offer an answer to Welf's doubts.

There were many reasons—one being that suspicious adventurers often flocked to this floor—but very few parties passed through during the night and early morning hours. Even adventurers who used Rivira as a base camp preferred to avoid operating during this time of day. Lilly explained how hungry monsters would gather from far and wide when prey was scarce.

"......"

"Lady Wiene?"

"This place is...familiar...but scary...and cold."

The vouivre timidly wrapped her arms around her body as she scanned the Colossal Tree Labyrinth.

Haruhime wasn't faring much better, fox ears and tail visibly shaking. Even so, seeing Wiene so afraid was worse. Putting on a brave face, she reached out and held the girl's hand.

Bell glanced at the girls in the center of the formation before resuming his constant vigil. Mikoto, who had slain the many types of monsters they had encountered thus far, never forgot to activate her Skill periodically as they advanced. Lilly and Welf were just as quiet as the rest of the party, inspecting the walls around them as if the bark might crack open at any second to reveal another wave of monsters.

The ceilings inside this sylvan domain were surprisingly high, and small hollows dotted the walls. While birds or small animals might have called these alcoves home on the surface, they were the perfect places for monsters to stage an ambush. Clusters of plants indigenous to these floors popped up all over the place, fascinating the adventurers who passed through.

Bizarre mushrooms with red and blue spots, grasses with golden thistles sprouting like cotton, and an astounding amount of vines hanging off the walls like snakes filled the passageways. Bell caught a glimpse of a dead-end room with beds of silver flowers, and it was so beautiful that he would have loved to paint the scene if he had the talent.

Everyone knew it was only a matter of time before the next encounter. These moments of peace were just the calm before the storm, so they stayed in tight formation and gained as much ground as possible.

...We're still being watched. And...

There were more of them.

Bell studied the surrounding fauna, his head on a swivel, as goose bumps broke out along his skin.

Had the unknown watchers from aboveground followed them this far?

There were more of them here on the nineteenth floor. Of that he was certain.

The hollow alcoves above his head, the treelike network of branching paths, the dark spaces behind massive leaves—Bell's gaze traveled from one suspicious spot to another, seaching for any movement in the shadows. While he saw nothing, he knew their observers were concealing their presence somewhere nearby.

Just who were they? What were they trying to do?

The ominous air made Bell's heart beat a little harder.

His shallow breaths quickening and dread saturating his veins, Bell knew he had no choice but to keep pressing forward.

He tightened his grip on the Hestia Knife in his right hand.

"...?"

Without warning—

An unexpected obstacle halted the party's considerable progress.

It completely blocked their path. Confusion ran rampant through the group at the very sight of it.

They came to a stop in front of a motionless *wall of mushrooms*.

"No way forward…"

"A-are we going the right way?"

"Hey, Li'l E, what gives?"

"P-please wait a moment. This shouldn't…"

Stretching from wall to wall and floor to ceiling, a colony of gigantic mushrooms sealed off the route.

A silent barrier of red- and blue-polka-dotted mushrooms stood in their way.

Mikoto and Haruhime voiced their disappointment at reaching a dead end. Lilly defended herself from Welf's frustration as she pulled out the map and opened it for a closer look.

"This is…*weird*."

Welf sniffed and grumbled under his breath.

An inexplicable feeling of recognition overtook Bell upon hearing those words.

……

And he realized immediately why those warning bells were ringing in his head.

However, this was more than a sense that something was off or baseless déjà vu.

It was the knowledge of the lessons drilled into his head by a certain half-elf "older sister" of his.

If you think you're in trouble—it's already too late.

Many of the gigantic mushrooms making up the colony *opened slits that looked remarkably like eyes* beneath their large umbrellas.

"……"

Dropping the act, the mushrooms of many sizes revealed their dark-purple bodies at once and moved as a unit.

"It's not a wall—they're dark fungi!!"

A wave of cold fear swept through the party as Lilly screamed loud enough to injure her throat.

Dark fungi.

The mushroom-like monsters had evaded Mikoto's Skill due to the fact that she had zero experience dealing with them. These monsters preferred to wait for prey to come to them, hiding among the gigantic fungi that naturally clustered together inside the Dungeon.

Just as infamous as the many species of insect monsters inhabiting the Colossal Tree Labyrinth, these creatures produced enormous clouds of poisonous gas.

"‼"

The mushroom caps swelled right before their eyes.

Their clouds of toxic spores made the purple moths' poisonous pollen in the upper levels look like child's play. It was potent enough to inflict Status ailments on contact and could even bring large-category monsters to their knees with little resistance.

A series of explosions rang out a second later as the fiends expelled their gas.

It was too late for Lilly and the others to get out of range as the purple clouds flooded into their path.

In the same instant—

"Firebolt‼"

—Bell made his move.

As the only one equipped with Eina's lessons, it was up to him to keep the venomous clouds at bay.

Nine bursts of electrifying flames burned through the cloud. As waves of extreme heat surged through the dense mass of spores like a tsunami, the Swift-Strike Magic slammed into the colony of dark fungi directly behind it.

The purple clouds that threatened to engulf the party went up in smoke.

"~~~~~~!"

Susceptible to fire, the mushroom monsters writhed in pain as they perished in the flames.

The conflagration engulfed fungus after fungus, and even the actual gigantic mushrooms ignited to become towering torches in the passageway.

Bell's quick reaction bought Lilly and the others time to escape the edges of the poisonous gas cloud even as bits of the spore cloud burned in midair—but the Dungeon wouldn't allow them to escape so easily.

A dark shadow suddenly appeared on the other side of the inferno, and a colossal boar burst through a moment later.

"A battle boar?!"

Nearly two meders tall, this was truly a large-category monster.

The wall of flames parted in its wake as the monster charged through with sheer brute strength. Its eyes locked on the adventurers, and its fur bristled.

It wasn't alone, merely leading the charge of its peers. It roared at the top of its lungs as a swarm of bugbears and other monsters followed it through the flames.

"Damn it!!"

Welf planted his foot on the ground and charged back into the poisonous purple haze.

Casting aside his greatsword, he grabbed the large shield hanging from Lilly's backpack on the way.

He held it directly into the boar's path to protect his friends.

"OOOO!!"

"!!"

The silver shield, forged by his own hands, collided with the monstrous boar.

Only with the strength granted to him by Haruhime's Level Boost did Welf, twinkling lights still hovering around his body, manage to stay on his feet and absorb a blow that would have sent many upper-class adventurers skyward. Digging in his heels, he lost only a few steps' worth of ground before bringing the monster to a complete stop.

That was when Mikoto rushed into action.

"HYAAA!!"

Jumping clear over Welf's head, she drew Chizan, one half of a set of twin daggers that she always kept on her person, and drove it into the monster's neck from above.

It was a clean strike, sending a gush of blood into the air, but it was not enough to behead the battle boar. Mikoto carved several more slashes into its hulking body as she spun through the air. The monster collapsed to the ground at the same moment the blood-spattered girl landed at its side.

"—HA!!"

Bell dashed by the boar's body and straight into the oncoming rush behind it.

He brandished his double knives—a flash of violet light slashed through a bugbear's neck, sending its head tumbling through the air, as a crimson streak rode the momentum to strike another monster down in the same moment. Bell's trademark agility caught the oncoming horde by surprise; they were powerless before him as he drew them into the fray.

He tore into the bugbears, slaughtering them one by one as Welf and Mikoto arrived with bigger blades, greatsword and katana; the three of them joined forces to take care of the rest.

"Haa, haa…!"

Bell slew the last monster as the combat came to an end.

The three humans struggled to catch their breath, faces illuminated by the burning mushrooms.

Haruhime gawked at the piles of corpses surrounding them and was about to rush to her companions' aid when Lilly grabbed hold of her wrist. "It's not safe yet," said the prum, her eyes following the last wispy trails of poisonous spore clouds.

"Sorry, but could a guy get an antidote…?"

"Y-yes, right away!"

Welf groaned as he staggered his way back to the supporters, skin glistening with sweat.

Haruhime quickly retrieved a vial of green liquid and handed it to him. Inhaling the toxic spores inside the purple cloud had poisoned Welf. He downed the concoction in one gulp.

"Seriously, Bell roasted most of them, and I still got hit…Guess this means upper-class adventurers can't just blindly charge in and hope for the best."

"Consider yourself lucky. There are worse cases of poisoning, and those take much longer to recover from..."

Lilly continued by explaining how the unlucky ones would have died on the spot and rummaged through her backpack as Welf's breathing returned to normal. Pulling out a few items, she turned to the others.

"Mr. Bell, Miss Mikoto, how are you feeling...?"

"It hurts, but I can stand up..."

"Everything feels heavy, no energy."

Mikoto and Bell returned to the supporters, their faces off-color.

Unlike Welf, the two of them both possessed the Advanced Ability Immunity. However, it wasn't effective enough to completely nullify the poison yet, and they became painfully aware of the dark-fungus spore cloud's potency.

Sharp claws and fangs weren't the only things adventurers had to worry about in the Colossal Tree Labyrinth.

"Lady Wiene... You look perfectly normal."

"...? I'm fine."

Being a type of dragon and born in the middle levels, Wiene must have been born with a high resistance to Status ailments. All the adventurers were looking at her with concern, but she couldn't understand why.

Lilly sighed before instructing Haruhime to drink an antidote, just to be on the safe side, and then followed suit.

"Lady Mikoto, Master Bell, what will you do...?"

"Conservation is of the utmost importance. Sir Bell and I will share one."

Living in poverty as a member of *Takemikazuchi Familia* for so long had taught her to scrimp and save whenever possible. Mikoto didn't give it a second thought when answering Haruhime's question.

Bell took the antidote—stamped with *Miach Familia*'s emblem—from Haruhime and said, "I-in that case..." After drinking half of it, he handed the bottle to Mikoto.

Her heart skipped a beat. With the half-empty vessel in her hands, the realization that Bell had just drunk from it shot through her like lightning. She stared at it for a moment before her face became bright red. Only then did it hit Haruhime, fox ears standing up straight as she quickly covered her eyes.

"One, two, and..." Mikoto whispered to herself, cheeks still flushed, before drinking the rest.

Even Bell started blushing. *A cunning strategy...* Lilly thought to herself, fists clenching as she watched with jealousy in her eyes.

"......"

Then, once everyone had recovered...

Wiene's ears started twitching.

"I hear...something."

"You do?"

Wiene turned, her elfish tapered ears guiding her.

Their surroundings were quiet. Bell followed the girl's gaze down the path from which they had come. There was nothing out of the ordinary.

Welf and the others started to wonder if something was wrong with Wiene when...

"...Ah."

"I hear it as well..."

Bell and Mikoto definitely sensed it.

A strange sound.

One that they hadn't yet encountered during their time on this floor.

Wiene possessed enhanced monster senses, far superior to the adventurers'. Fear flashed across her face—an omen of what was to come. The vouivre girl took a step back.

"Are those wings? No, not quite..."

It wasn't the telltale signs of other adventurers locked in combat, nor was it a monster's howl.

The unusual sound reached Lilly's ears. She, too, thought it was the flapping wings of a bird at first, but it was too metallic. A bead of sweat rolled down her neck. She adjusted the straps of her backpack as Welf lifted his greatsword into a defensive position.

The peculiar noise grew louder.

Something was approaching along the path.

The entire party took a few steps back as the ominous tension became too much to bear.

When their nerves had been wound tighter than a bowstring—the sound's source revealed itself.

"Are those…bees…?"

Haruhime asked her question in a shaky voice as black shadows began to appear at the very edge of her vision.

Their insect-like bodies were covered in thick black plates resembling armor. Angular and menacing, each shadow was as tall as an adult human. Pincers shaped like scissors jutted from their jaws, but the adventurers were more concerned about the other end—a poisonous stinger shaped like a pike.

"…Deadly hornets."

Bell turned pale as he said the species's name.

They normally appeared on the twenty-second floor and below as one of the monsters that prevented third-tier and second-tier adventurers from advancing into the deep levels.

Its fearsome pincers were one thing, but the deadly hornet's stinger was powerful enough to pierce heavy armor and even kill Level 2 adventurers in one thrust. Those who survived its sting usually succumbed to blood loss soon after. With armor strong enough to deflect attacks that didn't land just right, they were like killer ants with wings.

Killer ants were known as "novice killers" in the Dungeon's upper levels; in the same vein, deadly hornets had a nickname of their own: "upper-class killer bee."

Each of the lethal monsters was equipped with four wings, two on each side. More and more shadows emerged, their number surpassing twenty.

"—RUN!!"

Welf's scream was the signal.

The whole party turned their backs on the deadly hornets and took off as fast as their legs could carry them.

"Hornets—really, really big hornets!! And too many to count!"

"Please stay focused, Lady Haruhime!!"

"Bell, I'm scared!"

"So am I!!"

Racing past what was left of the gigantic poisonous mushroom colony, the party sprinted down the middle of the wide main path.

The screams of the terrified adventurers joined the near-deafening buzz of their deadly insectile pursuers as they fled. Many had painful memories involving bees, such as a grandfather drawing off a swarm to help him escape or the searing pain in her tail when she had been stung at her family's home, but nothing compared to this very moment.

If the hornets caught up, they would be impaled before those massive pincers devoured them.

Bell's party raced across the wooden ground, their bodies soaked with sweat.

"Why do deadly hornets have to show up now of all times?!"

"This ain't a time for questions, Li'l E! Run for your life!!"

"LILLY *IS* RUNNING!!"

Lilly screamed, lamenting the Irregular that had ascended several floors to meet them. Welf howled back, greatsword resting on his shoulder.

The supporters were the slowest members of the party, and the others had no choice but to keep the same pace. Lilly and Haruhime were going as fast as they absolutely could.

"...I'll slow them down with Magic!"

"No, Bell! It won't work!"

The insects were too fast. A ranged attack would never land against monsters that could move so freely.

In this wide and cavernous passageway, taking down any one of the extremely agile deadly hornets with Firebolt while on the run would be next to impossible. What was worse was that magic swords weren't an option because there was too much space overhead, nearly ten meders. They could easily dodge the blast.

But above all else, there were too many.

Welf yelled out that it would be like trying to empty an ocean with a bucket.

"And we do not have time for that…!"

"！"

Mikoto screamed as she saw something farther down the passageway. Bell's head whipped around, his eyes going wide.

Dark shadows shaped like mad beetles slid over the walls up ahead, right in their path. Mikoto and Bell sped up, their faces contorted in desperation.

It was up to them to eliminate the obstacles and clear the way for the rest of the party.

"Hah! Haa, haa…!"

Run. Run. Run.

Their formation was in shambles. Welf was in the back, furiously pumping his arms and legs.

The supporters raced past the corpses Mikoto and Bell left in their wake, sprinting deeper and deeper into the Dungeon.

Their lungs burned as their ragged breaths echoed through the hall. Their pursuers were gaining; the swarm wasn't going to let them escape.

"Lilly, what's up ahead?"

"This is a straight path to the twentieth floor! Should be almost there…!"

Bell slipped under a bugbear's claws, his counterattack slicing the creature in half as Lilly's desperate, almost pleading voice reached his ears.

The party ran through the curving path and, just as Lilly had predicted, they spotted a large hollow alcove at the other end.

It was the entrance to the next floor.

Their goal suddenly in sight, everyone's eyes flashed as they dashed toward the hole with even more vigor.

However…

Crack!

"—"

Crack! Crack!

The sounds were coming from their destination as well as the walls on both sides of the path. A mere fifty meders stood between them and the entrance, but ominous cracks spread out like spiderwebs. Their environment was crumbling before their very eyes.

The party fell into stunned silence as a massive horde of monsters was born simultaneously in the passageway.

A monster party.

The most underhanded of all Dungeon gimmicks.

Mikoto reflexively triggered Yatano Black Crow. Forty-four enemies.

Mad beetles, bugbears, gun libellulas, dark fungi, battle boars—a nightmarish parade was advancing toward them.

They were trapped in a pincer attack from ahead and behind. The Dungeon had bared its fangs yet again, sending the adventurers into the deepest pits of despair.

"Aahh—"

Wiene's face froze in fear, the deadly appendages reflected in her eyes.

The rest of the party wasn't faring much better, terror threatening to overtake them.

That's when—

"—KEEP GOIIIIIIIIING!!"

Welf didn't let it happen.

He screamed at his allies, ordering them forward just as they started to slow down.

Bell, Mikoto, and the rest decided to put their faith in the voice urging them from behind.

Kicking at the ground, they sped up.

Right into the jaws of the ferocious beasts roaring in their path.

"!!"

Welf sheathed his greatsword and jumped into the air.

With a clear view over his allies' heads, he grabbed a longsword's hilt with his right hand—removing the magic weapon from the other sheath strapped to his shoulder.

He brought the crimson blade down in one swift motion.

"Breakthrough...!!"

Roaring flames.

The magic sword came to life in response to its creator's call with a burning howl of its own.

Torrents of flames crashed into the monsters barring their path. Even their dying howls of agony couldn't escape the inferno.

The rest of the party watched in awe, their eyes opening as wide as they could.

Their path had been transformed into a smoldering gorge.

The Dungeon itself seemed to scream out in pain, the magic sword's overwhelming power incinerating the walls and ceiling and every plant in its path.

Bell led the party straight into the charred wasteland at full speed. Enduring the heat and holding their breath to avoid burning their throats, they raced through the passageway's charred remains.

At the same time, a *crick!* sounded from the magic sword.

Releasing that much energy at once took its toll on the weapon. Cracks appeared along the blade, now close to its limit.

"Come on, buddy, hang in there...!"

Welf called out to the sword in his hand, fearing the worst.

Even as it started disintegrating, the magic sword continued to glow as if to reassure its wielder that it would fight to the end.

"_____!!"

The swarm of deadly hornets closed in.

There was almost no space left between them. The closest ones flapped their wings at a frantic pace, the echoes reaching a crescendo as if building suspense before the kill.

Their prey was in range—the fleeing adventurers right in front of them. They raised their stingers.

"!!"

In that moment, Mikoto leaped off the ground.

The farthest ahead, she dove the final four meders and landed inside the hole.

Bell, Lilly, Haruhime, and Wiene were right behind her, jumping through the threshold one after another.

As his companions bounded down the stairwell composed of tree roots, Welf made it inside.

"Of course you'd follow! Take this…!"

The deadly hornets didn't hesitate. They swarmed into the hole en masse, determined to catch their prey.

Welf twisted his body mid-leap to face the tenacious monsters, lips creased into a grin.

His unblinking eyes on the deadly hornets, he gripped the magic sword with both hands and lifted it high above his head.

Flight was meaningless.

In this narrow tunnel, no amount of agility could save them in this constrained space.

For the second time, Welf roared along with his weapon.

"GOOOOOOOOOOOOOOOOOOOOOOOOOOOOOOOOOOO!!"

A massive fireball engulfed everything in its path.

Every deadly hornet began glowing like hot steel in a forge.

"———Ahhh!!"

The swarm of lethal insects, having been drawn into the connecting tunnel, were vaporized into nothingness.

At about the same time, the magic sword let out a high-pitched ring and shattered.

"—Thanks."

This was no apology but gratitude.

Welf smiled at the hilt still in his grasp as he performed its last rites.

The shards gave off one last crimson sparkle as if offering their own farewell.

Then, the explosion launched Welf, Bell, and the rest of the party into the air, as if to hurl them out of the wooden cavern.

"""""""""?!"""""""""

Torrents of wind carried them down the stairwell.

Light appeared at the end of the tunnel, causing one boy to experience a serious case of déjà vu. Suddenly, the adventurers flew through the exit.

Thud! Thump, thump! Thud, wham! Dull impacts rang out one after another.

"The twentieth floor…"

"Finally, we made it…"

"W-we…we're here…"

"Hurry up and get off Lilly!!"

"Ooph, oh…"

"Ouch…!"

Mikoto tried to regain her bearings; Welf smiled through his bumps and bruises; Bell was filled with relief and Lilly with anger while Haruhime and Wiene shook their heads in pain.

The party slowly untangled themselves after landing in a big pile. And an unexplored labyrinth filled with looming trees spread out before them.

It all happened so fast.

She remembered speaking to someone wearing a black robe before a black fog enveloped them. After she coughed a few times, some kind of fabric had been slipped over her head, muffling any noise.

After that, there was just steady swaying like she was being carried, and then she was here.

"…Was that some sort of magic just now?"

"Nothing that impressive. Just a simple magic item and a shortcut, Goddess Hestia."

The cool air inside the stone passageway chilled her skin.

Hestia trudged along behind the black robe's shadow through the man-made tunnel.

The tunnel itself was rather cramped, barely wide enough for three people to stand side by side, along with a low ceiling. While she couldn't tell what material the walls were built from in the dim light, she could see the seamless surface was engraved with many patterns. Without any windows or doors to speak of, Hestia was certain this was a secret passage of some sort.

*Well, I sure got outplayed...*Hestia thought to herself. From the moment her "guide" told her to follow, she had done so without complaint. Taking the immaculate planning and execution of her captor into account, she knew it was useless for a powerless goddess like her to resist.

She still spoke with her usual casual tone, but both knew who was really in control.

"Very few individuals are aware of this shortcut. It's possible to count on one hand the number who have used it."

It went without saying that the black-robed figure lighting the way with a portable magic-stone lamp had their back to Hestia while speaking.

Her guide seemed confident that the goddess wouldn't try to escape. Either that or knew that Hestia could be easily caught if she did make a break for it. Probably both.

Hestia held in a sigh, frowning slightly at the mysterious figure. Whoever it was, they didn't seem to have any interest in hurting her. So she focused on the passing walls instead.

"A shortcut, you say..."

If her captor had been telling the truth, she must have been carried into this "shortcut"...That meant the entrance was extremely close to their meeting point in the fourth block.

Visualizing a map of the city, Hestia thought about where the main streets and landmarks were to get a general idea of her current location. Then she asked another question:

"Is this a shortcut for *your master* to use to escape in an emergency?"

"......"

Hestia was confident in her theory, but the black-robed figure's response was only silence.

Except she got the funny feeling this person was smiling beneath that hood.

Not planning to answer me, I see... That's fine. If my guess was right, then soon...

She would learn everything she wanted to know.

Her captor's master would tell her.

Hestia didn't pry and kept up.

"Oh? A dead end?"

They reached the end of the tunnel a little while later.

Hestia raised a suspicious eyebrow as the black-robed figure reached out to the wall and ran a hand across the grooves carved into the surface.

"—"

As soon as a few words like an incantation came from beneath the hood, the wall started sliding away with a low rumble.

Did whoever this is say "Open sesame"...? Hestia jokingly thought to herself as the hidden door opened, disappearing into the adjacent wall to let them pass.

It connected to a chamber shrouded in darkness.

"......"

Hestia followed the robed figure up a small flight of stairs and into a stone hall.

She looked around the room as details emerged from the gloom.

The floor was covered with large slabs. The ceiling was high overhead, its shadows seeming to hover in the air around her. The stones that composed the walls were showing their age. Perhaps it was once a temple, built in the Ancient Times and long forgotten.

Disregarding the "shortcut," there was only one other entrance to the chamber. It was located at the top of a stone stairwell, signaling to Hestia that they were underground.

Then her gaze fell toward the middle of the chamber.

"He" was present, sitting on an altar among four lit torches that provided the only source of light.

"—Ouranos."

The guide led Hestia to the front of the altar. She turned to face the deity, looking him square in the eyes.

The majestic yet wizened god sat on his throne—a large stone structure fit for a king. Over two meders tall when standing, he exuded an intensity, a presence, and a divine authority that were in a league of their own, unmatched by other deities. Heralded as a "Supreme God" while residing in the heavens, he was one of the truly influential deities.

White hair and a similarly colored beard spilled from beneath the hood of his robe. His robust arms were propped on the throne's armrests—a god immovable. He simply existed in that spot, surveying the chamber like a ruler and a statue at the same time.

A towering, unyielding king, the *true leader of the Guild* lifted his chin to look down on Hestia.

"It's been a long time, Hestia."

"Yeah, Ouranos...I haven't seen you in, what, over a thousand years?"

There was no joy in this reunion. Ouranos maintained his calm expression and aimed his booming voice toward the young goddess.

Hestia wasn't the least bit intimidated by his overwhelming presence and addressed him like an acquaintance from days long past.

The goddess had only recently arrived in the mortal realm as a participant. She didn't know much about Ouranos—especially over the last thousand years—other than he was often referred to as the "Father of Orario."

She did know a few basics, such as the fact that he was part of the first group to descend to this world, one of the gods who brought an end to the Ancient Times and settled in Orario.

He had worked together with the mortal children to plug the "Great Hole" in the ground that constantly spewed monsters—helping to build the "lid" that turned the Labyrinth City into the first line of defense.

With his familia eventually becoming the Guild, he oversaw both the city and the Dungeon. However, he realized that someone with that much power must maintain a constant stance of neutrality. Therefore, he bestowed his followers with political power rather than Falna.

The last thing Hestia knew about Ouranos was that he spent his days beneath Guild Headquarters, offering constant "prayers" to the Dungeon.

These prayers—powered by his immense divine authority—kept the Dungeon in check. It was his will that prevented hordes of monsters from reaching the surface and plunging the world back into the original state from the Ancient Times. That was how it was explained.

Given Ouranos's presence here, Hestia reasoned that she must be in the Chamber of Prayers beneath Guild Headquarters.

The two deities observed each other with the same shade of blue eyes, directly under Orario's governing facilities.

"This ends my role here, Ouranos."

"You have done well, Fels."

Behind Hestia came the sound of fabric shifting.

Then the person called Fels started to take his leave.

"Well then, I shall excuse myself. I'll be late if I don't set off soon."

With those words, Fels returned to the hidden door.

"Please make yourself at home, Goddess Hestia."

Fels said a final good-bye before disappearing into the darkness.

Hestia watched until the figure vanished, and then she returned her attention to the god before her.

"I have a lot of questions, Ouranos. Mind if I get some answers first?"

"I'll allow it."

Hestia had known Ouranos was the one who ordered the mission the moment she saw the hieroglyph message on the document.

While she didn't know how it would happen, she had had a feeling that the two of them would meet face-to-face at some point.

"Was this mission only your idea?"

"It was indeed. No Guild employees have been informed."

"Are Bell and the others safe?"

"They're in the Dungeon. There are no guarantees."

Hestia's first order of business was to ensure her followers were safe. She frowned at the god dodging her question, but her shoulders relaxed.

I can still let him have it after I find out everything he has to say, she promised herself before she reined herself in.

"Such an elaborate scheme…What's with the roundabout process?"

"It was necessary to take expedited measures to ensure our

meeting remains absolutely secret. I was prepared for you and your followers to be wary."

Most likely, Ouranos didn't want anyone else to know that he had summoned Hestia to the Chamber of Prayers. This forceful method was probably chosen as the least risky course of action.

Hestia felt that they were being tested at the same time.

Ouranos knew from early on that Hestia and her familia were harboring Wiene.

Everything that had transpired up to today, including the mission, happened under his watchful gaze.

He saw their decisions, their reactions.

It was all to determine whether or not she was worthy of an audience with the deity.

"Am I correct in assuming that you've called me here because of the vouivre girl—because of Wiene?"

Hestia changed her course of questioning.

The large, wizened god looked down at her from atop his altar.

"Just what is she? Do you know something, Ouranos?"

"……"

"What is happening in the Dungeon right now? What are you hiding?"

Ouranos remained silent as Hestia piled on more questions.

Her voice reverberated around the dark chamber. Before her last words faded, Hestia asked the most important question yet.

"What is your will?"

Crackle! Sparks burst from one of the torches.

Ouranos slowly opened his mouth, his majestic form illuminated on all sides by the flames.

Eyes as blue as the midday sky locked onto Hestia.

"I shall inform you, Hestia, of our secret…"

The clash of swords echoed through the labyrinth.

Slashes and their answering counterstrokes. A cutting edge stopped in mid-swing, met by a blade and a burst of red sparks.

A shield immediately blocked the subsequent reprisal. The warrior wielding the weapons felt the impact. Waves of pain shot through its arm, and it let out a bloodcurdling roar through its pulsating throat.

The deep, beastly roar filled the passageway and shook the battle party to the core.

The Dungeon, twentieth floor.

Bell's party had made good progress, pressing even deeper into this floor they were seeing for the first time.

Not much different from the nineteenth, this level of the Colossal Tree Labyrinth was overflowing with plant life. Its walls covered in tree bark, the twentieth floor was a green maze that dazzled adventurers who traveled through its halls. Their faces were illuminated by the steady, dreamlike blue glow emanating from the moss-covered walls.

Lilly guided the party through the halls using her map. The monsters they encountered were similar to the ones upstairs, with mad beetles and dark fungi, among others. Mikoto's Skill, Yatano Black Crow, kept them safe from ambushes, while Bell and Welf knew how to deal with them on the front lines. The group's efficiency had improved, making their journey much safer and faster than before.

However, a new enemy had appeared.

It was currently crossing blades with Bell and Welf.

"RUOOOHH!!"

"OO! OOOOOGH!"

The lizard warrior howled as it charged the party on two powerful legs.

A blade's flash catching their eye, the two young men blocked it at the same time.

"These things are pretty damn good!"

Welf growled to himself, not taking his eyes away from the red-scaled monsters called lizardmen.

Standing upright and wielding weapons in both arms, the two monsters attacked much like adventurers would. About 170 celch tall, they could look Welf in the eyes. Bell had fought against many creatures in the Dungeon, but this was the first time he felt as though he was engaging other adventurers in battle.

Mainly because these two monsters attacked with swords.

Their clawed fingers were wrapped around sword hilts and shield grips.

"Flowers as nature weapons...?"

The two lizardmen were carrying "landforms"—naturally occurring weapons that the Dungeon supplied.

These metallic flowers grew straight from the Dungeon walls. Removing the stem from the flower resulted in a round shield measuring fifty celch in diameter. What's more, each of the petals could be individually plucked from the flower, becoming daggers as wide as swords and worthy of the nickname "cutters."

The nature weapons they had encountered up to this point included tree-stump clubs and stone tomahawks, but this was the first piece of equipment that provided monsters with the offensive and defensive support equivalent to an adventurer's sword and shield. Welf parried a cutter away from his body as a lizardman blocked Bell's knife with its round shield.

"SHAAAAAAAAA!!"

The two adventurers were forced to simultaneously deal with the tenacious lizardman assault and the ranged attacks of a gun libellula mob coming from behind. The monsters used powerful side sweeps, quick downward slashes, and sudden forward thrusts to overwhelm them. The blows shattered the floor beneath them, and the two humans' limbs trembled under the strain of receiving the attacks.

Their technique might have relied mostly on power, but it was unmistakably swordsmanship.

"Monsters with sword skills...Well, guess what?!"

Welf yelled back at his unusually skilled foes.

The tables turned as soon as Mikoto and Lilly finished wiping out the gun libellulas with a slew of arrows.

Welf blocked the lizardman's following strike and, with a well-timed twist of his blade, sent the creature's flower-petal dagger flying. He exploited the second it took for the disarmed lizardman to regain its balance, raising his greatsword high into the air.

Surprised realization passed over the monster's face as it lifted its shield up to defend. Welf smirked at the useless gesture.

He then used every muscle in his body to bring down an over-arching slash that cut straight through the shield and plunged into the monster's body.

"GEH—!"

Welf's sword tore right through its magic stone. The lizardman crumbled into ash before the halves of its shield hit the ground.

As the remaining lizardman reacted to seeing its companion slain, Bell kicked off the ground with the speed of a rabbit.

"GAH!"

A crimson arc carved straight through the creature's midsection as the boy slid by, holding Ushiwakamaru-Nishiki in a backhand grip.

The blade tore red scales off its body as it bit deep into its flesh.

The creature staggered for a moment with a massive gash in its torso before loudly collapsing to the ground behind Bell.

"That was a real surprise at first, but they're really rough around the edges. Those weren't techniques."

"Bear in mind that if monsters like that appear in greater numbers… the way forward will become much more arduous."

Welf returned his greatsword to his shoulder, scoffing at the fallen monsters like a seasoned veteran, while Mikoto exchanged an empty arrow quiver for her katana. Lilly and the supporters quickly set to work, collecting magic stones from the battlefield.

"I wonder if any of them live long enough to learn how to do more than just swing."

"While Lilly can't guarantee there aren't…it wouldn't make sense, Mr. Welf. Once it was identified, the Guild would immediately issue a bounty for such a monster and send exterminators to eliminate it."

Bell listened to his allies' conversation and thought about the look of insatiable bloodlust in the lizardmen's eyes. The battle over, he led his party deeper into the Dungeon.

"Lilly…how far do we have to go?"

"According to the map, our destination is close. Please turn right up ahead."

They had diverted from the main route quite a while ago.

Lilly's eyes never left the red circle over a room close to a pantry in the back corner of this floor, their mission's destination, as she spoke.

Every party member could sense their anxiety increasing with every step.

Backpacks over their shoulders, Lilly and Haruhime desperately tried to hide their exhaustion and keep their nerves under control.

Even Welf, who always lightened the mood with a few jokes, was unusually quiet.

Mikoto's Mind was little more than fumes after triggering her Skill so many times. She took out a Dual Potion, drank the whole thing, and silently wiped her mouth.

Bell led the group at the front, holding idle thoughts at bay while keeping his eyes and ears wide open. He glanced back over his shoulder.

Wiene looked up, her trembling amber eyes meeting his almost as if on cue. They seemed to exchange thoughts and feelings in that long moment.

The inside of the girl's hood was glowing red with the light of the red jewel in her forehead.

The party encountered several more groups of monsters after that.

The path required them to climb over a series of thick, matted tree roots, up a hill, and through a thicket of lush plant life.

Until finally…

"We're here…"

They had arrived at their mission's destination.

The room was a long rectangle about ten meders wide, and the ceiling was just as tall. Tree bark covered the walls and canopy, just like every room they had passed by on the way, and it was all carpeted with Lamp Moss.

Green grass and an assortment of small white rings came together to form a flower bed growing out of the floor like a patchwork garden.

However, they were not what the party noticed first.

"Quartz..."

Maybe because the pantry was nearby, but the deep-green quartz that resembled emeralds stuck out from the floor, walls, and ceiling in every direction. The verdant light of the rock formations reminded Bell of the quest that he and Lilly once undertook at Nahza's request. For others like Haruhime, this was their first time seeing quartz in every size and shape like this with their own eyes. The sight took their breath away. The largest cluster was situated at the other end of the room, directly facing the party—and covering the wall almost like a miniature iceberg.

Other rooms located close to pantries had the same manner of quartz formations.

"I'm glad to hear this is it, but..."

"There's nothing to see and no one here..."

The group came to a stop at the entryway, Welf scanning the chamber as Mikoto frowned.

There were no monsters waiting to greet them, let alone a party of people. Everyone agreed that the quartz was beautiful, but nothing special enough to designate this room as their mission's destination.

Bell and his party stood in the room's only entrance.

Of course, a way to go even deeper into the Dungeon from that spot didn't appear to exist.

"Lady Lilly, are you certain our location is accurate...?"

"I am absolutely sure. This...has to be correct."

Lilly again examined her map, along with the one provided with the mission document, as an uneasy Haruhime asked for confirmation.

Bell paused in front of the tranquil room, the moss's blue light mixing with the quartz's green in front of his eyes. He set foot inside.

The room was brighter than the path they had taken thanks to the quartz. The party followed Bell, staying in a tight cluster in case a monster came out of the Dungeon walls. They also kept their eyes open for a clue as to why their mission had brought them here.

But it was all for naught.

"There really is...nothing..."

"Dammit, Guild, what did you want us to do?"

At a loss for an explanation, they returned to the entrance.

Welf voiced the frustration everyone was feeling and massaged his neck. Haruhime's Level Boost was nearing its time limit, so the motes of light hovering over his body were vanishing as they spoke.

The fatigue they had been hiding, the exhaustion from relentlessly pressing forward through the Dungeon, had reached a breaking point and weighed heavily on everyone's shoulders. Meanwhile, the white flowers at their feet gently swayed back and forth.

—*Now that I think about it, the ones watching us...*

Bell raised his head from his spot in the middle of the party.

All the gazes he had sensed after they entered Babel Tower, which had only increased once they arrived on the nineteenth floor, had vanished.

There was no mistake. Whoever had been observing them was gone.

Bell racked his brain, trying to figure out what it could mean, when—

"_____"

Twitch.

Wiene's pointed ears twitched again.

"I hear..."

"Huh?" Everyone's attention suddenly focused on Wiene.

She looked over her shoulder to the opposite side of the room. Her gaze fell on the wall of quartz on the other end.

*No way...*The party was in denial as they watched the vouivre girl focus on sounds only she could hear. But once they tried...

"_____"

...they could hear it, too.

It was a song none of them had ever heard before. Growing louder, the reverberations rang in their ears.

Every eye went wide as the adventurers tried to find words.

"A song in the labyrinth..."

The tone was pure and steady, forming a melody that conjured images of the ocean under a calm night sky. Lilly whispered to herself, having heard about this somewhere before.

"Is it...calling?"

Wiene's eyes opened fully as her gaze raced along the quartz iceberg, trying to locate where the song was coming from.

The others had figured it out, too. The sound waves were coming from even deeper in the Dungeon, from behind the cluster of quartz crystals.

No one said a word as they climbed to their feet and drifted to the wall as if the melody were magnetic.

They came to a stop in front of the gorgeous quartz formation.

It looked like one solid piece at first glance...but then they found a dim spot among the crystals.

The song had grown so loud that now even the quartz vibrated ever so slightly in time with each note. Exchanging glances, everyone nodded.

Welf stepped forward, took aim with his sword—and brought it down in one swift motion.

Crash! The quartz broke into pieces, shattering like glass to reveal an alcove in the wall.

"...Well, how were we supposed to find that?"

Welf groaned, whispering at the opening.

The Dungeon always healed itself, repairing the damage it sustained during battles, but quartz grew back abnormally fast. In fact, the process was already under way. The party quickly strode through the opening as new crystals formed before their eyes.

Shards of broken quartz littered the path under their feet as they watched the entrance seal itself behind them.

"...Let's go."

The song was gone, as though it had served its purpose.

Peering down the slope into the depths of the tree, Bell urged his allies forward.

Tension held them in its grip once again as the party formed a line and pressed onward.

"Could this place be...?"

Lilly's quiet voice trembled in through the dim, bark-covered passageway.

While everyone knew exactly what she was trying to say, no one spoke. Breathing as quietly as possible, the party was so on edge that they became drenched in sweat.

The path was narrow, but there didn't seem to be a danger of monsters bursting from the walls. There was no Lamp Moss on any surface. Small quartz crystals dotting the passage provided just enough light for the adventurers to see one another and their immediate surroundings.

Bell led the way. Wiene, directly behind him, reached out to take his hand.

The boy didn't say anything as he felt her thin fingers wrap around his, giving them only a tight squeeze.

Having accepted the portable magic-stone lamp from Lilly in one hand, Bell pointed forward with the other as the group continued their descent.

"...A spring."

A body of cool, clear blue water awaited them at the bottom of the hill.

The bottom of the wide pool appeared to be five meders deep. It could have easily passed for a small pond.

The little light the quartz crystals provided glinted off the water. Bell used the lamp to scan the room, sweeping the beam from one end to the other.

"Looks like the path ends here..."

"That can't be...The song came from here, did it not?"

Haruhime didn't want to believe what Bell just said.

Casting light on the ceiling and the walls revealed only solid bark. There were no openings that could possibly lead to another path.

Lilly and Welf tilted their heads, examining the room in an effort to puzzle out what had happened to the mysterious singer.

"...?"

That was when Mikoto discovered something on the water's surface.

A single floating golden feather.

The idea came to her as she stood transfixed by the feather's speckled, golden sparkle.

"Sir Bell, the light."

Mikoto approached the shore with purpose in her stride.

The light from Bell's lamp passed through the clear water, reaching the bottom with ease.

As every detail came to light, Mikoto caught a glimpse of an opening in the submerged wall leading away from this apparent dead end.

"I have a theory…"

Mikoto spoke as she removed her katana, armor, and the rest of her equipment from her body.

Down to a single layer of battle cloth, she dove into the water. Trained in the unforgiving rivers of the Far East, she used her ninja-like coordination to glide through the water toward the opening like a fish.

Wiene, Bell, and the others watched with bated breath…Bubbles rose before Mikoto's head breached the surface a few seconds later.

She pushed the wet hair plastered to her face out of her eyes before giving a firm nod to her allies above.

They all exchanged glances and began to disrobe.

Mikoto briefly emerged to collect her katana and knives. They followed her example, leaving everything but the essentials behind before entering the water. Lilly and Haruhime removed their Goliath Robes and backpacks, filling small pouches with as many items as they could fit.

Joining Mikoto and Ouka on trips to nearby rivers in her youth had served Haruhime well. She swam with relative ease while Welf walked along the bottom, weighted down by the massive sword he refused to leave behind. Lilly held her dagger-length magic blade tight against her body as she zipped through the water like a minnow. Wiene, who had been reluctant, held on to Bell's arm as he helped her in.

The water blurred their vision and chilled their skin as they filed into the hole.

It opened into a long submerged passageway that was illuminated by quartz crystals poking out of the bottom as if to guide the way.

Their Statuses allowed them to hold their breath much longer than the average person could. Mikoto led them to a fork in the underwater path. Once there, the group noticed light filtering down from above and changed course.

Kicking their legs as fast as they could, the party made a break for the surface.

"—Pwah!"

Their heads popped out of the water one by one only to find what resembled a limestone grotto instead of the wooden alcove from whence they came. With black stone walls extending in every direction, only the dim quartz light remained consistent. The party climbed out of the water, Wiene and Haruhime shaking their bodies to dry off.

Bell was quick to find a new path in the blackness—one leading even deeper into the rocky labyrinth.

"So this is..." said Lilly, appalled, as she peered into the dark, unexplored corner of the Dungeon.

"...'Frontier.'"

The Guild possessed a great deal of Dungeon map data.

While it was being used to assist modern-day adventurers, it was the adventurers who came before them as well as the brave explorers from the Ancient Times who had originally gathered it. These people had blazed the trail with no knowledge, putting their lives on the line to discover new routes and make maps of every floor. These were grand achievements.

However, there were still areas yet to be explored.

The Dungeon was far too immense to ever be completely mapped.

People sometimes overlooked branching passageways in the never-ending journey deep into the Dungeon.

There were also special cases like this one, where pristine terrain had yet to be touched by explorers.

"Frontier."

Just as the name suggested, no one had ever been here before.

It wasn't recorded on any map—not even top-class adventurers knew this area existed. Lilly, Bell, and the rest of the party gaped at the thought.

"……"

A large opening connected to what seemed like a dark abyss.

Bell's party quietly took their first steps.

They fell into formation around Wiene. Bell held the magic-stone lamp high as everyone followed his path.

Quartz crystals provided nothing more than a slight glimmer. The lamp's beam was all they had to cleave through the darkness. They were so on edge, a few confused their own heartbeats for far-off footsteps and the rock crunching beneath their feet as a sign of danger. The passage was quiet, but the party heard every little sound. Without the occasional familiar monster cry in the background, the silence was deafening.

There was no way to know what creatures they would encounter.

Should an as-of-yet-undocumented Dungeon gimmick or an Irregular occur, death was a very real possibility.

This was pure, unbridled "unknown."

Their throats were dry, but their skin was slick with perspiration. Their five senses were focused beyond their intended limits. Their minds had never endured such stress, and yet, at the same time, they also felt sharper than ever before. Nothing was more reassuring than a familiar hilt in their grasp. The "unknown" revealed more of itself with each step, just like it had for their forebears.

Bell led the party farther and farther into the Frontier. Just as everyone's anxiety hit its peak, the rocky tunnel's end came into view.

"It's dark…"

And it opened up.

Bell and Welf were suddenly freed from the claustrophobia that plagued them in the tunnel. This new space was extremely wide, overwhelmingly so. The words that fell from Welf's lips resounded off into the darkness.

This was probably a large room. However, it was pitch black.

The lamp's illumination couldn't penetrate far enough into the darkness to find the opposite wall.

"......Um, Mikoto."

"Sir Bell?"

"Are there any...monsters in here?"

"N-no, not as far as I can tell..."

Bell struggled to control his trembling voice as he asked.

Something was there.

There was definitely something in here.

More somethings than he could count were watching them.

They hid in the darkness, masking their presence while observing the adventurers' every move.

Terror crept into Bell's veins as he realized how very many eyes were looking at him.

Mikoto's Skill couldn't detect them. That left only three possibilities: these were people, they were monsters they hadn't encountered before, or they were simply lurking just outside Yatano Black Crow's range.

A fresh wave of cold sweat ran down Bell's neck as his mind raced. He had to issue orders, get Haruhime to recast her Level Boost, make sure Wiene was protected, and so on.

However, there wasn't time.

An incredible killing intent swelled within the darkness.

"«««««««!!»»»»»»»

It swept over Bell, Lilly, Welf, Mikoto, Haruhime, and Wiene like a jolt of electricity.

The animosity was intense enough to halt these upper-class adventurers in their tracks.

Suddenly, *thud thud thud THUD THUD THUD!!* The unmistakable sound of feet charging directly at them reached their ears.

At the same time, *whoosh!* Several feathered wings took flight.

"‼"

Bell's left hand guided the lamplight toward the closest oncoming sound.

The beam cut through the darkness, but Bell could make out only one thing—scarlet scales.

"—RUOOOOOOOOOOOOOOOOOOOOOOOOOOOOOOOOH‼"

Bell's eyes flew open as he recognized the reptilian-warrior howl.

—*A lizardman?!*

A lizardman with bloodshot eyes didn't give Bell a chance to attack as it stepped deep inside his space.

The lizardman wielded a long curved blade in its left hand—a scimitar. A flash of silver scythed down with blinding speed.

"_____"

The invisible swordsmanship stole Bell's breath away.

The Hestia Knife in the boy's right hand had moved to the right place out of sheer luck.

The two blades collided directly in front of his chest.

Immediately after, he felt the impact with his entire body, making his vision swim before hurling him to the side.

"Bell!"

The boy slammed into the ground, rolling away from the party as Welf's yell reverberated through the room.

The lamp fell from Bell's grasp, and a reptilian foot crushed it beneath its talons.

With the light source gone, the area was plunged back into darkness.

"What the hell is going on—?!"

"HYAA‼"

"—?!"

Welf's heart was racing in his darkened surroundings when a small shadow zipped toward him.

He promptly raised his greatsword overhead, where it crashed into something with a high-pitched metallic ring. The impact was strong enough to drive him to his knees.

Sparks scattering from the collision briefly revealed the attacker: a diminutive monster wearing a red hat.

"A goblin?!"

The plump bottom-rung monster disappeared into the veil of darkness. Welf watched with stunned eyes, unable to believe its strength.

"!"

"!!"

Even farther back in the rear guard, Mikoto recognized the sound of projectile weapons whistling through the air. Jumping over to land by Wiene, she deflected the shots with a sweep of her katana.

"—Feathers?!"

In the instant it took her precise blade to repel the projectiles, she realized what they were as they fluttered before her eyes.

Still recovering from the shock, she realized another volley of feathers was heading right at her from the same direction.

"Everyone! Wiene!"

"GAAAAAH!!"

"!"

Bell had gotten back on his feet while yelling in his party's direction, but then another flash of silver descended upon him.

He dodged the lizardman's blade by the slimmest of margins, and the monster howled as it pressed the attack.

Bell moved to engage an opponent he could barely see.

"Wh-what in the world is...?!"

A metallic ring echoed in the chamber; a burst of sparks scattered through the air. The bestial howls combined with the adventurers' panicked gasps in the chaos.

Bell's party was forced into a desperate last stand, relying only on sound. The battle left Haruhime powerless to do anything. In the obfuscating dark, the pandemonium reached a fever pitch.

"!"

At that moment...

Lilly's hand, which had plunged into her spare pouch the moment combat began, brushed against what it was so desperately searching for. While fighting against fear and panic, the devoted supporter of the party made a quick decision and grabbed what she needed to overcome their trial.

She pulled a small bag out of her pouch, opened it, and flung it forward with all her might.

"Lamp Moss!"

"!"

"?!"

The bioluminescent substance spilled out, spreading across the ground.

It was the Lamp Moss Lilly had harvested on the nineteenth floor.

Pieces of the Colossal Tree Labyrinth's primary light source lifted the shroud of darkness surrounding them.

Friend and foe alike were caught by surprise as the battlefield came into view.

"...!"

That's when Bell's party definitively learned the true identity of their attackers.

"Huuooo!"

"OooOOooOO...!"

A lizardman, a goblin, and a harpy flapping its wings in midair appeared.

The species of monsters might have been different, but they each had one thing in common: all of them had equipment, whether scimitar or hand ax, shield or armor.

"Monsters...!

"...With weapons...!"

Bell and Welf could hardly believe their eyes.

Both clearly remembered the posting on the Guild's bulletin board:

A report stating that monsters had been seen stealing equipment from adventurers or looting it from dead bodies in the Dungeon. It had even displayed a sketch of them with the gear. Both young men felt as though that drawing had come to life.

"H-how many of them are there...?!"

At the same time, Lilly was more distracted by the other monsters farther back.

In addition to the harpy, a gargoyle and a griffin circled the space above their heads. Meanwhile, on the ground were...*lamias, al-miraj, formoires, war shadows, the humanoid spider called arachne, unicorns*...The horde was composed of myriad monsters hailing from the upper, middle, lower, and even deep levels of the Dungeon. The space almost seemed big enough to fit the surface's Coliseum, and the number of eyes watching them in the room made Mikoto and Haruhime turn pale.

Wiene fearfully looked around at the numerous monsters that had many of the same features she did.

"OOOOOOOOOOOOOOOOOOOOOOOOOOOOOOOOO!!"

The lizardman facing Bell let out a ferocious roar, and the other monsters started to move all at once.

The blue-green light emerging from the ground illuminated claws and fangs as well as the raised swords and axes.

"All these guys...!!"

"They're after Lady Wiene?!"

The attacking monsters' weapons were all aiming for the vouivre girl at the center of their party.

Breathing ragged and eyes filled with bloodlust, they headed for Wiene with drool spilling from their mouths. Welf and Mikoto desperately tried to hold back the onslaught threatening to overwhelm them.

"The magic sword isn't an option like this...!"

The battle had transformed completely into a wild melee in the darkness. Engaging the monsters in hand-to-hand combat, Welf and Mikoto could potentially get caught up in the blast.

The chamber's entrance, their only escape route, had been blocked off at some point during the fight. Lilly yelled in frustration, frowning as she loosed a barrage of arrows into the air only to have the harpies overhead launch a volley of feathers in her direction.

"Lilly! Haruhime!"

"Lady Wiene!"

As the attack neared the supporters, Wiene shielded them with her one wing.

Haruhime and Lilly embraced the girl as her peculiar append-age spread open. The pain and shock from the attack drew a groan from her.

"I-it hurts…"

Another round of feather missiles descended on the girl—but then Bell turned toward them from his distant location.

"—FIREBOLT!!"

A roar.

Swift-Strike Magic streaked across the chamber to protect Wiene and the girls.

Several thunderous bursts of flame cut through the darkness and collided with the harpy and the griffin in midair. Shrieking in pain, the monsters fell to the ground in a trail of smoke. The gargoyle, along with the other airborne fiends, used their wings to shield themselves from the magical attack like Wiene had done earlier.

"SHAAAAA!!"

"!"

The snarling lizardman charged forward and slashed at Bell as if to remind him who his opponent actually was.

Bell had been interrupted in the middle of launching more ranged attacks and only barely managed to dodge.

The lizardman carried two weapons: a longsword in its right hand, a scimitar in its left. A breastplate was firmly strapped to its chest over its scarlet scales. Metal plates covered its forearms, waist, shoulders, and knees, protecting the vital areas. The equipment might not have been the highest quality, but the lizardman could be described as fully armed and armored, standing a head and shoul-ders taller than Bell.

Bell grimaced as he drew Ushiwakamaru-Nishiki and faced his opponent with double knives.

This lizardman…It's strong!

Not only was its first strike fast enough to create afterimages, it was smart enough to exploit the darkness for offense and defense.

Being on the receiving end of the monster's onslaught, Bell was well aware of the creature's potential. There was no comparison between this lizardman and the one he fought earlier on the twentieth floor. Its strength, speed, and skill with the sword were in a different league. Welf might have been joking around about one of them honing its technique, but this monster fit that description. The possibility that this could be some subspecies of lizardman popped into the back of his head.

In terms of Level, the monstrous warrior could be beyond him—while only a guess, Bell couldn't shake the thought.

Bell's rubellite locked onto his foe. It glared back at him, running its tongue eagerly back and forth behind its sharp fangs.

He would never reach Wiene and the girls without winning this fight.

Silencing every doubt, the boy held nothing back as he charged forward to defeat the lizardman.

"Hya!"

"GRWAAA!!"

The Hestia Knife slashed forward, leaving an arc of violet light in its path while the monster's longsword came down with its full strength behind it.

The two closed upon each other and collided.

""!""

The blow confirmed Bell's suspicions. The lizardman was incredibly powerful.

At the same time, the lizardman was taken aback by the boy's incredible speed.

Rubellite eyes met reptilian pupils.

The faintest of grins appeared on Bell's lips, and the lizardman bared its fangs in what resembled a ferocious smile.

""—OOOOAAAAHHHHH!!""

Bell and the lizardman roared at the top of their lungs as they crossed blades again in a flurry of strikes.

"Li'l E—do it!"

—Elsewhere, Welf stood as the last line of defense holding back the advancing horde.

He yelled over his shoulder, using the flat part of his blade as a shield against the onslaught.

"But—"

"JUST DO IT!!"

The formoire laid into his makeshift defense with a metallic club. Knowing that the next block might be his last, Welf wasn't about to let Lilly object. The prum was hesitant, glancing to the other side only to see Mikoto fighting for her life against several monsters at once.

Tightening her grip on the glistening dagger-shaped magic sword, Lilly bit her lip before finally hardening her resolve.

"FIRING!!"

With that, she swung the red dagger with all her might.

A river of flames surged from the Crozzo Magic Sword in a straight line.

Welf and Mikoto noticed a sudden wave of red light in their periphery and immediately dropped to the ground. Using their incredibly quick reflexes, the monsters jumped out of the fire's path at the last moment. The beasts shrank away as a corner of the room erupted into a ball of flames.

"AHHHH!!"

"RUOOO!!"

Bell's battle with the lizardman continued unabated, the two going blow for blow as flames danced in the background.

Their profiles were cast in a soft orange light as longsword and knife collided. The scimitar streaked through the air, only to be intercepted by a crimson blade. Then as a violet slash arced forward, the longsword halted its advance.

The monster had displayed a powerful fighting style that included fierce kicks and an approach to swordsmanship that made good use of its combat instincts, all backed by sharp, unyielding counterattacks.

Bell's body became a blur, and the lizardman's blades sliced through empty air. Sparks erupted from the armor that stopped the boy's attack. The monster knocked him backward, but not before a line of scarlet scales was ripped from its body in a spray of dark-red blood.

Then...

"SHAA!"

"WHA—?!"

Their stalemate was broken.

Bell was trapped between the scimitar and the longsword. Caught in simultaneous attacks on the left and right, he blocked both weapons with his knives. In that moment, something flew in from an impossible angle and nailed him in the stomach.

—*A tail!!*

The third strike came from an appendage as thick as a log.

The completely unforeseen attack from a creature that shouldn't be very experienced fighting adventurers sent Bell reeling.

It was the perfect final blow. Striking from an angle that the boy never thought to defend, the lizardman's tail knocked Bell off his feet. Now was the monster's chance to finish him off, and it used the opportunity to drive its clawed foot into Bell's chest in a powerful kick.

The boy hurtled backward through the air.

"GAH!"

"OOOOOOOOOOOOOOOOOOOOOOOOO!!"

The lizardman declared victory with a roar as Bell's body bounced deeper into the room like a river rushing through broken levees.

He lost his grip on the Hestia Knife and Ushiwakamaru-Nishiki, and the weapons flew from his hands.

The lizardman warrior wasted no time in turning around, shifting focus to its original prey. Its bloodshot eyes landed on the vouivre girl surrounded by adventurers, and it charged.

"_____!!"

Wiene reflexively cringed in fright at the pounding footfalls and savage roar.

Cutting straight across the scorched battlefield, the lizardman raised its longsword high overhead.

The monster's long shadow fell over the girl unable to stand when...

"No!!"

"!?"

Haruhime jumped in front of her, arms open wide as Lilly embraced Wiene, placing her own body in front like a shield.

Two more shadows jumped into the fray as the strike hurtled toward its target.

"Oh no you don't!!"

"I won't let you!!"

A terribly battered Welf and Mikoto brought their greatsword and katana crashing into the longsword.

Two blades came together in time to catch the longsword. Their weapons audibly groaned as the two adventurers fought the incredible power and weight—and then it stopped.

The longsword came to a halt a tiny distance from Haruhime, who was positioned directly in front of Wiene.

Rattle rattle rattle! The lizardman tried to force its weapon forward, its orpiment-colored reptilian eyes wide with shock at the strength of the humans holding it back.

"_____"

Just then...*ring, ring.*

The lizardman's ears picked up a chime.

Shifting its gaze to the source of the sound, it saw an adventurer bounding toward it like a blood-splattered rabbit. And then a punch of bright white light.

A five-second charge.

Bell's eyes flashed as he unleashed every bit of anger with his entire body.

"HAAAAAAAAAAAAAAAAAAAAAAAAAAAAAAAAAAAAAAA!!"

Impact.

"GOHOO!"

The glowing fist collided with the lizardman's cheekbone.

Several broken scarlet scales soared through the air. Now it was the lizardman's turn to be sent flying.

The blades fell from its grasp and loudly tumbled across the floor.

It worked...!

Bell had used his Skill, Argonaut, while moving at high speed.

Seeing Wiene in danger had provided him with an extra spark of emotion and determination. Up until now, he'd been able to charge Argonaut only with his feet firmly planted on the ground. The situation had forced him to do a Concurrent Charge.

The lizardman bounced off the ground and hurtled through the air into a pitch-black stalagmite a good distance away, finally coming to a stop.

The other monsters had fallen back, forgetting to even bellow after seeing the magic sword's destructive potential. Silence hung in the air.

At the same time, Bell paid no attention to his numerous injuries and stood with his back to Wiene, ready to face the next challenger.

"GEH—"

Clawed fingertips digging into the floor, the lizardman pulled itself up using the stalagmite for support.

Still seated on the ground, the monster made a noise in its throat—when it suddenly lifted its head and cried out toward the ceiling:

"GUH-GYA-GYA-GYA-GYA-GYA-GYA!!"

Bell, Wiene, and the rest of the party watched in disbelief.

The murderous aura and rage that had been washing over them just moments ago were gone. It was almost comical to see a lizardman holding its gut and cackling like this.

Scanning the room again, the party realized that the other monsters' threatening glares had disappeared as well.

"GYA-GYA-GYA-GYA-GYA—!"

Slowly but surely, the cackling cries began to change.

"—HA-HA-HA-HA-HA-HA-HA-HA!"

They started to sound much more like a person's laughter.

"Eh...?"

"Wha...?"

Haruhime's and Lilly's astonishment at the sound was plain on their faces. Welf, Mikoto, and Bell were just as dumbfounded.

Unable to comprehend what they were seeing, there was nothing to do but stand and stare.

Realization started to set in. Each member of the party glanced at Wiene before returning their gaze to the lizardman.

"That's new! Never met adventurers like these before!!"

Never in the familia's wildest dreams had any of them expected a lizardman to start speaking, let alone with this level of fluency.

The monster happily slapped its knees a few times before climbing to its feet.

"Adventurers willing to sacrifice themselves to save a monster! Haaah! Don't know what this feeling is, but I like it!"

"—Didn't I tell you, Lido? These ones are different."

Flap! A new set of wings took flight.

A single golden feather fluttered to the ground from overhead. One of the winged monsters—a siren—glided down.

"I know that voice..."

"There's no way..."

Bell and Welf flinched as soon as they heard the new voice's unusual inflection. The golden-winged siren landed with a smile on its face.

"So we meet again."

One look at the monster's sky-blue eyes was all Bell and Welf needed to be certain.

It was the strange robed person—no, monster—they had encountered on the nineteenth floor.

Seeing her face for the first time, they were shocked at just how warm and friendly she seemed. Neither Bell nor Welf could string words together to respond.

Just like Wiene's, her beauty was breathtaking. Her long, dull golden hair was light blue at the tips. Not unlike the half-human/ half-bird harpy's, both of her elongated forearms formed beautiful golden wings. Similarly colored feathers covered most of her lower body, the exception being the birdlike talons on her feet.

As she wore a battle cloth that Amazons would have approved of over her pronounced bust, her un-feathered stomach was completely exposed.

The siren standing in front of them was a far cry from the ferocious beasts they had heard of that froze adventurers in their tracks with earsplitting screams.

"Yeah, it's just as you said, Rei! These guys are different!"

The lizardman addressed the golden-feathered siren, Rei, as it giddily approached the group, its thick tail swaying back and forth.

The two monsters walked right up to Bell as the other party members watched in various states of shock. Lilly was perfectly still, slack-jawed. Mikoto was confused beyond words, and Haruhime tried to figure out what to do.

"Sorry about that. You were too fast for me to hold back."

"Umm…huh? I…um……"

It took Bell several moments to understand that the lizardman was talking about the battle that had just ended.

And for good reason. The monster that nearly killed him moments ago was suddenly more interested in having a conversation than cutting him to shreds.

"First off, let me apologize. We've been testing you from the start."

"Test…ing…?"

"Yeah. We had to know if adventurers had truly taken in one of our comrades or not. Would they abandon her at the first sign of danger? Use her as a decoy to make their escape…?"

Those words surprised not only Bell but the entire party. Wiene was no different.

"We'll explain the details later, but…I'm sorry for scaring you like that and inflicting so much pain."

"……!"

"Thank you for protecting our comrade all this time."

The lizardman no longer felt like an enemy. In fact, it apparently had never intended to kill them in the first place.

Its lowered reptilian head and sincere voice all but confirmed it.

Next, the lizardman shifted its gaze to Wiene and opened its mouth to speak. However, the startled girl dashed for the safety of Haruhime's shadow.

The lizardman chuckled to itself, not reproaching her in the slightest. Giving up on the endeavor for now, it turned back to Bell.

Urhh...

Bell was in serious agony, with open cuts all over his body and a throbbing pain in his chest where the creature's foot had connected that showed no signs of dulling. But the ache couldn't be farther from his mind.

Sharp claws and fangs; skin covered in scales. These were not familiar traits for a person. And yet the lizardman was interacting with Bell, a human, without making him fear for his life as any other monster would.

A lizard warrior equipped with adventurers' gear.

A talking monster.

The same as Wiene.

"I'm Lido; as you can see, I'm a lizardman. Nice to meet you, Bell Cranell."

"H-h-how do you know my...?"

"Ahh, I heard it from Fels."

—Well, they were the same to a point. Wiene had a mostly humanoid form, making her appearance easier to accept.

That was the main difference between the lizardman looking down at him from just above eye level and the vouivre girl. He bore a perfect resemblance to others of his species. If a wolf walked up to a lamb and tried to start a conversation, the peaceful grazer would probably have the same reaction.

Bell's mind was moving too fast to pay any attention to the word that sounded like a name. On the verge of passing out, he managed to come back into the moment.

"Hey, mind if I call you 'Bellucchi'?" Lido asked.

"Uh, um, sure…G-go ahead."

The lizardman narrowed its reptilian eyes, focused on Bell.

Smiling…perhaps? It wasn't the hungry stare that hunters wore in front of their prey.

Many thoughts ran through Bell's mind as he looked into the lizard's squinting eyes, but it was difficult to make sense of any of them.

"Bellucchi."

"Y-yes?"

"Let's shake hands."

Huh?

Bell came back into the moment as its right hand appeared in front of him.

It was covered in red scales and protected by a metallic glove, its fingers ending in sharp claws.

Pupils shrinking to nothing but red dots, Bell stared at the hand hovering in front of him.

He knew what following through on the gesture would mean, and it made him feel faint.

"M-Master Bell…" "Sir Bell…" "Bell…" "Mr. Bell!"

His allies couldn't bear the tension and called out to him, but they didn't move from where they stood.

Haruhime was pale as a ghost, Mikoto dizzy and on the verge of becoming physically ill, Welf unable to hide his anxiety, and Lilly struggling with her growing alarm.

All of them knew that what they were seeing defied logic. They called out to their leader, voices like hands desperately reaching out to stop a fall.

"……"

Sweat poured from Bell's skin. It wouldn't stop flowing.

A handshake. A sign of friendship. A bridge between man and monster. Unprecedented. "Unknown."

Bell couldn't help but feel that he was making a mistake somehow. It seemed like the instinct to refuse that right hand and turn away was overwhelmingly correct. His completely nonfunctioning mind thought so.

He wanted nothing more than to run away from a decision that would turn all common sense on its head.

However, the lizardman was patient.

He waited for Bell to either make a move or reject the offer.

He was afraid.

Bell was terrified.

Of those fangs, those claws, all those scales. Of the reptilian gaze, of the creature's terrifying visage.

Every fiber of his being wanted to put as much space as possible between himself and the lizardman looking down at him.

Logic screamed in his ears that it would be easier to listen to reason and flee.

But.

Bell glanced over his shoulder.

"Ah…eh, uh……"

He saw the vouivre girl's bewildered eyes.

He thought back to when they first met, remembering how he felt during that fateful encounter.

"…"

Finally…

Bell smiled.

A bit clumsily.

—If this is a mistake, I'd rather make it for the right reason.

"A-hem." He cleared his throat.

And worked up his courage.

"………P-pleased to meet you."

Bell stiffly stretched his lips and took hold of the extended hand.

Haruhime and Mikoto watched with bated breath. Welf flashed a grin and let his shoulders relax. Lilly looked up at the ceiling and let out a long sigh.

Bell shook hands with a monster.

"—Pleasure's all mine!"

The lizardman—no, Lido—bared more of his fangs in a broad grin and gave Bell's hand a firm shake.

One heartbeat later—"WOOOOOOO!!"

The adventurers nearly leaped out of their skins as a burst of sound roared through the room.

The monsters that had been just as anxiously watching Lido and Bell as the adventurers—they were celebrating.

The red-cap goblin applauded. Harpies on the ground skipped excitedly. The formoire pumped its fists into the air, albeit slowly. al-miraj hopped around in circles. The cheers continued.

Friendship between man and monster—this day would go down in history, and all were elated to be a part of it.

"Hey, over there, hit the lights!"

Lido's booming voice cut through the celebration to issue orders.

Hellhounds and other agile monsters brought the magic-stone lamps out from hiding places in the rock landscape and flipped them on using claws or fangs.

"Monsters…using magic-stone lamps…"

Mikoto was dumbfounded at the sight of monsters operating the man-made devices.

Harpies had already taken to the air and started pulling back pieces of thick cloth to reveal the quartz crystals hidden underneath.

Every detail of the limestone cavern-like room came to light in a matter of moments.

"—A g-green dragon?!"

"One of those was in here the whole time…?"

Far away from the entrance where the party stood, a dragon more than ten meders long lay at the base of a quartz pillar. Its body covered in scars, the wizened beast observed the adventurers with quiet eyes that seemed to contain the wisdom of countless years. Lilly and Welf recoiled at the presence that had been watching them from the shadows.

"Please, let me greet the surface dwellers!" "Uuuu…" "Me too!"

Some who could speak, others who could not, as well as those who had difficulty with pronouncing words—every sort of monster gathered in front of Bell.

"I have heard stories about you. It is an honor to make your acquaintance, Signor Bell."

"S-Signor?"

"To be able to shake your hand, I am very happy!"

"Th-thanks."

"I'm Laura. Good to meet you."

"N-nice to meet you, too…"

"……"

"Eep!"

The red-cap goblin who called him "Signor" was the first in line as monsters approached Bell one at a time to shake his hand. His face had gone entirely stiff, and at times he would quietly shriek—such as when a silent large-category monster, a formiore, held out its massive hand toward him.

"I apologize for the late introduction. I am Rei, a siren."

"I'm…B-Bell Cranell."

"Yes, I am aware…Bell, thank you for saving my comrade."

The siren from before came to exchange greetings with the young boy as well. She offered her wing, the tip extended out like a finger. Bell clasped it.

Feeling the soft feathers in his hand and noticing Rei's ravishing smile, he blushed bright red.

"They're all happy, too. They're glad to meet a person who doesn't reject us."

The lizardman warrior, smiling from ear to ear, watched the monsters approach Bell one after another, sometimes shaking his hand again and again.

Bell looked around after hearing Lido's comment.

The gentlemanly red-cap goblin, the harpies bursting with emotion, the lamia that spoke in halting sentences, the silent war shadow…It didn't matter if they could speak or not, or even if they were humanoid or monsterlike, Bell could see consciousness in every one of the monsters who came to shake his hand. Some had tiny palms, others were large and covered in fur, but every one of them was warm.

As an indescribable feeling swelled within Bell, the monsters chanced glances over in the direction of Lilly and the other adventurers.

However, Welf and the others uncomfortably avoided the incoming gazes.

"…Uuuu."

As for Wiene…

She watched the cluster of monsters surrounding Bell like a child whose treasure was about to be stolen from her.

"Kuuu…"

"A-al-miraj…"

She watched as a new, smaller monster briskly stepped up to Bell. It wore a loose blue battle jacket and had a broken pocket watch hanging around its neck like a pendant. The white rabbit looked up at the boy with cute round red eyes. Bell bent over, the same awkward smile on his face as he held out his hand.

"Kuuu!" The al-miraj wiggled its long ears and leaped at him.

"H-hey, wait, that tickles…! Wh-why are you licking me?"

"Aruru…She cannot speak, but it seems she's taken a liking to you."

"When you say 'she'—it's a girl?!"

The al-miraj had already jumped onto his chest and was happily licking his cheek when Rei offered an explanation. Bell almost screamed hysterically. Lilly and the other adventurers weren't sure what to say as they watched the indescribable scene of two "rabbits" frolicking together—and that was when the dragon girl finally exploded.

Rushing out from her hiding spot behind Haruhime, she ran straight for Bell.

"N-no! You can't have Bell, no!!"

"Kuu?!" The al-miraj yelped as the vouivre girl physically pulled her away and latched on to Bell's arm.

The monster came bouncing back, hopping adorably to protest. But Wiene let out an "Uuuu!" and wouldn't retreat even one step, which was when she noticed—

—that she was surrounded by monsters, and they were all looking at her.

The creatures that were as fantastical in appearance as she, the ones she'd been too afraid to face, were now right in front of her.

The siren Rei stepped forward, and Wiene tightened her grip on Bell as she approached.

"Would you please share your name with me?"

"…Wiene."

"Wiene…It's a very good name."

Rei smiled at the quiet voice.

Wiene blushed, squirming as though she were being tickled after the compliment on the name Bell and the others had given her.

A few moments passed before a winged hand was extended to her.

The vouivre girl hesitated, fearfully reached out with her own hand several times, then quietly settling into a grip.

The golden-winged siren smiled with her blue eyes.

"A pleasure to meet you, our new comrade. No one here will hurt you. We welcome you."

Just as the boy and his familia had done, she had been accepted as a "comrade." Wiene's amber eyes opened wide.

Touched by the kindness and acceptance, she quietly wept.

After the soft wingtip reached out and dried her tears, the smallest of smiles bloomed on the girl's face.

The surrounding monsters howled to the ceiling, as though giving their blessings.

"…Um, please tell me."

Around the time the echoes started to die down…

Still not fully grasping the situation around him, Bell spoke while still hugging Wiene.

"All of you, and Wiene—what are you?"

It was what they'd been trying to find out ever since the day they met the fantastical girl. Bell and the party wanted to know the answer to that question more than anything else.

Every monster turned to face the adventurers.

As the representative of the group, the golden-winged siren answered.

"We are Xenos."

"—Xenos?"

Hestia whispered under the light of the crackling torches.

Ouranos, still seated on his throne, nodded in response.

"That's how we refer to them…Monsters endowed with intelligence."

In the Chamber of Prayers beneath Guild Headquarters, the elderly deity, who knew everything about the situation, informed Hestia as to Wiene's true identity.

Xenos…A word that gods and goddesses used to describe heretics.

They were anomalies expunged from the established system.

"You're saying that Wiene is also one of these Xenos, or whatever you call it?"

"Indeed. All of them share one thing in common: an intellect that far exceeds what is normal for monsters…They possess the capability to understand—but more important, they all have hearts that are in no way inferior to our children in terms of will and emotions."

"……!"

"Abnormal monsters that aren't dominated by the urge to murder and destroy…"

Hestia almost forgot to breathe as she listened to Ouranos bring these facts to light.

His voice continued to resound in the Chamber of Prayers, adding that the human-shaped monsters looked almost no different from the people who inhabited the mortal realm.

"As for when the Xenos first appeared, it is not known. However, those of us who have observed them with our own eyes and come in contact with them have ever since offered them support under the pretext of 'protection.'"

"Support…? The Guild is supporting monsters?!"

What the hell are you thinking?! Hestia was about to embark on a rant when something occurred to her.

She and her followers had done exactly the same thing for the vouivre girl. They had harbored and continued protecting her.

It was just as Ouranos said. That pure, innocent girl had a heart of her own, no different from Bell or any of her other children.

The elderly god did not budge as he watched Hestia's mouth snap shut. Then he continued.

"This mission's purpose was to return a Xenos who had reached the surface back to her allies in the Dungeon. That Xenos is none other than the vouivre girl you and your children have been protecting, Hestia."

"…I won't bother asking how long you've known. Just tell me where Bell and my children are going right now…"

"They should be headed to where the Xenos reside—their Hidden Village."

The mission had been to take Wiene home.

The unrest spreading throughout the city after the other night's commotion must have been the impetus for creating the mission.

Hestia let that idea sink in. At the same time, a new question arose. The goddess couldn't stay silent.

"Ouranos, why did you bother asking us to carry it out at all? Couldn't you have kidnapped Wiene and brought her back by force? Why let us learn about these 'Xenos' at all?"

"There are several reasons, including that Bell Cranell and your children have already become aware of monsters that could communicate using language. However, the most important one is…"

Ouranos paused for a moment before he told Hestia.

"I decided it was possible your familia, no matter how minuscule the chance…could become our hope."

"Hope?"

"Yes," said Ouranos with a nod.

"To bridge the gap between people and monsters and lead to the *path of coexistence.*"

"This is a dream, right...?"

"Would you like Lilly to pinch your cheek to check...?"

Welf and Lilly spoke as though they were in a trance.

Bell heard their mutters, unable to hide the cold sweat running down his own cheeks.

"Food! Drinks! Bring out everything we have! Today, we need to celebrate our new comrade and the first people we've ever had as guests!"

The monsters erupted with excitement as soon as they heard the lizardman Lido's booming voice—the room shook from all the noise.

A wide array of food, including fruits, nuts, and herbs found in the Dungeon, was circulating. Barrels of alcohol carved with marks that read RIVIRA were rolled out. People and monster alike sat in a large circle encompassing several bright magic-stone lamps.

The whole scene was reminiscent of the night spent with *Loki Familia* around a campfire. It was truly a banquet.

"Bellucchi, eat all you like; don't be shy! Try this!"

"Wh-what is it...?"

"You humans call it 'mruit.' Supposed to be a real delicacy on the surface!"

Lido, seated on Bell's right, held out what looked to be a red fruit in the palm of his hand. Very slowly, Bell picked it up and took a cautious bite. It felt like he was biting through a thick slab of soft meat, but his taste buds disagreed as a mellow, fruity flavor washed over his tongue. The texture was unlike any beef, pork, or chicken and he could describe it only as the finest steak of some sort, eliciting his surprised reaction. "It's so good..."

Honey-cloud fruits and more were placed in front of Lilly, Welf, and the other adventurers as well. Smaller monsters like the red-cap goblin and al-miraj were in charge of distributing giant mushrooms grilled by hellhound flames atop wide leaves in lieu of plates.

"Um, sorry for hitting you so hard back there…"

"Don't even sweat it. Everything'll grow back soon enough. And I didn't exactly hold back, either."

Bell gingerly brought up Lido's left cheek—specifically the painful-looking wound his fist had made. He apologized guiltily, but the lizardman warrior merely brushed off worn-out scales with his arm.

"Nothing to lose sleep over," said Lido, his sulfurous yellow eyes forming crescents. Most likely, he was smiling.

Bell was getting to the point that he could recognize their facial expressions, even if they didn't look like people. It had been a real struggle at first, but the young boy felt as though he was getting the hang of it.

Lido's low voice and ferocious appearance made him seem much more intimidating than many of his comrades, but he was surprisingly personable. It was thanks to his constant laughter that Bell was able to stay somewhat calm despite their company.

He felt proud of himself for adapting so quickly—then again, he might've also just become numb.

Those thoughts made him want to laugh in spite of himself.

"Now that I think about it, you guys drink liquor…?"

"Yeah. At first I thought, *What the hell is this?* but then I got a taste for it, and now it's become a habit! People really make the most interesting things!"

Lido was drinking from what was most likely a bottle that had been discarded somewhere in the Dungeon. His breath smelled of alcohol as he slapped Bell on the back several times. Around them, a stunningly beautiful lamia was as red in the face as the lizardman, and several other monsters were not far behind, either.

"Never been less drunk in my life…"

At the same time, Welf and the other adventurers weren't as social. A troll passed by, giving out wooden tankards filled with the cheap brew. Welf had hoped liquid courage would save him, but to no avail. Lilly sat next to him, sinking further into silence.

Mikoto and Haruhime sat on their heels, incredibly tense, as a group of harpies gathered around them with eyes gleaming in curiosity. They seemed most interested in Haruhime's scent, sniffing the air around her as the renart seemed on the verge of passing out.

"And then Bell came back to save me."

"Did he? That makes me jealous. Bell is certainly stra—Ahem, very kind."

"Yep!"

Wiene sat on Bell's left. Receiving warm welcomes from all the monsters, despite her bewilderment, she would every so often flash an unworried smile. At the moment, she was speaking with the siren Rei, recounting the events up to the current day.

While it was a little bit embarrassing for Bell to hear his name mentioned a few times, the entire party was overwhelmed by the monsters' hospitality.

"So then this alcohol and equipment...Is all of it from adventurers...?"

Their hosts continued rolling out more food and drinks. Bell watched in awe, glancing at the armor covering Lido's body before cautiously asking.

The Guild had posted notices on the bulletin board about monsters seizing adventurers' equipment. Bell was pretty sure he was looking at the culprits right now.

"Weeell, yes and no. The alcohol was a gift, but these blades once belonged to an adventurer who suddenly attacked me."

Lido let his gaze fall on the scimitar and longsword lying by his feet as he set his bottle down on the floor.

"But he dropped them and ran away as soon as I started fighting back...Thought I might as well try them out. Adventurers take monster claws and fangs home after slaying them, right?"

"Th-that...Yes, it's true."

"People seem to want them back even after they're dead, so we try to return what we can…But adventurers get angry at us for carrying their weapons. It's hard to know what to do."

Lido spoke with a nostalgic air, as if remembering a specific incident in the Dungeon. Bell couldn't respond.

"I gotta tell you, liquor is amazing, but crafted weapons are really something else! They cut better than those flowers over there and are a whole lot harder. There's no way we could make those!"

Words excitedly pouring out of his mouth, Lido spoke with tremendous respect for people and their creations.

Many other monsters wore some type of battle cloth, Lido included, even if they didn't have armor. A few of them wore normal clothing, like the scarf that the red-cap goblin had wrapped around his neck.

Perhaps they were trying to imitate people…copying what they saw.

Bell felt that each of them had grown fond of the handiwork of surface dwellers for one reason or another.

"—Lido, stop this nonsense at once."

The speaker hurling venomous words toward them weaved through the banquet's commotion.

"They're people. They aren't worthy of trust!"

"Are you still on about that, Gros? You saw how Bellucchi and his friends protected Wiene with everything they had. We only had to go through all that because you insisted on testing them. Ain't that right?"

Standing apart from the monsters who had joined Lido in welcoming the party, there were others who had separated themselves from the group.

A gargoyle, an arachne, and a griffin, among others, were seated atop a nearby cliff. All of them were glaring at Bell. Its body composed of ash-colored rock, the gargoyle called Gros implored Lido to see reason. Instead, the lizardman turned back to Bell and waved off Gros's words. "Don't mind him," he said reassuringly.

"Sorry, they…All of us have been through a lot. The news that people would be coming here had everyone on edge."

"Th-that's, um…It's okay."

"From what we've seen of you on your way here and in battle, we know that all of you are different from normal adventurers. That includes them."

"Wait a second, on our way here…? You were the ones watching us in the Dungeon…?"

"Oh, you noticed? That's right, our comrades kept an eye on you until your arrival."

Lido went on to say that, in addition to testing them, Xenos members had trailed the adventurers to make sure that they could rescue Wiene in a worst-case scenario.

That explained why Bell felt they were being watched in the Dungeon.

"Were you guys only watching us in the Dungeon? Was anyone on the surface…?"

"Nope, Lett and his team started observing you upstairs, on the nineteenth floor."

Lido scratched his scaly chin, clearly stating that he didn't know of anyone going any higher than that.

Bell's mind began turning again once he realized that those first watchers were someone else.

"…Hey, was that true, what you said a second ago? Are you in league with the Guild?"

Slam!

A wooden jug was set on the floor with more force than necessary.

Welf had been following their conversation and couldn't hold back any longer.

Surprised that Welf had spoken up on his own, Lido blinked a few times before flashing his fangs in a grin.

"Yeah, all true. They've pulled a lot of strings to keep us hidden, as well as provide us with food and equipment…They've done more than enough for us."

"…Lilly cannot take you at your word that the Guild would dirty its hands to keep this secret. The risk of discovery is too great, and the benefit…What benefit could there be?"

"We are not simply parasites that rely on the Guild's charity. We accept their requests to investigate situations or strange incidents while suppressing uprisings in the shadows...Our relationship is 'give and take,' as they say on the surface."

Lilly made her skepticism known while Rei stepped in to support Lido's explanation.

The Guild asked the Xenos to respond to Irregulars before adventurers were alerted to the danger or when the situation was too difficult for adventurers to handle by themselves.

"We got similar goals, that's all." Lido casually dismissed the notion.

"But I'd say that we're more connected with a god named Ouranos than with the Guild itself. Most Guild employees have no idea we're down here."

"L-Lord Ouranos..."

Orario's founding deity. Several of the adventurers gasped at the name.

The Guild claimed to lack any form of military power, yet here sat their—no, Ouranos's *private army*. Suddenly, Lilly and the others realized where Lido and the rest of the Xenos stood in the hierarchy.

"So then, it's just as you said. This mission..."

"That it is, Bellucchi. Lord Ouranos contacted us, and we agreed to test the people who lent a helping hand to one of our comrades."

The mission hadn't been issued by the upper levels of Guild management but from Ouranos himself, its true head.

They'd been dancing in the palm of his hand—being appraised. Bell and his party knew the whole truth now.

"However, hearing about you got our hopes up a bit."

Just as Bell was about to ask for clarification—

A booming voice came from the other side of their makeshift magic-stone campfire.

"REI! SING!"

"OOOOOOOOOOO!!"

A couple of drunken monsters started demanding a song, and more howled in approval.

The siren, still seated close to Bell, sighed and looked up at Lido. He nodded, eyes twinkling with expectation.

Rei grinned and stood.

"I suppose I must. I shall sing and add some color to this banquet."

Taking a few steps forward, *whoosh!* One flap of her wings and Rei landed on top of the tallest magic-stone lamp with the grace of a feather.

She turned on her heel to face Wiene, Bell, and the others, wearing a delicate smile.

"A new comrade and guests from the surface are here. Let's make this one special."

With that, Rei closed her eyes and drew a breath.

Silence hung in the air for a fleeting moment before a beautiful voice replaced it.

"Wow...!"

"This song..."

Hearing the high-pitched notes, Wiene suddenly smiled with joy, while Bell and the others reacted with surprise.

It was the gentle soprano that had guided them through this Frontier.

The siren brought one of her golden wings to her chest, singing happily and enjoying her solo with a smile on her face. There were no instruments or lyrics. The pure melody alone was enough to ensnare the hearts of her listeners.

A single siren, weaving a song with her eyes closed, ringed by people and monsters sitting side by side.

The scene, illuminated by quartz and magic-stone lamps, was so elegant and beautiful that it seemed to come from another world.

This hardly seemed to be the same dark labyrinth filled with monsters deep underground—but then again, perhaps it was one of those moments when the Dungeon would allow its audience a glimpse at sacred mysteries and illusions.

The song reverberated deep into the maze.

Bell and the others had never heard a song so captivating, so beautiful, and the passage of time left their minds.

"Let's dance, surface dwellers! May I have this one?"

"Eh? Wha...wai—Please don't, I'm not a dancerrrrrr!"

"M-Mikotooo!"

A young harpy girl dragged Mikoto out, leaving a wailing Haruhime to chase after them. In the ring's center, two shadows danced together. A curious and energetic monster girl twirled hand in hand with Mikoto, or perhaps it was more accurate to say she swung her partner about. A human hand and a winged hand were clasped tightly together.

The singing siren chuckled to herself for a moment before changing the tune.

Her beautiful ballad became an upbeat, toe-tapping rhythm similar to a waltz.

Completely drunken Xenos rushed to join Mikoto. They called out to one another, pairing off. The red-cap goblin and a lamia joined hands, hellhounds ran stride for stride with al-miraj, and the formoires joined the trolls, using their gigantic fists to pound the floor like drums. Other monsters came up to Wiene and whispered in her ear to join. "Okay!" she replied cheerfully, heading toward Haruhime. Meanwhile, the gargoyle and his group watched the tumult from their distant seats, unamused.

The song, cheers, and laughter wouldn't stop.

Wiene pulled along a flustered Haruhime all the way to where Mikoto and her partner were, before starting their own dance.

The long shadows of people and monsters stretched across the floor, mingling together.

"...Things never get this crazy."

Lido's eyes were filled with delight as he muttered. And his lips were definitely turned up in a smile.

Bell, Lilly, and Welf were convinced they were dreaming and still at a loss for words. But before they realized it, all of them were laughing.

The siren's soothing song and the echoes of joyful howls serenaded them.

"Lido, what did you mean earlier when you said we got your hopes up a bit...?"

"Hmm? Ahh..."

Bell watched Wiene and the girls for a time before turning back to Lido.

The reptilian warrior didn't look away from his dancing comrades as he responded.

"You gave us hope—that maybe things can change..."

"People and monsters coexisting...?!"

Hestia wasn't sure how many jolts of surprise shot through her body after what Ouranos had just said.

The elderly deity's face was as stoic as ever. He did not turn away from her stunned expression.

"Do you understand what you're saying, Ouranos...?!"

"Of course."

People and monsters living together in peace was impossible.

Hestia had already reached that conclusion, and yet Ouranos responded with a deep nod. He knew what that meant.

Those born in the Dungeon were the greatest enemy of surface-dwelling races. People killed monsters and monsters killed people. With such overwhelming fear and ingrained hatred on both sides, they would like nothing more than to avoid each other. They could not be together.

The various races residing in the mortal world were fated to kill and be killed by monsters.

That was their destiny ever since monsters first emerged from the "Great Hole" back during the Ancient Times.

They were doomed to fight for all eternity.

Then Ouranos arrived with the divine will to turn that undeniable truth on its head...Hestia frowned, unable to overlook such a desire from the Guild's master, of all people.

"However, the Xenos do not attack people instinctually but instead wish to engage with them in dialogue."

"!!"

"Rather than with fangs or claws, they wish to use words and logic to make their voices heard. They want to walk on the surface. They want to know our children…to learn more about people."

Wiene's face appeared in the back of Hestia's mind.

"Self-aware Xenos are constantly under threat even from normal monsters. They live in alienation and exile. They have no place to belong on the surface or in the Dungeon."

"…"

"With no one to hear them, their easiest choice as monsters was to resign themselves to oblivion. However, they possess determination as well as the means to express their thoughts and wishes. Just like our children," he said. "Then I discovered them."

Ouranos lowered his eyes ever so slightly.

"As the one who offers prayers to the Dungeon…No longer could I withstand their lamenting as they perished."

Someone sure is diligent—Hestia tried to force herself to poke fun at Ouranos but she couldn't manage to get the words out.

Because she had met Wiene.

Could she really bring herself to abandon the vouivre girl now?

Could she become a treacherous and deceitful goddess for her familia's sake?

Hestia's thoughts swirled, trapping her in a whirlpool of choices and decisions. After a few minutes of heavy silence, she lifted her face and started asking Ouranos another question.

"Are you serious about bringing harmony to the children and monsters?"

"The will of the divine has been set. However, it is an impossible demand. The truth is that it is beyond my control."

Ouranos had no qualms about confessing everything in response to Hestia's question.

"If our goal is harmony between our children and monsters, then we must question the reason of their existence in detail."

—Prove that monsters themselves were important.

From birth, they were constantly stigmatized because of their physical features that diverged from what was considered normal.

Threatening physiques, claws and fangs that were symbols of bloodshed, death-heralding flames, and voices tinged with savagery.

In order to break free of their reputation as icons of slaughter and violence—as well as for the sake of establishing peace—there was no choice but to demonstrate their role in this world to the children of the mortal realm. In order to realize their dream of basking in the surface's sunlight, it was imperative to overcome people's hatred and fear by proving their significance.

One option was the cruel subjugation method known as taming. Although it would allow them to be recognized by the masses, it required living with a collar of thorns. What's more, that path would never lead to true peace.

"…So basically, in your quest to prove the meaning of their existence, you thought there's a possibility Bell and my other children could become a bridge between the two sides?"

"That is correct."

Hestia let her head hang limply at the revelation. The elderly deity was so unbelievably open about these secret plans it was almost refreshing.

She understood Ouranos's reasoning. After getting to know Wiene, she also wanted to help the Xenos find happiness.

However, this path put Bell and their familia in a very precarious position.

Ouranos mentioned alienation and exile. If the fact that *Hestia Familia* had assisted these "monsters" became public knowledge, not only would their standing in Orario be at risk but their place in the entire world. Just like the Xenos.

Perhaps it was impossible, but Hestia preferred to not have their fate hanging in the balance.

Even if that means running away, the goddess thought to herself.

"Is what you just said the Guild's opinion on the matter as well?"

"Currently, it is mine alone."

That made sense.

Declaring peace with monsters would shake the world to its core.

Even Ouranos, the one heralded as the founding deity of Orario, could not help but lose political power as cracks formed in his base.

"The highest levels of Guild management, including Royman and his closest advisers, have been kept in the dark on this matter."

His employees had been ordered only to deliver the mission to *Hestia Familia*. Most likely, Royman believed that Bell's rapid growth had caught Ouranos's attention and the deity intended to test the boy's strength with the mission.

Ouranos explained this to Hestia.

"So the only ones who know are…"

"Among deities other than myself, Hermes, because he accepts my requests…and Ganesha."

"G-Ganesha?!"

Hestia was completely taken aback at the unexpected name.

"You must be kidding," she said, wide-eyed.

But then, her shoulders jolted.

"Don't tell me the Monsterphilia is…?"

"Correct. It was conceived five years ago in order to soften people's hatred for monsters, no matter how slight, and has continued ever since."

The Monsterphilia: an event that turned taming monsters into a spectacle.

The festival had been proposed and organized by the Guild. It hadn't been the brainchild of deities who craved entertainment. It was still relatively new, and Hestia had heard that the Guild didn't offer much explanation about it during Denatus.

Now she was able to connect the dots.

Ouranos had been the driving force behind the event. Putting on a show despite the dangers of bringing monsters out of the Dungeon was all his idea.

He wanted to soften the public's opinion of monsters by showing the majestic tamers interacting with them, making the beasts less alien, providing a foundation for future change.

It was all to lay the first stepping-stones that would lead to a day when the Xenos could revel in the sun's rays.

It wasn't just "Monster Festival" but "Monster*philia*."

But that merely served as the first stage, and its impact was rather limited.

"I informed Ganesha in order to gain his support."

While the Guild oversaw the event, it was *Ganesha Familia* that provided tamers for the show.

Ouranos would never have gained Ganesha's confidence by being manipulative. So the elderly deity had no choice but to reveal his divine will.

Never thought it'd be Ganesha...

Out of everything she had heard, that had been the most surprising. Hestia wiped the sweat off her neck with visions of the friendly god wearing an odd elephant mask popping up in her head.

She promised herself right then and there to take some time to get to know him better.

"Is that everyone working with you?"

"No," Ouranos responded plainly to Hestia's question.

The god looked down at his feet as if he were gazing deep into the Dungeon far beneath.

"Fels is also with us."

"Well...this certainly exceeded my expectations."

A serious voice devoid of any shock or mockery reached the banquet, still as lively as ever with singing and dancing.

Bell and everyone else who heard the remarkably monotone voice turned toward the entrance of the room to see where it came from.

"Fels, you made it!"

What they saw seemed like a living shadow, wearing a long black robe and black gloves adorned with intricate patterns. Bell and the adventurers were quick to react to this mysterious individual, instantly ready for a fight, but Lido opened his arms and gave the newcomer a friendly wave.

Fels. A name that both Lido and Rei had mentioned quite a few times.

The adventurers still watched the hooded figure for a bit as he approached. However, Fels seemed more interested in watching Wiene and the other dancers.

"You're here earlier than I thought you'd be."

"I came as fast as I could. But please, Lido, I could do with a quick explanation. To tell the truth, I'm quite startled."

Fels asked the lizardman warrior climbing to his feet to recount what had happened.

The adventurers followed suit, standing as Lido brought the stranger up to speed. "Oh-ho?" A light chuckle emerged from the hood. "You all may be more important than we thought."

Fels looked down toward Bell and the others, offering words that were difficult to discern as praise or ridicule.

The black-robed figure stood just a little shorter than Welf. Examining each member of the trio in turn, the shadow come to life continued speaking.

"First, allow me to introduce myself. I am Fels. I act as a liaison between Ouranos and the Xenos—a messenger, if you will. I also take on odd jobs as necessary."

"O-odd jobs?"

"Yes, that's right...Perhaps you would understand if I were to say that I was the one keeping tabs on you and the vouivre girl?"

"!"

Bell, Lilly, and Welf were stunned.

Something resembling a laugh spilled from the darkness of Fels's hood as a gloved hand rose into the air.

"Bell Cranell, Lilliluka Erde, Welf Crozzo...as well as Mikoto Yamato and Haruhime Sanjouno. I've been observing your activities over the past week."

Those were the only words they needed to hear to put the pieces together.

The person in front of them was the Guild's "eyes" who had taken the liberty of thoroughly investigating them without their knowledge.

"Are you…Are you a monster, like them?"

Lilly knew that something was odd about this person; something felt off. Fending off her confusion, she pressed for answers.

"Nah, Fels is a person," Lido replied, and Fels's black hood fluttered up and down again.

"*Formerly* a person may be a better choice of words."

Huh? Bell nearly whispered under his breath.

"I'll show you."

Two black gloves took hold of the hood and pulled it back.

"—"

For Bell, Lilly, and Welf, time came to a screeching halt.

The eyes that were supposed to be there didn't exist—just two pitch-black cavities, empty eye sockets.

The skin they expected to see was also missing. Perfectly aligned teeth protruded from the exposed jawbone.

The face simply didn't exist.

A white skull of death stared back at the adventurers.

"A…a skeleton?!"

"Hold up, hold up, hold up…!"

"A spartoi?!"

Three voices shrieked.

There was no doubt that it was a skeleton's head—no eyes, no nose, no ears, no hair, just bones. The horrifying personification of death itself was proof enough that this being was no living person.

Bell was reminded of the skeleton monsters from the deep levels called the spartoi. But Fels slowly shook his skull side to side to refute the boy's terrified scream.

"Sorry, but I am not a monster. As I said, I am *formerly* a person."

"F-formerly a person…?"

"What…what the hell happened…?!"

Lilly could only echo Fels's words as Bell struggled to speak, mouth opening and closing again and again. Meanwhile, Welf clenched his teeth together in a desperate attempt to remain calm but couldn't hide the fear scrawled across his face. Fear was a natural reaction to a voice originating from a skull with no skin or throat to speak of.

While the three of them stood dumbfounded, it was Lido who spoke up with an answer:

"Fels is the Sage. An awesome Magus."

Those words.

It was as though Bell and his companions had been doused by water, all of them going silent.

That is, until a moment later, when Lilly let out a cry.

"The Sage?! As in THE Sage?! The one who created the Philosopher's Stone in the Kingdom of Magic—the only one to ever successfully create the *elixir of eternal life*? That Sage?!"

"Y-yeah...Probably that Sage, I guess...?"

The lizardman was unfamiliar with what was considered common sense on the surface, so the prum's red-faced outburst caught him by surprise. Overwhelmed by this demi-human girl only half his size, Lido took a step back as a stunned Bell remembered the story Eina had once told him about the Sage.

Just as Lilly said, that legendary person created the Philosopher's Stone, a magic item that granted the user eternal life.

Mastering the Advanced Ability Enigma, the Sage became the most powerful Magus in history.

He brought his creation, the Philosopher's Stone, before his god only to watch the deity smash the stone on the floor...

If that story were true, then the being standing before him was worthy of being named among the heroes in fairy tales and legends. Bell's eyes opened as wide as they would go.

"Another correction, if I may. I am what became of the one once called the Sage."

The Magus shocked the adventurers further, explaining with a shade of self-deprecation.

"As my story will be handed down to future generations...and as it is told even today, I came to loathe the deity who destroyed my precious stone. I became more driven than ever before in my pursuit to acquire more knowledge, to unlock the secrets of immortality… and became what you see now."

The skeleton recounted the traumatic experience with that god while running black gloves up and down the robe that hid the rest of his body.

"My methods took their toll, causing my skin and flesh to rot off my bones. Now I have become something more revolting than a monster. I've forgotten the sensation of hunger and thirst…I am no more than a living ghost."

Fels finished by saying that all his experimentation produced was a "curse."

Learning the other side of the story, one that had been lost in history, the adventurers gulped as the Sage's fate came to light.

At the same time, they were in awe at how cruel the deusdea could be, completely ruining the lives of their followers.

"I now go by the name Fels the Fool."

"Fels." A fitting name for someone who had once been known as "Sage," only to have been reduced to a farce.

Incapable of expressing even the slightest emotion, the skeletal Magus who could no longer even smile now went by that name.

"…Mind explaining how the Sage ended up in a place like this?"

"It's a long story, to say the least. Suffice it to say that Ouranos took me in despite my wretched state after I wound up in Orario."

Welf certainly looked uncomfortable, but he posed his question without fear. Fels responded openly, making the peculiarly indistinct voice friendlier in tone.

"Now I'm privy to a front-row seat in the 'center of the world,' the driving force behind the changing times."

Pulling the hood back up, Fels spoke as though satisfied with the state of things.

As Bell stood frozen in place, he had thought nothing could surpass the shock of encountering Lido and the other Xenos. Now his eyes were spinning from a second knockout blow.

*   *   *

"The Sage, huh…Well, of course I've heard of him. So that kid from earlier has become your right-hand man, Ouranos?"

"I do not deny it. Outside of my agreement with the Xenos, Fels is the one piece I can move at will…My private soldier."

Ouranos nodded at Hestia's inquiry.

Several familias, including *Ganesha Familia*, worked closely with the Guild to create a public face. Meanwhile, Fels, a Magus—a being who had a firm handle on the intricacies of Magic—worked in the shadows, conducting dirty jobs and taking on secret missions.

"I take it Fels played a major role in keeping the Xenos a secret up until today?"

"Indeed. We have already worked together for centuries."

Fels also filled the role of Ouranos's personal bodyguard. Many Guild employees had witnessed his movements through Guild Headquarters, with rumors of an elusive "ghost" circulating among their ranks through the generations, each with a common thread.

"Monsters with the capacity to think and feel…I first encountered Lido and his kind fifteen, maybe sixteen years ago."

Fels continued to speak even as the siren sang among the happily dancing monsters in the background.

At that time, members of the familia close to Ouranos captured them. The deity managed to keep their presence a secret from the rest of Orario by issuing a strict gag order. That familia fell into ruin and no longer existed.

Fels obeyed Ouranos's divine will and had served as a messenger ever since, eventually becoming the Xenos's first contact with the world aboveground.

"After talking with Lido and his companions, we decided to dub their group of heretics 'Xenos.' They now live as a community under the same name."

"A community?"

"Yeah. Others like us are born throughout the Dungeon. We make contact with our comrades to form our own organization."

Bell asked for clarification from Fels, but it was Lido who provided the answer.

"We gather in Hidden Villages like this one and travel between different floors in the hopes of finding comrades nearby."

As soon as Lido explained that most of their activities took place in the lower levels, Lilly jumped back into the conversation to ask about something that had been stewing in her head for some time.

"…This has been bothering Lilly for a while, but…do monsters not spawn in this room?"

"Oh? You noticed, Lillicchi?"

"L-Lillicchi…?"

As the prum struggled with how to feel about being addressed in such a strange manner, Lido glanced out over the chamber dotted with dark-green quartz jutting from the walls and ceiling.

"This place…You might call it a safe point. There are plenty more just like it."

"Eh?!"

"Of course, adventurers haven't found them. That's why we call these places Hidden Villages."

Lido ignored the astonishment on Bell's, Welf's, and Lilly's faces and carried on with his explanation.

The Xenos frequented undiscovered Frontiers in the middle levels all the way down to the deep levels—places adventurers didn't know existed—using them as base camps in their search of monsters who shared their unique gifts.

They were a community of monsters, a traveling brigade.

"There are about forty Xenos at the moment…The numbers go up and down, but Lido, Rei, and Gros were members from the start."

"It has been a long time, yes?"

Fels glanced at the siren and gargoyle while the lizardman flashed a toothy grin.

"…That would make you the leader, wouldn't it?"

Welf finally asked what he and Lilly had suspected for a while now.

"Yeah. Gryuu used to hold that title, but his dragon body can't move like it used to. So I'm leading everyone in his stead now."

"Then the strongest member is…"

"Of course! You're looking at him!!"

Lido proudly puffed out his armored chest.

Bell thought that might be the case after fighting the lizardman one-on-one. Lido was most likely holding back at the time, but it still summoned flashbacks of *Ishtar Familia*'s first-tier adventurer, Phryne, during the battle. Therefore, the boy had suspected that the lizardman's potential strength could very well exceed hers.

"…Well, that's what I'd like to say."

—However, Lido let his reptilian head droop, shoulders slumping right away.

"One of our newest comrades took the title from me in no time flat…"

"O-ohhh…"

Welf wasn't sure what to do with the clearly depressed lizardman. Bell, however, was stunned.

The question had to be asked.

"Um, so, what's this new member like?"

"He isn't here now. He's a strange one, I tell you. Went off to the deep levels on his own for training."

"Th-the deep levels…Do…do you think that's okay?"

"Knowing him, I think worrying would be a waste of time."

Lido drily chuckled to himself as if he was exhausted just thinking about it.

"…Mr. Fels."

"What is it, Lilliluka Erde?"

After some time had passed…

Tired of singing and dancing, the revelers were starting to seat themselves on the floor. Mikoto, Haruhime, and Wiene were among them.

Lilly had been lost in thought when, finally, she looked up at Fels.

"When the siren Rei…Miss Rei spoke with us, she described the Xenos's relationship with the Guild as 'give and take.'"

"Yes, this is true."

"Lord Ouranos provides support, and in return the Xenos scour the Dungeon for new members…Is that really everything?"

Her chestnut-tinted gaze bore into the darkness beneath the Magus's hood, but his only answer was silence.

"Lilly can't help but feel that this relationship is too one-sided. There's something oddly urgent about these heretics' chosen words and actions…"

A group that used several unknown Hidden Villages and had members capable of traveling alone in the deep levels possessed considerable power. The brigade of monsters called Xenos should be able to take care of itself with or without assistance from Fels and Ouranos.

Lilly acknowledged that the Guild, in charge of the city and Dungeon management, would want to keep an eye on them to prevent mass panic from spreading through Orario. However, from what she could tell, the deal was incredibly unfair.

Above all, the Xenos members seemed to yearn for something more.

Lilly spelled it all out.

"If this is simply charity, then Lilly will drop the suggestion now… However."

Averting her eyes and hesitating for a moment, she made her point.

"Are they in this relationship because they want something only Lord Ouranos and Mr. Fels can provide?"

She'd kept these misgivings to herself ever since arriving at the Hidden Village, voicing them only now.

Bell and Welf stayed silent, ears perked and waiting.

A look of quiet contemplation grew on Lido's face.

As their conversation reached a standstill, only Wiene's laughter and playful monster howls could be heard.

"—To walk on the surface."

Just then...

A voice cut through the still air, clear as day.

"Miss Rei..."

"That is our desire."

Rei stepped lightly as she approached the group, winglike arms folded as if she were hugging her own body.

Bell, Lilly, and Welf gazed at the siren's resolute blue eyes in amazement as her words sank in.

"...I have dreams."

Lido's soft voice brought them back into the moment.

"Dreams about a ball of red light sinking behind a massive pile of rocks...A sky that can't be found here, burning red, so red and beautiful it makes me tear up. Getting redder and redder as time goes by..."

"Wouldn't that be...a sunset?"

The lizardman warrior looked up at the dark shadows that hid the Dungeon ceiling from view, but his gaze seemed to reach farther, going beyond.

Bell could easily visualize what he was describing.

"You may be right," Lido answered with a nod.

"But is that just a dream...? You've been outside on the surface, haven't you?"

"Not even once. Which means that maybe sometime in *a past life* I broke out of this dark hell and spent some time above."

Lido's suggestion made Bell and the others freeze.

"In...a past life...?"

"You couldn't mean..."

Lilly and Welf whispered in astonishment. Then Bell's voice shook as he asked:

"*Reincarnation...?*"

Lido and Rei didn't respond, staring off into the distance.

"You know, Bellucchi, that Wiene's a real talker."

"Huh...? Oh, y-yeah, she is."

The seemingly abrupt change in topic caught Bell off guard, but he recovered in time to nod his head affirmatively.

Lido watched the laughing young vouivre girl play with Haruhime and Mikoto as well as chat with harpies and al-miraj.

"Some of us can use language, but some can't speak a word. There are those who know how to express themselves while others have no clue. Don't you find that strange?"

Lido amusedly mentioned that was where the individual differences ended, though.

"Here's what's crazy. The really good ones can speak right from the start. Almost like they're *recalling something they already know.*"

"!"

"Maybe they'd watched people for a long time *in the past*…Jealous of them, yearning after them."

—*"Lots of people, just like Bell…Protect someone from me."*

—*"I see those people, and I feel cold."*

—*"But those people were beautiful."*

The vouivre girl's words, whispered under the covers of a very cramped bed only a few days ago, came to the forefront of Bell's memory.

A surge of disbelief accompanied them.

Wiene and those like her really did—

"—*A powerful longing.*"

Fels's voice interrupted his thoughts.

"Each of the Xenos has their own unique thoughts and feelings. However, they all have one thing in common: an intense yearning for people or the surface world."

The Xenos *remembered* in their dreams their jealousy of the people who resided beneath the sun and the sky and their desire to do the same.

They had seen beautiful things among the violent hostility and murderous intent.

Humans desperate to save one another's lives. A dwarf courageously standing tall despite the numerous injuries covering him head to toe. An elf on the edge of death and still carrying herself with pride to the end. Or perhaps ones who showed mercy, sparing a monster's life. Even something as simple as a beautiful blue sky and the setting sun.

The Xenos remembered their "past lives" in their various "dreams."

And each possessed an intense desire that gave them a strong reason to keep living.

"I want to live in that world with a beautiful sunset one more time."

"I want to spread my wings in a world filled with light, but in exchange, these arms can never hold...I want to be held by someone I love."

To be with people in the sunlight. That was their wish. What these men and women desired.

They were looking for a way to make it happen, with help from Fels and Ouranos.

All to accomplish a goal that would have been so simple if only the Xenos were human.

They were also fully aware how difficult it was, how long a road they would have to take. Both Xenos stopped speaking, letting their words hang in the air.

Lido and Rei smiled wanly as Bell and the stunned adventurers came to the same realization.

"We know what we are. Our place is in the shadows—halfway between man and monster, neither side accepting us...Even so, we want to keep dreaming."

They wanted to follow those dreams and the permission to do so.

Lido cast his gaze at the labyrinth ceiling once again as he spoke.

"Maybe Mother wanted beings stuck in the middle like us to have a place to go when she made Hidden Villages like this...The thought crosses my mind every now and then."

"M-Mother...?"

"Mother—you know: Mom. The one who gave us life."

"In other words, the Dungeon."

Rei's words astonished the adventurers again.

"We still do not know how Mother feels about us...Why those who should be our brothers and sisters attempt to take our lives. Even so, we are allowed to exist. It is our quandary."

Lido and Rei seemed to be asking the Dungeon despite knowing there would be no answer.

On top of everything, they still wanted to pursue their dreams.

"So that's why...we couldn't be happier to meet you, Bellucchi, and everybody else."

After looking off into the Dungeon with Rei, Lido returned his gaze to the adventurers.

At about the same time, Wiene and the others stood up and rejoined the rest of the group.

Bell heard someone happily call his name and glanced over his shoulder to acknowledge it before turning his attention back to the Xenos.

"We're not asking for help or favors. It's enough to know that there are people who accept who we are...That alone means the world to us."

Lilly and Welf stood motionless with Bell at their side.

The Magus watched from underneath the shadowy black robe. The siren smiled.

Lastly, the lizardman shyly scratched his nose.

"I'm glad I met all of you."

"—Ouranos, last question."

In the stone chamber illuminated by crackling torches...

Hestia's voice echoed.

"What's happening in the Dungeon?"

"..."

"These 'Xenos'...Do you know why Wiene and others like her were born in the first place?"

Rogue monsters, subspecies, Irregulars. If these were all it took to explain the situation, then that was that.

However, she was convinced there was something more to the

Xenos due to the simple fact that not even the deities could explain their existence. Hestia had to know why.

After a long silence descended upon the chamber, Ouranos slowly opened his lips.

"What do you think happens to monsters after death, Hestia?"

"......?"

Hestia frowned at having her question answered with another question.

The elderly god didn't wait for her response and carried on.

"The souls of our children return to the heavens, are judged and sorted by our kind, and then many are reborn into the world...So what about the souls of monsters? No, it would be better to phrase it as...If these monsters who are not our children have souls, where do you think they would go?"

Shudder.

Hestia felt her heart tremble.

"Could it be...?"

"This is only my speculation, but I also have confidence it is correct."

Ouranos was gaining momentum.

"After death, monsters return to the mother from whence they came, the Dungeon...They're given new form somewhere deep inside the labyrinth and then are born again."

A cycle of death and rebirth—monster "souls" were in constant circulation inside the Dungeon.

The motionless, elderly god declared it while his deep-blue eyes narrowed.

"Monsters have...souls...?"

"Yes. They have shown change during their centuries of death and rebirth."

Specifically, they became self-aware and capable of learning.

The "change" started to manifest itself in individual monsters after so much time had passed that the Ancient Times felt like a distant dream. Strong feelings of attachment and desire accumulated in each soul as it completed countless revolutions in the cycle.

Hestia's dumbstruck voice tumbled out.

"I can't believe something like that…What could possibly be the cause?"

"The driving force is either the monsters' strong yearning and desire…or—the Dungeon's will."

Ouranos's words vanished into the shadows enveloping the chamber.

The banquet at the Xenos Hidden Village was coming to an end.

Bell and the others were making preparations to return home. Lido and the rest of the Xenos were planning to move to another Hidden Village soon after.

Haruhime and Mikoto wore awkward smiles as they shook hands with their dance partners and said their good-byes to monsters who had become something close to friends.

The magic-stone lamps were extinguished one by one until only the glow of quartz illuminated the area.

"……"

Enveloped in their green radiance, Bell watched his allies exchange words with the Xenos around the dim cavern.

He hadn't had time to think about it before, but the monsters with human characteristics were all genuinely attractive individuals. Some spoke with ease while others couldn't say anything at all. It was just as Lido said. Every one of them was different. Even their body types were incredibly varied. They each had their own personality, their own way of living.

He had learned that they had aspirations. He had heard they had hope.

And he had also discovered that before they gained these feelings, they were bloodthirsty beasts incapable of even shedding a tear.

That was just as true for the openhearted Lido as it was for the beautiful Rei.

—Can I point a blade at monsters the way I used to ever again?

The thoughts he'd been keeping locked away started resurfacing in the corners of his mind.

As Bell stared into the palm of his hand, he could almost hear the whirlpool of anguish inside him.

"...Bellucchi!"

Lido spotted the boy lost in thought. He waved one hand high above his head and approached him.

Bell looked up to see the lizardman warrior slowly wagging his thick tail back and forth as he pulled something out from beneath his breastplate.

"You know what this is?"

"That's a magic stone...isn't it?"

Lido nodded as he pinched the purple stone between his claws.

Suddenly, he brought it to his open mouth and plopped it inside like candy.

"!?"

"Do you know what happens when we Xenos...we monsters eat magic stones?"

Crunch! Crunch! Bell wasn't sure how to react as he watched Lido purposely chew louder than necessary.

At the sight of a lizardman gulping down a magic stone, one of the facts that Eina had drilled into him rose from his memory.

"Enhanced species..."

It was like how adventurers became stronger by receiving excelia and updating their Status, but for monsters.

They gained a power boost by consuming another monster's "core"—a principle of the monsters' world where only the strongest survived. The ones who gorged themselves on magic stones and became too powerful were identified by the Guild and subsequently marked for extermination via missions.

Bell couldn't respond as he watched the phenomenon firsthand.

"We kill any monsters that aren't our comrades. Then we pluck out their magic stones and eat them."

"‼"

"I'm sure you already knew that other monsters attack us on sight. We aren't about to lie down and let them kill us without a fight. We kill to survive and eat to see tomorrow."

They had meticulously honed swordsmanship and the potential to match top-class adventurers...Bell reflected on their earlier battle, the strength and power the lizardman possessed, and knew at once that Lido was telling the truth.

The Xenos were forced to commit cannibalism every day to stay alive in the Dungeon.

Purely because their lives depended on it.

Blood drained from Bell's face as Lido made his point.

"So please don't waver. Don't hold back for our sake. Those things are scary as hell, and they'll kill you if you hesitate for even a moment. You'll die, Bellucchi."

"Lido..."

"And even if they can speak, if they attack you, kill them for me."

This den of monsters is already littered with corpses and ash.

While he didn't say it directly, the lizardman warrior truly wanted Bell to prioritize his life above anything else.

"Don't you ever die. I want to see you again."

The Xenos themselves had killed countless other Dungeon-dwellers and would continue to do so.

So don't you hold back, either. So we can meet once more.

Bell's eyes trembled at Lido's argument.

"Bellucchi."

"......?"

"Let's shake hands."

Reptilian eyes smiling, Lido stuck out his right hand.

Bell paused for a moment, looking between the lizardman's face and his hand...but then he managed a grin.

Hearing the same words as when they first spoke, the boy smiled at the row of fangs right at eye level.

He took the hand offered to him.

Bell felt Lido squeeze back, scaly skin rough on his own.

"...So, why did you arrange for us to meet them, exactly?"

The prum was busy tying an item pouch to her waist when she caught a glimpse of Bell and Lido's handshake. Then she turned to the Magus standing beside her, looking up at the concealing hood as she spoke.

Fels didn't meet her stare, but a response emanated from deep within the dark confines of the robe.

"We wanted you to know them. That's all...at least for now."

At the deep, cryptic answer, her chestnut-colored eyes narrowed.

Her glare said it all: *We'd rather not have more trouble to deal with, so please excuse us and leave us out of it.*

The black-hooded figure shrugged good-naturedly.

"I don't think I need to remind you, but please keep what you saw today to yourself."

"Would anyone believe Lilly if she told them?"

Clenched fists trembling in frustration, Lilly stomped away toward the center of the room where Welf and the others were waiting.

Bell and Lido weren't far behind. The people and monsters gathered at the quartz pillar before going their separate ways.

"Bell, let's go home."

Wiene immediately broke away from her conversation with other Xenos as soon as she saw him coming.

Turning around with a smile on her face, she reached out to take his hand.

Bell weakly smiled in return and was about to let her.

However, Lido got in the way.

"Your place is here, Wiene."

"Huh?"

He grabbed hold of her bluish-white arm and dragged her back toward the Xenos group.

Shocked, Wiene yelped and started struggling.

"Lido! No! Let me go!"

"No. You're staying here in the Dungeon."

"I don't wanna! I want to be with Bell!"

Her thin arms stood no chance of breaking Lido's grip. Tears of desperation began forming in her amber eyes.

Bell watched, unable to speak as the lizardman knelt down to the girl's height.

"If you're with them, Bellucchi, Lillicchi, everyone will wind up crying."

"!"

"Bad things happened to you on the surface, yes? Only this time, that might happen to Bellucchi."

All those angry, jeering voices. Cold, hard stones striking her skin and the weapons maliciously pointed her way.

Wiene's slim shoulders trembled as memories of that night came to mind.

"...We cannot live on the surface yet. But no one will be cruel to you here. You can live here with us."

The siren's voice reached them. The young girl's dragon wing, the feature that clearly identified her as a monster, quivered.

A flurry of emotions flooded the vouivre girl's mind as she looked at each of the other monsters in turn.

"Lady Wiene..."

Bell didn't move.

He heard Haruhime behind him as she did her best not to cry. The moment of separation came much more abruptly than he'd expected, and surprise was written all over his face.

No—it was just an act.

The moment he met Lido and the other Xenos and learned there were others like Wiene who considered her a friend, he had done his best to ignore the possibility. Immersing himself in the new discoveries and revelations had allowed him to run away from reality.

The reality that Wiene had a place here.

That saying good-bye would be the obvious conclusion.

"There is a group of hunters that indiscriminately try to capture the Xenos."

"!"

"After all, they're monsters who can communicate with language. The ones with humanoid features possess enticing beauty. If they're rare enough, anything becomes exciting for these hunters. After capturing Xenos, they apparently smuggle them out of the city and sell them to gourmets."

Lilly and the other adventurers were as genuinely shocked as Bell at Fels's explanation.

The black-robed Magus spat out the words with disgust.

"They put out tidbits of information, calling the Xenos 'monsters wearing armor' and the like, but they never leave a trail to follow. They must have a base of operations, a place to hold their captives, but…"

Fels cast his gaze toward Bell from beneath the concealing hood. *Staying with Wiene will only result in disaster.* Bell got the hint.

Ikelos's ominous smile appeared in the back of his mind, sealing off his last hope of escape from the reality. He turned to face the young girl.

"Beeeell…"

As the lizardman and siren gently held her shoulders, tears rolling down her face, Wiene cried Bell's name as though hanging on to him.

A realization hit Bell as Lilly, Welf, Mikoto, and Haruhime watched with worried eyes.

—I won't let her be alone. I won't let her die.

He could keep the promises he made to himself without being there to protect her personally.

"Bell! I…!"

A large group of intelligent monsters stood directly behind her.

Behind him was the family he'd gone through so much with up until now.

Bell was surrounded by those precious to him, before and behind.

For this girl's happiness…

And his familia's, everyone's, his goddess's—

"…See you, Bellucchi. We'll head out first."

Lido said his good-byes before turning his back on the adventurers.

Bell couldn't stop him, couldn't even take a step forward.

The monsters began to disappear into a corner of the cavern shrouded in darkness, Wiene with them. She looked around one last time.

He could see her amber eyes glistening with tears. Bell clenched his hands and shouted even as his expression was on the verge of breaking.

"This isn't good-bye! We'll see each other again!"

He left her with that reassuring promise, unsure if he could keep it.

Wiene sobbed, mouth opening and closing as if trying to tell him something, but she couldn't turn her feelings into words.

It wasn't long before every Xenos faded into the darkness.

"……"

With his allies silently watching over him from behind…

Bell only stared at the spot where he last saw the vouivre girl.

Morning fog filled the air.

The puddles dotting the stone pavement suggested rain must have fallen the previous night. Wide-leaved trees appeared to be shedding tears as water droplets fell from their branches every so often. Another one splashed on the stone surface and vanished.

The sun wasn't out yet. Only the smallest traces of light were starting to appear on the horizon.

Silence hung over the sleeping city.

It was early morning at the base of Babel Tower.

Bell's party returned from their mission a little more than a full day after their departure.

Fels, who accompanied them to the surface, had already disappeared. The party of five stepped out from beneath the white tower's entrance.

Hestia waited for her followers outside the gate alone before sunrise.

Noticing that they numbered one fewer than when she saw them off, the goddess's shoulders sank in sadness as she said, "Welcome back," with a weak smile.

"Goddess…"

"…What is it, Bell?"

The group was completely alone in Central Park. Bell opened his mouth to speak.

"What…is the Dungeon?" he asked, turning to face Hestia.

Welf and his other friends quietly watched as she averted her eyes.

"The Dungeon is…the Dungeon…"

She gave him the same response deities had given the children of the world from the beginning.

The goddess wouldn't say more than what had already been said.

Bell stood like a statue as her words faded away.

The boy stared at the ground as if the world itself weighed on his shoulders.

Dawn broke on the other side of the city wall, ushering in a blue sky.

EPILOGUE

Boundless

Malice

© Suzuhito Yasuda

"Damn bastard!"

Wham! A loud kick landed on the cage.

The sound of the rattling chains that restrained four limbs and shrill screaming halted at precisely the same moment.

The one who had been howling and pleading, saying "It hurts, let me out from here," had fallen completely silent as though fearful of its master's furious voice.

A man's sharp, angry breaths echoed off the stone walls.

"Glenn, keep it down, would you? Want me to feed you to the monsters?"

"Gah…s-sorry, Dix. But come on, we were so close to finding their nest…!!"

A hulking human named Glenn howled in frustration, fists clenched at his sides.

The goggled man, Dix, sat on top of a black cage while resting the shaft of his red spear against his shoulder.

"Tailing *Hestia Familia* and the vouivre monster was going so well, too!"

Surrounded by a ragtag group of animal people, humans, and Amazons, he let out a sigh loud enough for all to hear.

Thanks to his deity investigating *Hestia Familia*, as well as assuming that the female vouivre had caused the ruckus in town, Dix had instructed his subordinates to stake out *Hestia Familia*'s home.

Of course they noticed when Bell's party left the building with the disguised vouivre in tow. They had planned on jumping them right away, but they quickly deduced that the group was headed for the Dungeon after seeing their equipment. So they had decided to wait. Returning the beast to the Dungeon—had the vouivre told them where the talking monsters' nest was located? Were they on their way there? That was Dix's theory and why they hadn't made a move.

In fact, they almost hit the nail on the head. They followed the party into the Dungeon, drooling at the idea their target would lead them directly to the nest.

Unfortunately—

"Burn in hell, *Hermes Familia*! Who would've thought *we* were being followed?"

Dix and his companions had been denied their prize by a second familia tailing them.

They were so focused on Bell's party that another group of adventurers went unnoticed.

Since *Hermes Familia* members were equipped with magic items, Dix noticed their pursuers only by lucky coincidence. Bugbears were known for their keen sense of smell—and a few of them seemed to be looking for *someone who wasn't there*. Getting a bad feeling, he ordered them to give up the chase and split up.

Once the enemy's presence was revealed, they had scattered through the Colossal Tree Labyrinth to make a clean getaway. Now they had regrouped.

That was the true identity of the many "eyes" Bell had sensed outside Babel Tower before the mission began.

Some of them belonged to Dix's group, members of *Ikelos Familia*; the rest were *Hermes Familia*'s.

"Damn that god of ours. Just when he finally makes himself useful, he pulls shit like this."

Dix grumbled and complained about his deity.

"Hermes's kiddies may have noticed…" Ikelos had mentioned in passing, smiling in anticipation. However, the deity was not present now. Most likely, the idea of a three-sided struggle enticed him—and he was keeping a close eye on the show involving his own familia from someplace close by. The god thought of his followers as nothing more than pieces on a board that he could manipulate for his own amusement.

Dix was all too familiar with their deity's hunger for entertainment, having experienced this kind of thing many times before. "Damn that god," he muttered with his lips curled back.

"So it's *Hermes Familia* that's sniffing us out...meaning they know about our dealings. Is the Guild on to us, too? Tsk, such a pain."

There was yet another side to Ouranos's secret mission.

Bell and the party, in addition to bringing Wiene to the Xenos Hidden Village, had served as bait to draw out the hunters, Dix and his subordinates.

That was the mission in its entirety.

"Thinking logically, they didn't jump us when we were trailing the brats...meaning we were stronger. My bet is they were trying to find this place."

The pursuers had been more interested in the location of their base than themselves.

Dix ridiculed their opponents while analyzing their actions.

"Wh-what are we supposed to do, Dix? At this rate..."

"The hell *is* there to do? There's no way we're gonna stop doing something so interesting. You all are having plenty of fun all the same, ain't that right?"

Dix chuckled from deep in his throat as he looked out at the not-quite-humanoid figures locked inside the cages.

Several of the captives trembled upon hearing his cruel laugh.

"If the Guild is getting involved, I doubt they want word about talking monsters spreading around the town. There's only so much they can do...We continue the hunt."

Dix stood up and paced back and forth while spinning his spear around in his hands.

"We pretty much know what floor the nest is on. Maybe we should use it for the first time in a while."

Walking down the line of black cages, Dix took about ten steps.

Holding his breath, he came to a stop outside one particularly silent enclosure.

Hyy! A small, fearful cry emerged from among the bars.

"You'll do nicely—better prove yourself useful!"

He thrust the wickedly curved spearhead deep into the cage. An earsplitting shriek of pain flooded out not even an instant later.

【BELL ✦ CRANELL】

BELONGS TO: *HESTIA FAMILIA*
RACE: HUMAN
JOB: ADVENTURER
DUNGEON RANGE: TWENTIETH FLOOR
WEAPON: HESTIA KNIFE
CURRENT FUNDS: 81,200 VALIS

Lv. **3**

STRENGTH: D 527   DEFENSE: E 466   DEXTERITY: D 533
AGILITY: B 701   MAGIC: E 499   LUCK: H   IMMUNITY: I

《MAGIC》

【FIREBOLT】

- SWIFT-STRIKE MAGIC

《SKILL》

【LIARIS FREESE】

- RAPID GROWTH
- CONTINUED DESIRE RESULTS IN CONTINUED GROWTH
- STRONGER DESIRE RESULTS IN STRONGER GROWTH

【ARGONAUT】

- CHARGES AUTOMATICALLY WITH ACTIVE ACTION

《DUAL POTION》

- RESTORES PHYSICAL STRENGTH AND MIND ENERGY SIMULTANEOUSLY.
- AN ORIGINAL POTION CONCOCTED BY *MIACH FAMILIA* LEADER NAHZA. THEIR ECONOMIC RIVAL, *DIAN CECHT FAMILIA*, DESIRES THE RECIPE, BUT NAHZA FLAT-OUT REFUSES TO OBLIGE. SHE HAS TINKERED WITH THE FORMULA, MAKING IT MUCH MORE POTENT THAN THE FIRST BATCHES.
- WITH BELL AS A REGULAR CUSTOMER, THE "BLUE PHARMACY" HAS BECOME A HOUSEHOLD NAME RIGHT ALONG WITH HIM, AND DUAL POTION IS THEIR BESTSELLER. THE PRICE RECENTLY ROSE.
- ALTHOUGH BELL DIDN'T EXPLAIN WHY, HE PURCHASED A GREAT DEAL OF ITEMS, INCLUDING DUAL POTIONS, FROM NAHZA FOR THEIR SECRET MISSION.

Afterword

I believe that it is best for a novel's main story to be resolved between the covers, and I do my best to make that happen.

Normally, light novels take at least three months to write. While that time span remains constant, I've noticed that three months feels like less and less time with age. However, I'm sure that many young people would disagree with that statement. At the very least, I remember three months feeling like an eternity back in my teenage years.

Of course, the fact remains that readers want to know what happens next regardless of age. That urge to "read the next chapter" is a trait we all share. Which is why I understand fleshing out a story is very important—but at the same time, I try to bring the story to a close by the end of each volume, even if that means increasing the page count.

After saying all that, I must admit that no, that was not possible this time.

Volume nine and the next, volume ten, are parts one and two of the same story. To all my readers, I offer you my sincerest apologies. Here I was, talking about the beginning of the "Third Act," making all these bold claims, and I wind up with something this embarrassing. What have I done...?!

Painfully aware of my own needlessness, having to resort to this makes me want to swear off it for good.

Allow me to lightly touch on this novel's content. I think it opens a brand-new world.

I've wanted to write this particular episode since I started the series back in Volume 1 if an opportunity arose. As an author, this new world is my own "adventure." Fantasy building on fantasy. That being said, longtime readers who have been with me since the start of this journey may feel blindsided.

I believe that every event that has taken place in the main series can retain its meaning while this new addition adds an entirely new flavor to the story. Also, characters who got a running start in the side story have joined the main cast. I'll try my best to keep everything thrilling.

Changing gears for a moment, I forgot to mention something during the previous volume. Chapter 4, "Beloved Bodyguard," was originally printed in *GA Bunko Magazine* under the same title and updated for volume eight. My apologies.

This afterword was really all over the place, but the time has come for me to express my gratitude.

To my supervisor, Mr. Kotaki; to the one who always takes time out of his busy schedule to provide beautiful illustrations, Mr. Suzuhito Yasuda; to everyone involved, thank you for making this volume possible. Lastly, I would like to express my deepest appreciation to every reader who picked up this book.

Concerning volume ten, a certain heroine who barely appeared in this volume will most definitely have a role to play. A certain other heroine, who has gone "dark" if you believe the rumors, will also make an appearance. They will bring forth devastation the likes of which has never been seen before.

Since the story had to be divided into two halves, I am working night and day to make part two available as quickly as possible. Thank you for your patience.

Thank you for reading this far.

Let's meet again in the next installment.

Now I will take my leave.

Fujino Omori